THE MAN WHO TRAVELLED
ON MOTORWAYS

By the same author

The Relatively Constant Copywriter
The Adulterer
The Hard Game
Rule of Night
Rock Fix
The Sexless Spy
The 'Q' Series
   Seeking the Mythical Future (Book 1)
   Through the Eye of Time (Book 2)
   The Gods Look Down (Book 3)
The Svengali Plot

THE MAN WHO TRAVELLED ON MOTORWAYS

by

Trevor Hoyle

JOHN CALDER · LONDON
RIVERRUN PRESS · DALLAS

First published in Great Britain, 1979, by
John Calder (Publishers) Ltd.,
18 Brewer Street,
London W1R 4AS

First published in the U.S.A., 1979, by
Riverrun Press Inc.,
4951 Top Line Drive,
Dallas, Texas 75247

Extracts from *The Man Who Travelled on Motorways* have appeared in *New Yorkshire Writing, Men Only* and *Word Works 7.*

ISBN 0 7145 3732 2 cased

Typeset in 11/12pt Times by Pentagon Printing Group, London
Printed by M. & A. Thomson Litho Ltd., East Kilbride
Bound by Hunter & Foulis Ltd., Edinburgh

Contents

The form and technique of the following were suggested to me by *Letters From The Underworld* in the volume also containing *The Gentle Maiden* and *The Landlady* by Fyodor Mikhailovich Dostoyevsky (in the translation by C. J. Hogarth published by Everyman's Library in 1913), to whose memory I tender my grateful thanks.

TH

Writing is a form of therapy; sometimes I wonder how all those who do not write, compose or paint can manage to escape the madness, the melancholia, the panic fear which is inherent in the human situation.

Graham Greene

A VISIT TO A PAPER MILL

With every piece of knowledge gained
(An additional neutrino sparks our brain)
We reckon to become better, improved men,
As in preparation for a second game.
Staring into space, the shock
Cracks home that this place,
This time, the only place and time —
And this our only face.
Then do we, anguished, contemplate
The secrets of the past:
One instant is all eternity,
This same instant is our last.

Anon.

I

I was then thirty years old, and so far, had lived a dull, ill-regulated existence, and I was called upon one day to investigate the goings-on in a paper mill. This paper mill was situated at the bottom of a street called, of all things, Cock Clod Street. I arrived there, and on the first day, which was a Sunday, they let me park my car inside the green wrought-iron gates because the workers were off and there was room to move about, park cars, etc., without getting trampled underfoot or in anybody's way. I saw that the Mini belonging to Eloise and Dmitri Zeilnski was already there. The inside of this car was in a dreadful state: Dmitri Zeilnski was a photographer and he kept the car littered with discarded 35mm canisters and cartons. Dmitri Zeilnski inhabited life like a suit of second-hand clothes; that's to say he was in a different spacetime continuum to the rest of us. One got the feeling that at any moment he would flicker before one's eyes into nothingness, slipping stealthily into the past or the future, reappearing at some other time — yet so preoccupied with his work as to be completely oblivous to any change in himself or his surroundings.

I went inside the huge building. It was quiet, except for the sound of splashing water somewhere. The Millspaugh papermaking machine was stopped: 215 feet long, a massive lump of machinery with huge drum rolls in the centre section which must be each, at least, ten feet in diameter. It's the kind of machine that makes a good analogy for life. Having been sucked in and spawned at the 'wet end' the victim is stretched, scalded, filtered, flattened, starched, smoothed and wound tightly onto a drum, weighed, trimmed, stamped and consigned to oblivion. The atmosphere in the long machine-room was close, the humidity catching the back of the throat with a cloying dryness. Steam drifted out of the guts of the monster, water splashed underfoot into gratings; there was a kind of concealed violence in the long silent-pounding room as though at any moment it might unleash a terrible mechanical power. Naturally it was the machine itself that was responsible for giving this impression.

Dmitri Zeilnski and his wife Eloise were on the gantry setting up their equipment. I hadn't realised until now how much they hated each other. Coming upon them like this, from below the gantry, unnoticed, I both saw and heard their bickering long before they heard my footsteps on the metal stair. As usual, Dmitri was totally preoccupied with his lenses and filters and other bits of accessories. Perhaps two-thirds of him was present in the spacetime vortex we were inhabiting.

Eloise, disgusting creature, was snuffling round his feet like a mangy animal, craven, subservient, utterly abject. She spat back, of course, but it was no kind of defence at all. If anything it betrayed the fact that her life was dependent on and dedicated to his. It is ghastly to see someone existing out of someone else: that if that life should fail their life too would go with it. It's parasitical.

Dmitri Zeilnski shouted something furious at his wife as I came up the steps, and she was about to deliver some absolutely cutting sliver of invective when she saw me and smiled in her ragged toothless way. (Eloise Zeilnski isn't toothless but she gives one that impression.)

Dmitri immediately grasped my arm, pushing his wife out of the way, and ordered me to help him set up the equipment. I was embarrassed because he had so crudely shown her up in front of me, though to tell the truth I didn't like her any more than he did. I was glad to be in the huge, warm machine-room with Dmitri, assisting him, because one got the feeling that this was the centre of something, i.e: things were happening here as opposed to somewhere else. As I've said, this was a Sunday, and Sundays are always so quiet and dead that surely (I imagine) there is a monstrous party going on not far away if only one knew where to find it. One does not, of course, ever find it. The monstrous party with its boisterous people remains forever hidden.

Here we are then, Dmitri and Eloise Zeilnski and myself in the huge, long machine-room, on the green-painted gantry, setting up the equipment and waiting for something to happen. The atmosphere was humid. My sweater was scraping on my back. Dmitri was perspiring lightly. Eloise's hair was a tangly mess.

'What are we shooting here?' Dmitri asked me. 'Precisely what?'

Immediately I am on my guard; I know that I must behave professionally, and this means giving the impression of behaving professionally.

'It isn't so much the machine as the felts we require,' I replied. 'Admittedly they're not very photogenic.'

'No.'

Eloise Zeilnski looked pained at this. Anything which displeases her husband or constitutes any kind of annoyance to him is an irritant to her, a snag in the unbroken fabric of their life together. She apes his expression.

'There are two ways of doing this,' I said. 'One, we use unusual light angles of shade and shadow, thereby creating peculiar patterns so that the felts look like felts taken from various odd aspects. Second, colour filters, mixed, interchangeable and overlapped. The advertisements will be in colour, so we might as well take advantage of the fact.'

Dmitri Zeilnski conveys the impression of having taken in everything you've said without having heard or taken note of a single word. It is an annoying trait that I determine to practise and copy. Eloise is looking critically at the felts on the machine as though — Heaven forbid! — she might be capable of making a worthwhile contribution. Her husband glances at her with the keenest contempt and irritability. I'm beginning to get annoyed with her myself.

'Will it make any difference, the machine being stopped?' Dmitri asked.

I have to consider this. 'No it won't.' In truth I don't know whether or not it *will* make any difference, but I have learned that the essential thing in this business is never to show any hesitation. He Who Hesitates Is Lost; how true!

On a papermaking machine the felts are in effect long conveyor belts which support the 'stuff' — the slushy fibrous paper — while at the same time allowing the drainage of water. When the 'stuff' hits the first felt at the wet end it is 95.5 per cent water, and as you will appreciate the object is to drain this away, leaving behind the web of paper, now self-supporting, to run at speeds of around 1000 feet per minute through the machine. It was our job to photograph the felts.

I say 'our job' but in fact this was solely Dmitri Zeilnski's task; my purpose was far more devious. I had to research, literally, the background to the plant. I was very anxious to know what went on 'behind the scenes'. You see, I have always been intrigued by the unseen things that make other things happen. Do you understand this? In our twentieth century, when on the surface everything appears to happen quite smoothly, in reality there is a fantastic amount of activity going on 'underground', so to speak. The paper mill is a perfect example of this principle. For instance, at first sight the mammoth Millspaugh (beautiful name for a juggernaut!) seems to move under its own volition. The enormous drum reels spin majestically, laws unto themselves; the paper web screams through at an incredible speed; the lights on the control panel — green, orange and purple — flicker on and off seemingly at will; yet of course none of this happens without some other thing making it happen. The question naturally arises (to one with a mind like mine): what is making these things happen? Contrary to initial impressions these events are taking place because something unseen is providing the primeval motive power. Then what is it? Possibly this doesn't fascinate you as it does me; I can only say that different things interest different people.

I was at this point in time anxious not to get too involved in the photographing of the felts. For this reason: Dmitri Zeilnski became so absorbed that he lost all sense of time and place, and if one were to assist him he came to take such assistance for granted. One's hands became simply *a pair of hands*, without human attachment, which he regarded as his property to direct and dispose of as he thought fit. This is not flattering. It makes one feel ugly and small and disfigured; but more than this, it erodes the personality to a point where the self becomes a nothingness, a shadowy negative form without shape or substance. Anti-matter if you like.

Anyway, I was determined not to become too involved. For my pains I would receive nothing: indeed less than nothing. To say that I hated Dmitri Zeilnski would be an overstatement. I neither hated nor despised him. His existence was a matter of complete indifference to me.

'I can't hang about for too long,' I said. 'I have other things to do.'

He sighed heavily. I knew he wanted me to stay so that he wouldn't be left alone with his wife. However, the benefit of my not being married to her was that I could leave her any time I chose. That was his problem, as they say.

'The electrician hasn't connected the power,' said Dmitri. It was my turn to sigh. For although it was his responsibility to take the photographs it was my responsibility to see to it that he had all the facilities he required in order to take such photographs.

'Very well,' I said despondently, 'I'll go and find the electrician.' I was reluctant to do this for reasons you can probably imagine: have *you* ever tried to find an electrician in a closed paper mill on a Sunday afternoon? No? Well let me tell you it is no easy task. Neither is it a very pleasant one. I shan't bore you with details of what it entails, you must take my word that my heart was like lead.

Evenutally I did find the electrician, who promised to connect the supply to the power points indicated to him by Dmitri. Having done this I made my way back to the machine-room by a different route so that I wouldn't be spotted by either of the Zeilnskis. I was determined to find out what *moved* the plant.

The making of paper is a fascinating business. During that winter I went on several occasions to the paper mill, each time becoming a little more fully aware of the magical way in which the raw wood pulp and esparto grass is transformed into smooth, unblemished, unbroken bands of pure white paper. In essence the process is simple enough; it starts to get complicated because nothing can be seen — everything happens inside vats, tanks, pipes, conduits, chambers, ducting, etc. In fact the whole complex assembly is one vast conglomeration of oddly-shaped metal containers, each with a specific if mysterious function. Can you see why it intrigued me?

Yet even the hardware described isn't the full story. I found this out by going off alone into the uttermost depths of the plant, climbing over hot blistering pipes and squeezing my tiny bulk through crude holes that had been knocked in the walls to permit the access of the pipes. Inside some of the vast subterranean rooms were the familiar throbbing vats and mildewed pipes, and these rooms led to other rooms, equally large, in which more vats throbbed and their pipes wound this way and that, feeding stuff into the vats and taking it away again. Yet still I wasn't satisfied. 'There must be more to it than this,' I can remember telling myself. 'What is the secret of the plant's volition; what is going on within the paper mill to give it the force of life?' These questions, I knew, were very important and needed answering.

Before I could progress any further, however, a distant hooter rasped faintly, and in the semi-twilight I could just make out the time by my watch. The problem now was how to return to the machine-room where I supposed Dmitri and Eloise Zeilnski would be taking down their equipment in preparation for going home. It was difficult to retrace my steps, for the rooms were to all intents and purposes identical, the vats and pipes too so similar as to defy individual identification. How, I wondered, could the people who worked here find their way about? Presumably the rooms were numbered, in case a breakdown occurred, to enable the repair team to locate the particular room in which the fault had taken place. Fortunately I had a gas lighter in my pocket and with this I began to search the rough brick walls for signs of a number or symbol – for anything that might give me a clue as to my position within the plant.

I don't suppose you have ever had to search for a number or symbol on a wall inside a paper mill: it is not an occupation I would recommend, I can tell you. It is so easy, so *easy*, to mistake a smear of concrete dust, or some white crumbling cement, for a sensible and decipherable legend. Oh how many times I held up the lighter, catching a glimpse of something out of the corner of my eye, stumbling towards it gratefully, straining my eyes upwards to see it, only to find I had been cheated by pale dust markings, shiny dripping water patches, or simply tricks of the unsteady light. It is no wonder men go mad when all their efforts are made an absolute mockery of.

Outside, without question, it was cold and blustery, for this was January, and January in Lancashire is an unwelcome experience. For no reason at all (at least none that I could fathom) the climate at this certain point in time reminded me of a cold, bleak drive through an oil refinery that I was to undertake, with the wind blowing the flaming jets to and fro, hither and thither, from side to side: lazy silent flames evaporating in the grey air. An oil refinery! Now there's a place to conjure with! What else has the atmosphere of foreboding, of a threatening world cataclysm? It is the end of all existence as we know it, a desolate burning hell with streamers of sulphurous smoke obscuring an eternal scudding sky. Do not think I am imagining such a place: I was to witness it with my very own eyes, and what's more it was devoid of human beings! That is my vision of hell on earth – a place bare of life, occupied only by a landscape of burning towers, erupting fire and smoke, *uncontrolled by an intelligence!*

I see a strained smile playing about your features. You think I am on the verge of sanity, that I'm skating on very thin ice. My answer to this is simple: doesn't life in our twentieth century push us all to the extremes of our minds? For myself, I try to lead a quiet life, I cultivate the calm pleasures, I refuse to read newspapers and magazines, yet even so the high-pitched scream of modern life penetrates my defences and strikes right into my skull. The scream is inside me, trying to get out – and I, who divorce myself from the world's harsh realities . . .

People today must perforce have the minds of oxen. If they do not they break, crack apart. I have been giving a good deal of thought recently to mental health. How can it be improved? If one is anxious to build up a good stout physique the body doctors have the answer. Eat the right food, take exercise, refrain from over-indulgence in smoking, drinking and other abuses of the constitution. Breathe deeply, perhaps, and get a sound eight hours' sleep every night. All of which a sensible person can follow if he so chooses. Now tell me how to achieve the equivalent in and for the mind. Exercise of the mind? It seems to me that the more one exercises the mind the more neurotic one becomes. Food for the mind? What kind of food is best for the mind? The theologian would answer: the spiritual kind, my son. Possibly true; but if in the exercise of the mind one comes to the conclusion that religion is a falsity, what course is to be taken? We can reject the evidence of the mind, embrace religion, and live our life through lies, or we can respect the power of our minds, throw God to one side, and thereafter go gradually mad with the thought of a barren universe.

The problem with Dmitri Zeilnski is that just when you think you have him pinned by the proverbials he fades into another spacetime continuum, his Nikon and Pentax slung over his shoulder. He is a swarthy man with heavy brows and dense black wavy hair. He wears thick-rimmed spectacles and his fingernails are cut very short and square. One of the most noticeable things about him is that his car is always in a mess. A conversation with him consists of not asking direct questions followed by his not replying. Nevertheless he is a fine chap, always providing that one doesn't do a tenth of what he asks. Eloise, of course, is a much more definitive figure. Servile, cringing, subservient, she is the kind of woman who would drive any man, not least her husband, to wander the world. A fact about the pair of them which has often perplexed me is their utter disregard for money. They spend money yet never seem to earn any. I should like to know how they do this, because it is a trick worth cultivating. Dmitri always has at least a pound in his pocket: perhaps it is always the same pound, which immediately it is spent reappears in his back pocket as if by magic. One has all the money in the world if one has just one pound note and that keeps reappearing in one's pocket.

We did a number of assignments together, in addition to the paper mill. Admittedly this was the most interesting, for the reasons I have explained. We even had plans to travel abroad but these came to nothing. He went and I stayed, and as you see I'm still here. What happened to Eloise Zeilnski is anybody's guess. (I heard the other day, on the phone, that after a suitable lapse of time she had followed him; what the current state of their relationship is I do not know.)

I come upon them, Dmitri and an Italian friend of his, in the saloon bar of a pub. Weak sunlight through the decorative windows of thickened glass, their lower parts opaque, gives their two faces a raw, fresh-washed look and makes their eyes appear amazingly translucent. Dmitri introduces me to his friend: I sit down. From the moment I do sit down there is a battle of wits, a contest of egos. Dmitri delights in asking me what I am doing so that he can knock me down; naturally the Italian is his ally. They drink halves of mild beer from dirty, lipstick-smeared glasses; I drink Guinness. It is midday and the pub is comparatively empty.

'So when are you going abroad?' Dmitri asks me. He asks me this in a friendly, interested tone of voice but he is waiting, just waiting, to knock me down.

'It will be sometime next year now,' I reply. He doesn't believe I will go; I am determined to go but I share his doubt.

He then launches into a long string of advice: his speciality. How to travel, where to go, who to see. I nod and look serious. I like him, though I hate him when he acts like this. His attitude is insulting. He is good at his job but not that good.

'My friend here knows of a cheap farmhouse you could stay at in northern Italy.'

'Oh yes?'

The Italian says in quite good but imperfect English: 'There is a small village twenty kilometres and more from the sea. My brother and his family live in a house next to the village. The rents are cheap.'

'The sea is the Adriatic?' I say.

'Yes,' the Italian says solemnly.

'Give him the address,' Dmitri says. 'I'll write it down and give you directions.' He is trying to be helpful and it would be churlish of me to refuse his help. Besides, perhaps one distant day I will indeed stay at a cheap farmhouse in an Italian village.

At this point we had very recently completed the paper mill assignment.

Dmitri writes down the address and draws a little map of how to get there. I thank them both for their advice and kindness. Dmitri Zeilnski has capable brown hands and I resent this. He travels all over the world while I'm stuck here with an emotional deadweight of guilt round my neck. The Italian is smiling faintly and I begin to feel I am losing control of the situation. After all, what is the Italian? What more has he to offer than me? People with nothing to offer are so insufferably, illogically superior.

Dmitri says, 'We must meet up when you're abroad.'

'We might even do a job together,' I say hopelessly.

'There are too many doing jobs like that,' Dmitri answers. He has found the chink he has been looking for. It is practically an open invitation. He is going to knock me down. The Italian grins. Dmitri says, 'To do a job like that you need an entirely new approach, something never tried before.'

'An angle,' is all my cliché-ridden mind can think to say.

Dmitri smiles. It is obvious that he believes me incapable of dreaming up such an angle. He considers me young, naive, and foolish. This despite the paper mill experience.

'When are you leaving?' I ask.

Dmitri smiles his smugly confident brown-faced smile. (I do him a disservice; he isn't really smug at all, just so damn knowing.) 'I have a few things to finalise in London and then I'll be away. I'm expecting mail from the States.'

Big deal, I almost say.

I cannot help wondering how the hell Dmitri came to meet the Italian in the first place. Was he passing through the Italian's village and happened to stop and they got into conversation? It was possible but hardly likely. Meeting an English-speaking Italian in a remote village in the depths of the Italian countryside was too much of a coincidence. Something else was bothering me: the Italian was expensively dressed. I had been led to believe that Italy was a poor country, yet here was a native of that country wearing better and more modern clothes than I. I felt like asking, 'Where did you get your money from?'

At this precise moment Dmitri says, 'He owned a large garage in a big town in Italy and has just sold it,' answering my unspoken query as to how the Italian comes to be dressed so expensively and in such good, modern taste. One would think this a coincidence; in fact one would think the world to be full of coincidences, to be choc-a-bloc with them, for million upon million of coincidences like this one to be happening all the time. But there is no such thing as coincidence.

I notice that the floor of the saloon bar hasn't been swept, probably for days, possibly for weeks. It is thick with litter: cigarette packets, cellophane wrappers, tobacco ash, broken beer mats, torn newspapers, ripped crisp packets, all mixed with gobs of spit and spilled beer. I look with disgust at the floor.

'Does nobody ever sweep up these days?' I ask abstractedly.

The Italian shoots his immaculate cream cuffs and I notice on his genuine gold cuff-links the initials *RK*.

'Well,' Dmitri smiles, 'so when are you going then?'

'Do you mean abroad?'

'Where else?' Dmitri continues to smile.

'Oh not too long, perhaps in a month or so. I'm waiting for the money to come through and then I shall be off.'

The Italian won't stop staring at me with his dark-irised eyes, and he is beginning to make me feel nervous. I don't like people staring at me with dark-irised eyes.

'Well,' Dmitri says, there being nothing further to say at this point.

'How is Eloise?' I ask, making my attempt to knock *him* down.

Dmitri's face crinkles in a brown grimace. 'We are still together – that is I stay with her when I am in the country. But . . .' He grimaces once more. 'Did nothing ever come of the paper mill project?'

'How do you mean, "come of it"?'

This pendantry annoys Dmitri: I can see it in his brown face. All he wants is a straight answer to a straight question. Ha-ha, never! If he thinks me a fool then I shall play the fool.

'Has the material been made into anything?' Dmitri says patiently.

'Not that I know of,' I reply, and it is evident that this non-answer angers Dmitri even more.

I go home feeling pleased with myself. Dmitri and his Italian friend have departed for South Wales, following *my* directions. They could end up in Glasgow. I need not tell you how I spent the next three days. Later, Dmitri went abroad and it is over a year since I last saw him. What has become of him? Whom is he now bullying?

II

We get many glimpses of a secret underlife during our years as thinking beings, yet we choose to ignore them. For myself, I find that more and more I am drifting, or rather sinking, deeper and deeper into a fantastic half-shadowed world of memory, reminiscence, nostalgia and the like which seems more 'real' than this everyday outside world I am forced to inhabit in order to make a living. This is badly put. I shall make another attempt: at certain times I feel I am living surrounded by a great stillness. I feel that events that have happened will happen again. Indeed, I'm convinced that once an event has happened it continues to repeat itself endlessly, like the continuous loop of a cassette tape or a never-ending series of television action-replays. So that we foresee events before they happen (because they have already happened) — and after our instant-self has passed through the spacetime in which the event is happening the event then continues to happen, as I've said, *ad infinitum.* Thus I am still sitting at the table in the pub with the weak sunlight pouring over me as through half-frosted windows. I shall continue to sit there for all eternity. Dmitri will continue to ask me questions, and I shall forever evade answering them.

To give another example. Once I returned in the early hours of the morning from a long nightdrive (from whence I came I can't remember). I went to the huge black ugly building where I had an office. It was early, about six o'clock, and the only people moving about were the cleaners, old charladies with grotesque hands and wrinkled stockings. I had a wash, made some coffee, and tried to make a flat place on which to lie down by placing two chairs together. Very ordinary events, you will agree, but the odd thing is that I am still having a wash, making coffee, and trying to make a flat place on which to lie down by placing two chairs together. At this moment I am doing these things. As I sit here writing I am doing them.

I mention this specific time, place and event because I was very conscious of the great stillness previously referred to. Of course it *was* still, actually still, because there is little traffic about at six o'clock in the morning, even in the centre of Manchester. But the point I want to make is that the stillness was doom-laden. This silly phrase is the one that comes nearest to describing my awareness at that particular point in time. I felt — quite literally — that the fabric of the air was about to be ripped from end to end. As a drowning man I saw the skyline silhouette of an oil refinery, a cold featureless hospital corridor, an anonymous animal smashed flat on a midnight road, a girl with sparse red pubics, a black-faced man on a ladder pointing the side of a house, a harsh cornfield that left indentations on the skin, an hotel room to which I had been led by a slim, swarthy man with a disfigured face, a pub standing erect in the centre of a wilderness whose bars were slopping with Guinness, an enormous August sun beating through the windscreen directly into my eyes, a darkened room in which I danced naked with a black girl, an exhibition stand crammed with gleaming motorcycles, a flat through whose blank windows clinical light scoured everything white, an occasion with wife and family eating fish and chips in the lost middle of Birmingham.

— All these events were happening at one and the same time. And I was participating in each of them. My entire life was enclosed in a series of giant glossy stills pinned to a cork board. The real events of my life had turned into photographs. More explictly, they had become fiction. My life was fiction; I myself was a fictitious character.

(Apropos of this, the thought occurs to me that if people inhabit fiction how can they believe in fiction when they read it? The simple truth of the matter is that people do not believe in fiction today because they no longer believe in the validity of their own emotions or that they themselves have a separate reality. How the idea amuses me!)

Round about this period in which I had the conversation with Dmitri Zeilnski and the Italian — whether or not this was before or after the experience in the office I cannot recall — I became heavily involved in a bizarre situation in a neighbouring town. I went to this town to drink; that is, to get drunk. As to why I should need to get drunk you can no doubt guess. The town in question reeks of beer. It is very easy to get beaten up in this certain town. It is noted for miles around as a town of sex and violence. If I were to describe it to you, which I shall, it sounds like this:

The Town is both flourishing and decaying all at once. In the centre, at the apex of a hill, where four main roads meet, they have constructed massive concrete walkways and subways which circumnavigate the traffic flow. This configuration is not beautiful, neither is it ugly: it is so frightening that it is a threat to human existence. These walkways and subways, some of which include shopping precincts, are bleak draughty hells upon whose walls are smeared obscenities, excrement, blood from used and discarded sanitary towels, beer sick and advertising signs. Every breakable artefact has been broken. Every lamp behind its toughened wire-impregnated glass panel has been smashed. The steel ballustrading leans at weary attitudes as though resting from the nightly onslaught. The dedicated benches have been ripped out of the ground and lie splintered in the flower-beds. Slim aluminium poles carrying spiky remnants of white light globes have had their spines severely distorted. There is litter and dirt and soot everywhere, ushered into heaped corners by the perpetual gusting winds. Some of the paving stones have been wrenched up. No one is safe after dark. Above and below the walkways and subways the Christian traffic shatters past, the dim interiors of perfumed peace reflecting the glow from flickering green needles in hermetically-sealed stainless steel casings. This traffic moves under its own volition, and is its own and everything else's justification for being. The tarmac of the roads is burnished to a deep brilliant black by the lisping tyres. It is truly an artery of the world — an artery that passes through a concrete bowel in less time than it takes to fart.

This is the flourishing part.

In the decaying part discarded hulks of cotton mills are strewn along the embankments of rusting railway tracks. Worthwhile slum clearance schemes have gone full ahead (to make more room for the Concrete Bowel) and now acres of family streets are piles of dust-laden nostalgia.

The Town is no more violent than it used to be but now the violence is openly on the streets. The people have finally learned — after many years of painstaking and expensive teaching, not to mention daily media conditioning — that materialism should be placed before and above everything while material objects themselves are worth nothing. It is a beautiful system, self-perpetuating, mutually sustaining, leading slowly but surely to its ultimate pinnacle of perfection: a factory where they make and smash objects on the same conveyor-belt.

In this environment I felt at home, because inside my head I too have a making-smashing device that keeps me company as I walk through this desolate society of ours. This device makes and smashes thoughts, ideas, hopes, aspirations, emotions even before they're fully formed. They are aborted; stillborn.

It was on a Thursday that I decided to visit the Town.

Needless to say I detested myself for having insufficient will power to resist the ugly temptations that were luring me there. As usual most of the street lighting was off, having failed or been broken. Gangs of youths roamed about, clomping their heavy boots up and down the walkways and subways. I hurried on quickly to the Pub. I remember particularly that there was a nasty stinging wind blowing ice-cold from the moors, sweeping down the street, gusting muck and grit into your eyes. 'If this is the best they can do . . .' I remember thinking.

As I approached the door of the Pub my mind was in a turmoil of indecision. Was it right, because one felt superior to certain people, to use them as a means of sating one's perverse desires? (Not that this really bothered me.) And what if she penetrated my flimsy disguise and caught a glimpse — only a glimpse! — of the person that was supposed to be underneath? It was a chance I would have to take. Other questions too assailed me, but these could wait.

III

As I entered the Pub I had a strange feeling that I wouldn't be very welcome. However, as I have this feeling wherever I go it was not something to take me by surprise. Rather, I was prepared for it — or, *rather,* I prepared myself for it. She wasn't at the bar or behind the bar, so I seated myself in rather a dejected mood and waited to see what went on around me. After a while a girl entered whom I knew: she had told me in the past that her name was Shirl, and I had no reason to doubt this. With her was a tiny man, diminutive in fact, whose name I didn't catch, but who bit his fingernails. This was something that gave me great personal satisfaction. Almost immediately Shirl began to talk directly to me, ignoring the tiny man, which, if the truth were known, had the effect of unsettling me. I like to know where I am with people; I like to feel that everyone has a proper station in life. Now by rights she should have been engaging both of us in conversation equally — if not the tiny man more than me, seeing that he was her companion — yet her biased attentions hinted that their relationship was not as it appeared. This, as you will agree, can be most disturbing, especially to someone of such tender sensibilities as myself. At first the tiny man seemed oblivious of this discrepancy, sitting back quietly in his chair and now and then sipping his beer. Slowly I began to detect in him a certain impatience, annoyance even, and endeavoured to draw him into the conversation, occasionally dropping the odd remark which perhaps he might seize upon and thus insinuate himself into the discussion. Though whenever I did this Shirl instantly snatched at the phrase or question or whatever it was and once more directed her reply to me, all but turning her back on him. Indeed, he was an odd creature. Shirl herself was highly attractive, physically, and her attractiveness was enhanced by the unavoidable comparison between the two of them. As stated, he was tiny, and amazingly thin. His face was very pale, and in it his eyes gleamed like pieces of polished coal. Was it my imagination that he never blinked? He gave the impression of being innocuous, yet there was a hidden streak of restrained obscenity somewhere inside that chilled the blood. He was the type of man that fascinates women.

My nervousness was increasing by the minute: the last thing I wanted was a scene or an incident; I dread the thought of becoming conspicuous or of disturbing any living creature. That is why I have such high regard for maintaining one's proper station in life. It is important to know who and what and where you are at all times.

'Strange that we should have met just here,' said Shirl. 'I didn't know you came to this place.'

Glancing at her companion, I said, 'I don't intend staying very long. Do you know what times the trains are? Or the buses?'

'Oh, but you're not going,' said Shirl. She laughed. She wore glasses. 'We're staying all night, aren't we?' she said, half to the tiny man, but not expecting or waiting for a reply, went on, 'This place isn't at all like it used to be. Don't you think so?'

'I can't really remember,' I said. I was hoping they'd go, for I had someone else to see.

'It used to get very crowded,' the tiny man said, addressing his remark to me.

'Really?' I said. Did he expect me to be surprised? I decided to show surprise, nodding my head to confirm the truth of his statement and raising my eyebrows to their fullest extent. He had the most penetrating gaze I had ever encountered. There was a handkerchief in his breast pocket on which his initials were embroidered, but I couldn't make them out.

'Oh yes,' Shirl said. 'Very crowded.' Her lips were sensually thick; they seemed to invite certain disgusting physical sensations. Through the oval-shaped lenses of her spectacles her eyes were fixed on mine. I hoped the tiny man wouldn't notice this.

Shirl said, 'You didn't come to my flat after all.'

I was astounded. 'Your flat?' I said. 'I didn't say I would come to your flat. Did I say that? I don't remember. When did I say that?'

The tiny man had leaned forward in his chair, no doubt so as not to miss a word of our conversation. His hands, I noticed, were pale and thin, covered in fine black hair. His sudden interest disconcerted me considerably. Shirl was not at all put out by this.

'I wouldn't have thought you were the kind of person likely to forget such a thing,' Shirl said.

'I'm sure I am not,' I said. 'Though I honestly can't

remember ever promising such a thing.'

'Evidently you did promise,' said the tiny man, 'and then you forgot.'

'Yes, yes,' I agreed, attempting to smile. 'It seems I must have done. But it is strange all the same, for I don't believe I know where your flat is.'

'Oh but I gave you directions,' Shirl said earnestly. 'I gave you the name of the street and the number of the house —'

It entered my head that possibly she was mistaken, but as there was little evidence of this apart from my own absence of memory it seemed that I must agree with the statement that I had indeed, at some time in the past, been invited to her flat. The tiny man's insistence was also a factor in my acknowledging the truth of Shirl's undoubtedly sincere conviction.

'And I was all prepared for you,' Shirl said. (What did she mean?)

'Are you in the habit of disappointing people?' the tiny man asked. He was now leaning so far forward that his head was level with the table.

'No, no,' I was quick to reply. 'Quite the reverse, in fact. Had I known — had I *remembered* —'

'You'll remember next time,' Shirl said, smiling faintly and narrowing her eyes.

'Well,' I said, nodding to the tiny man, 'yes . . . I suppose next time I *will* remember. I shall make a — er — point of remembering. Shan't I?'

I wished that the tiny man would stop staring at me. His eyes were really quite peculiar. And I still wasn't sure in my own mind what short of relationship existed between them. Was I expected to accompany Shirl to her flat? Or had the invitation been made before she struck up an acquaintance with the tiny man? But no! — Shirl had quite distinctly repeated the invitation, hinting at a 'next time'. Then what function did the tiny man fulfil? Surely he couldn't be her brother. Perhaps a distant relative? At any rate I wanted them to go, immediately if possible, because I had come to the Pub for a specific purpose and their presence was obtruding on the plans I had carefully laid for the evening.

'I detest people who give offence,' the tiny man said suddenly. At this Shirl laughed. 'Don't you?'

I wasn't sure who had asked the question; not that it mattered, for of course I agreed wholeheartedly with what had been said.

'Don't *you?*'

'It's the most unpleasant of things,' I said. I was surprised to find that this statement — could one call it an accusation? — had nettled me. It had made sweat break out on my body. Were they suggesting that it was I who had given offence? Was that what they were getting at? If so, I should have liked to have known what led them to this conclusion, and what specifically I had said or done that had apparently been sufficient cause to give offence. As I say, I should not disturb a mouse if I could help it.

I said brusquely, 'I also detest those who make wrongful accusations. There are plenty of them about if one cares to look far enough.' I guessed that my severe tone would check them in their stride; it would certainly demonstrate that they couldn't get away with everything, even if they thought they could.

'We must be off,' said the tiny man, finishing his drink and standing up all at once. So they closed ranks and retreated at the first sign of battle! Secretly I exulted. Such arrogance deserves to be stepped on instantly, as one would destroy without hesitation an ugly crawling slimy thing crossing one's path.

'Well, be seeing you,' said Shirl, rising with what seemed to be a disquieting amount of hesitation. What else was she hinting at? Was she trying to lure me? Did she, in fact, want me to strike the tiny man?

Something surprised me at this moment. Now having

risen, Shirl, it appeared, only came up to the tiny man's shoulder. Not that she was tinier than he, but rather that he was taller than her. This amused me for a moment; then it upset me, because in point of fact the tiny man was quite tall – still extremely thin, but much taller than I had at first supposed. I am very small myself, with a deformity of some sort on my back, and I have a natural antagonism towards people who are tall and straight. Shirl was not very tall (taller than me, however), but round and plump, with pertinent breasts. I began to hate them both for their tallness.

'Are you staying?' Shirl said. She plucked the tall man's handkerchief out of his breast pocket to dab her lips and I saw the initials *GD* embroidered in green, set slanting across one corner.

The tall man repeated Shirl's question. His tiny black eyes were fixed viciously upon me. How I wished that one of the roaming gangs would set upon him as he walked along and kick him and hurt him. It would teach him a lesson. I could see the boots going in – one of them my boot – knocking the senses out of him. Sometimes I have wished evil on certain people and evil has befallen them, and how I wished evil on the tall man! If he thought he could intimidate me he had another think coming.

Looking towards the door I saw Val catch sight of me. I had sensed that she was here somewhere (I have a sensitivity about such things). With Shirl and the tall man gone I could concentrate all my powers on the reason I had come to this dreadful room in the first place. And why had I come here? Even now, thinking back, to recall the purpose of my visit nauseates me more than I can say. A devil, or a demon, had driven me to seek out the one person who so repulsed me that all my being quivered in disgust and loathing, yet who also generated within me the most intense kind of exitement. All my life I have had to contend with these two opposing forces; they have warred incessantly and torn my insides to shreds, destroying in the process the good, noble ideals to which my being aspires. Why must each person be at civil war with himself?

Be that as it may, Val and I had an understanding. We met infrequently, usually after dark, and always scurrying away at once to remote, innaccessible places where we were certain not to be disturbed. In truth this was not the entire reason. I could not — would not allow myself — to be seen in her company a moment longer than was absolutely necessary, and so no sooner would we meet than I hurried her away down a dark street or hired a taxi to take us miles from anywhere, up there on the wild swinging moors. Even in broad daylight one could walk all day and not see another human soul. In the summer (which this was not) the sun beat hotly on the coarse rasping grass and in the valleys were the rigid smokeless shapes of mill chimneys, embarrassed by the unaccustomed clear air.

The first thing to find was always a hollow, a small depression, some shallow private place warmed by the sun and immune to prying eyes. Then I would tell her — without any preamble and as crudely as I could — to get undressed. She would obey without question, slowly, to my commands, removing her garments one by one, following the instructions I rapped out to her precisely to the letter: if she did not she knew the consequences. It was always my policy to have her undress completely, but to remain covered with certain undergarments so that I could see what effect they had, contrasting their flimsy, transparent appearance with the fullness they were supporting and partially concealing. As always on these occasions I took along an empty camera, the purpose of which was to deceive myself into believing that the exercise was one of pure art and objectivity. Having told her to partly remove a garment as far as the knees I then made her open her legs as far as the restricting garment would permit, and all but inserting the camera lens into the apex of her limbs, clicked the shutter several times to signify that her diseased cunt was now a matter of photographic record.

During all of this she remained pallid and mute, bending herself to my will as so much dull animal bulk, heavy with boredom and empty with incomprehension.

A fine bodily thing about her was the size of her breasts. The sheer enormity of her breasts. They were perfect in that each breast was in itself larger than her face; the shape and line of them were less important than this one primary fact. A favourite vantage point was to be had from directly below: she standing with legs apart above me and thrusting out her breasts for me to catch the outlines of her nipples against the sky. In this position, too, it was useful to have her bend outward at the knees, thus opening up to my gaze every innermost detail of her vulva, prepuce and clitoris. Not to study this disgusting spectacle, but in order to make the strain on her limbs grow to intolerable limits, I issued strict orders that she was to remain rigidly in this position until otherwise instructed. The sun being hot on my face, I would rise up and wander away for a while, taking a casual stroll to look down into the town or towards the wet black strip of road shivering in the heat, occasionally glancing back from various viewing points to see how she looked and to what extent detail was visible. It sometimes amused me to wonder at the reactions of a stranger, should one appear suddenly over the moor, coming upon this girl in a state of extreme impropriety. However, no one ever did appear, unfortunately.

Odd funny little gimmicks would occur to me from time to time, such as taking with me a candle to be inserted into her, and setting it alight, leaning back contentedly in the sun to watch the slow, steady progress of the invisible flame towards her pubic hairs. These, by the way, were reddish and sparse, and in some ways this displeased me, for I rate a woman's voluptuousness pro rata to the amount of body hair. It amused me to wait until the last possible moment before removing the candle, to see in Val's complacent expression a twitch of emotion, a shudder of hurt. Oh, my mind was full of devious little tricks! Another consisted of having Val press her breasts into the ground: the grass was sharp, and with any luck would slice finely into one or other of the white breasts, nicking it keenly and drawing blood. To aid this I would straddle her shoulders, or kneel into the nape of her neck, enjoying the knowledge of what this additional pressure might be doing to her. In this position I would read a chapter of a book or a magazine article, only shifting my weight to bear down more firmly, pressing her into the ground. The moment of greatest anticipation, of course, was when I released her and allowed her to rise; her ugly flattened breasts re-formed into their hanging shape, the nipples now raw and angry, and innumerable criss-crossed lines and indentations were imprinted in the bulky smoothness. I would bid her stand in front of me, and to her blank face would laugh at the pitiful sight she presented, making remarks aloud to myself and the world in general about her pathetic gross body, its features and failings, the misproportion of it, and what a complete and utter disaster she was as a so-called human being.

These experiences built up to a climax, as is normally the case; up to this point I had been most careful not to reveal any part of my own body. Now I told her to disrobe me, with the proviso that she cleansed each portion with her tongue as it was opened to the light. This procedure took some considerable time, leading gradually to the action of her kneeling between my legs and licking my private parts. Whether or not she appreciated the privilege of being allowed to perform this, I never dained to inquire, or indeed discovered. All this while I subjected her to constant abuse, a stream of patient, well-spaced vilification relating to the coarseness of her nature and the ridiculousness of a situation in which she was allowed even to approach me. But of course it was lost on her; I had long ago ceased to believe that contact between us was feasible.

With Val kneeling and in an attitude of prayer before me, and I standing, would jerk forward my abdomen and strike repeatedly at her pale, broad face with the blunt, heavy end of my cock. Eventually it would emit premature semen, thick globular strings of stuff which stuck in shiny patches to her brow and cheeks. Only when I experienced the approaching sensation of release and exorcism in my loins would I permit her to actually take the cock in her mouth and savour its full largeness and strength. At these moments I sought to empty myself into her, urging the pumping action with all the exhortations I could summon, striving to achieve the optimum disposal of stuff through the stiffened muscle and into the gaping orifice available for the purpose. Not a drop must be wasted. And Val, to her credit, gulped at it gratefully. There were times, I will admit, when I deliberately withdrew so that some of it spilled onto her chin, making it shiny-wet, splashing down to spatter her white swaying breasts. This was of the utmost necessity, because only in this way could I despoil her to the point where she became sub-human, or, to be more exact, non-human. As you will have gathered she was less than real to me: devoid of personality, identity, separate existence even. Therefore to enable her to fulfil a meaningful role (in other words, to become real) it was essential that Val be made to occupy a position of the most base and ignoble kind. She was to be human and yet non-human, existing and yet non-existent.

On other, still sunny days I would have her lie spread-eagled, naked, while I walked barefoot over her body. My only cause for complaint was that she rarely, if ever, complained. Standing on her open thighs, with my cock erect, I would savour the feeling of warm unstable fleshiness beneath my feet; then moving along would place my two feet on her two breasts, maintaining this position until either I grew tired of it or Val was having difficulty in drawing sufficient breath to replenish her lungs. Interestingly enough, standing thus, her face was masked by my cock, which in its aroused state interfered with my line of vision. It had the effect of considerably improving her looks. And when her chest had begun to heave with the effort of supporting me I would at once squat directly above her and lay my complete assemblage on her face. Her hot, rapid breathing was a pleasing stimulation, leading quickly to an abrupt, uncontrolled discharge which was directed onto various aspects of her features. Once, quite inadvertantly, it spat in her eye, causing some discomfort, but as this was hardly my fault I did not see how I could be held responsible, nor did I feel in the least contrite. I could hardly be blamed if another person insisted on keeping his or her eyes open under such circumstances.

It was in this very position too — I should mention — that most frequently the mystical revelation came upon me; it was here that I came nearest to perceiving the precise reality of the secret underlife to which I have referred. In this situation I saw with utmost clarity the planet we inhabit as separate from the space which surrounds it: the skyline itself was the finite limit, and beyond was an endless void into whose depths one could plummet at any moment: I felt in acute physical danger of falling from the surface of the planet, arms and legs splayed outwards with centrifugal brute force, tumbling headlong into the furthest, deepest reaches of blackness and infinity. At the same time I knew beyond doubt that Val had been born with no other purpose than to lie thus beneath me. She was of the planet, created out of it, and the strands of life which ran through the rocks, the earth, the air, also connected her to them and me to her. Time, space and human existence were all one and the same, indivisible, the one entity.

She came across to me in her lumpy sweater, scratched shoes shuffling in the debris, the hair on her head sticking out at all sorts of ridiculous angles. There were holes in her tights.

'Hello, stranger,' Val said, her eyes bulging through her thick glasses. No doubt she was without undergarments, for there, clearly to be seen, were the outlined protruberances of her nipples.

'You dirty fucking whore,' I said to her, unfailingly, as ever, disgusted.

IV

Committing to paper the tangled world in which we live is not the easiest of tasks — nor the most rewarding, I might add. But as we slowly progress, hacking our way through the undergrowth, I hope eventually a glimmer of light will appear, that you will begin to comprehend the alternative universe of which I speak.

In the office I maintained in the big black building it was my custom to remain behind after the other staff had gone home, and, sitting in the hushed lamplight, contemplate the mess my life had become. Not for a million pounds would I have changed places with any other living soul, for although my life was a ridiculous sham, nevertheless it was the most precious life there had ever been. Besides, self-pity is one of the few luxuries I permit myself. If one cannot feel slighted by the world what is the good of living?

On the desk in front of me were scattered the photographs taken by Dmitri Zeilnski at the paper mill: over four hundred in 35mm colour transparency form. They were in strips, each strip enclosed in a misted paper sheath. I gazed at the heap, wondering what on earth I should do with them. Fortunately, he had now departed abroad for a while, leaving me in peace, so there was time to think of something.

The ringing of the phone interrupted my morose thoughts, and picking up the instrument I prepared for the worst. To my surprise it was not who I had expected: it was Marl. Quite a lengthy period had elapsed since I had last spoken to her. She told me that she had managed, finally, to get a job.

'I don't suppose it is a very interesting job,' I said. Already, and rather to my annoyance, my breath was quivering in my throat.

'I demonstrate appliances,' Marl said. 'I go round from house to house demonstrating appliances. The idea is that I give a free demonstration and then the person is meant to buy the appliance. They are very expensive and there is a huge profit.'

She said this lightly, glibly, as though it were a clever thing to say. No doubt she was trying to impress me. I was sick of her type, and of her money-grubbing.

'Are you at home?' I asked gently.

She confirmed that she was.

'Is your husband there with you?'

Marl said that she was alone.

'Are you completely alone?'

'Yes,' Marl said, her voice adopting a puzzled tone, yet obviously intrigued at the same time.

'Have you sold any appliances today?' I inquired, changing the subject abruptly. I cannot stand it when people, women especially, anticipate me. Or rather, *think* they are anticipating me. It is insulting. It is degrading.

'Do you know, I heard a rumour about you the other day,' I said. I had heard no such rumour but it amused me to have her think I had.

'A rumour about me?' Marl said. 'What was this rumour? Are you pulling my leg?'

'What have you been doing to cause rumours?' I asked her. This was calculated to bring forth a confession or a denial.

'What was the rumour about?' She paused, and her voice became coquettish. 'It wasn't a bad rumour, I hope?'

'Do you?' I said, playing the game with her. The shallowness and insensibility of women never fail to astound me. They are so preoccupied with meaningless physical vanities that it is a struggle to conduct even a superficial conversation with them. Their tiny minds encompass the world, with the result that the world becomes tiny too. I should imagine there are women to whom this does not apply, but in my experience they are usually as ugly as sin, defeating the whole purpose of being women.

'Listen,' I said to her. 'This selling of appliances is just a way to make money, isn't it?'

'Could be,' said Marl. 'Amongst other things.'

The stupidity of this reply made me squirm in my seat. For her to suppose that such infantile innuendo could possibly hope to interest or impress me demonstrated (if such demonstrations were necessary) to what lowly levels her mind aspired. It entered my head to dismiss her at once, to have done with her − but no; one of my besetting 'sins' is that I am never rude to anyone, least of all women. I then said something which made her laugh:

'Tell me what you are wearing at this moment.'

'Can you see me in your mind's eye?'

'I know what you look like, if that's what you mean.'

It seemed to me, suddenly, that the office had become unaccountably warm. The receiver was moist in my hand. A torpid sluggishness was creeping from my stomach into my chest. This was the presentiment of a mystical experience.

'I wish I could understand you,' Marl said, 'but I can't.'

'Do you think women understand anything?' I said, attempting, successfully I hoped, to hide the contemptuous tone in my voice. To hell with her, I thought, having the arrogance to think that she had power over me. I had taught such women their manners before now.

'Shall I tell you what I am wearing?' Marl said, trying to subdue the eagerness in her voice.

'Yes, tell me,' I said shortly.

'Well . . . ' Marl began, 'I have on a dress — '

'What colour?'

'Blue. I am wearing a blue dress. It has a V-neck with white frilly lace along it. It is quite short; quite short.'

'Is it tight or loose?' I asked.

'Fairly tight. The material is thin and silky. Reasonably close-fitting, as I say.'

Of its own accord my hand had moved to rest on my thigh. The feeling of discomfort was growing. Why was the air so oppressive?

'Apart from that I am wearing flesh-coloured tights, seamless, with an elasticated band round the waist. Also, to aid support, I have on a pretty micro-mesh bra decorated with little flowers — '

'Which is adequate for its purpose?' I said.

'Generally speaking, yes.'

Who was that I could hear breathing into the mouthpiece?

'And underneath the tights I have on briefs of the semi-transparent kind, in a shade of green. That's about it.'

'You are alone, you told me.'

'Oh yes, alone.'

It stuck me as incredible, in this day and age, that such creatures should exist. Was there no shame left in the world? The age-old battle to overcome wickedness had been lost. We had not progressed one inch, not succeeded in the slightest degree. All the great preachers and prophets were of no more consequence than the whining of a gnat. Not for the first time did it strike me that not living in this world could be actually condoned and sanctioned. Modern people were vain empty vessels with the odds weighing heavily against them. It was I who aspired to be beyond evil, who sought 'the good and the beautiful', but a decisive percentage of me had always, and would forever, deny the possibility of ever achieving it.

'Are you still there?' Marl said

'Yes,' said I. 'With my cock full in my hand.'

She shuddered lightly. 'I am alone,' Marl said.

'I am alone, with my cock, my prick, my tool, full in my hand. It is encased in my fingers, its hot bigness standing up from my loins.'

'Tell me what I should do.'

'Do you feel the magic and power of it?' I had first of all to ask her. 'Do you believe in its magic and power?'

'Please tell me what I am to do,' Marl said.

'Do you believe in its magic?' I insisted on repeating. 'You must believe in its magic and its power.'

'Yes,' said Marl in a dull, low-pitched, mesmerised voice.

'The rod is magical; in its stiff hugeness is the secret, the mystery for which you have been searching.'

'Please, please,' said Marl. 'Instruct me.'

The office in which I sat was heavy with stillness. Behind the glass the dark sky moved restlessly. A million people inhabited the streets, seeking neat and tidy destinations. The city was in chaos: behind the impregnable buildings anarchy reigned. All was well, providing the traffic lights continued to function.

'Unfasten the dress you are wearing and remove it,' I said. The cock was right in front of me. 'Remove the dress from your body and discard it. Have you done this?'

'Yes,' said Marl in a whisper.

'Now put your right hand between your legs and press your fingers into the softest place.'

'I am doing it.'

'As you are doing it think of the thing I hold in my hand; it rises directly out of me, enclosed in my hand, erect with life. And as you think of it press your fingers rhythmically

into the place between your legs. You must now slide
forward on the chair and open your legs so as to permit
improved access for your fingers.'

'I feel it,' Marl said.

'Your legs are open,' I said.

'They are open.'

'Next you must consider it necessary to remove the
garments that are impeding the progress of your fingers.
Peel away the outer garment, sliding it down from your
thighs, over your knees, along your lower legs, disposing of
it completely.'

'Are you holding it now?' Marl said.

'Yes.'

'Is it still big?'

'Yes.'

'And very hard?'

'Exceedingly hard.'

I then said, 'Describe to me what you are wearing and
the position you are in.'

After only a momentary hesitation Marl said, 'I am
wearing my bra, micro-mesh with little flowers, and my
briefs. My legs are long, white, and open wide.'

'Take off your briefs,' I said. She did so. 'With the tips
of your fingers caress the inner sides of your thighs,
working closer and closer to the softest place – '

'Oh is it still big?' said Marl.

'Yes,' I said. 'Big and impatient. Starting to bubble.'

'My fingers are now inside.'

'It is moist, wet – '

' – Slippery.'

'Your cunt is beautiful open wide wetness,' I said. 'Rub
your fingers along it to generate the wetness. The hairs
surrounding it are smooth and slick with juice.'

'Let me remove my bra.'

'Not yet.'

'Let me.'

'First I must know if your breasts are swollen. They long to be held. Your nipples are hard, are they not? Your two breasts are confined tightly, swelling with the longing to be caressed with warm open hands.'

My cock was beginning to spit.

'They have become bigger,' said Marl. 'My nipples are stiff, protruding through the nylon mesh; their shapes are clearly to be seen. Tell me if your cock is still strong. Is it big in your hand? Describe your cock to me.'

'The skin is drawn tightly about it, infused with the core of magical power, and the rounded end has become wet. The whole length of it exceeds the width of my closed hand.'

'What is there at the base?' Marl asked.

'At the base are thick black hairs, out of which the cock rises with absolute rectitude, curving hard.'

'You do have thick hairs,' Marl said. 'I like to know that your hairs are thick and black. You must tell me to take off my bra.'

'Do you wish to be naked?'

'I want to free my breasts and lie with open legs, dreaming of your stiff cock.'

'Very well, take off your bra.' I said.

My cock was jerking in my hand.

'Enclose your breasts in your hands and squeeze them powerfully. Now touch the erect nipples with the tips of your fingers – '

'Is your cock really big at this moment?'

'Yes, yes; but now it is starting to come. The opaque sperm is pulsing from the broad, blunt end.'

'*Oh,*' Marl said.

'Shall I describe it to you?'

'Yes, describe it to me.'

'What is it I should describe?'

'Describe your cock to me and what is happening to it. You must say that it is big and hard, magical with power, and the sperm is starting to come from it.'

'A good deal of sperm is now being emitted, hot sperm running down my cock. Tell me where my cock should be at this moment and it will doubtless erupt with sperm. Where should it be?'

'Between my legs,' said Marl. 'My legs are open to receive it, slippery with wetness.'

'But where exactly should it be?' I asked.

'Inside me, large inside me.'

'Precisely where?'

'Inside my cunt.'

'Yes?'

'The full length of it up inside my cunt. I should be able to feel it thrusting upwards inside me. Is that what you want me to say? Is this making all the sperm come?'

'It is coming fast now,' I said.

'Coming from the end and running down your cock?'

'Sperm pumping out, lots of it.'

'Hot thick sperm?'

'Thick and slimy. Of course,' I said, 'the sperm should not be running to waste, it should be shooting up inside you with my cock tight in your cunt.'

'I am coming,' Marl said. She was moaning. 'I am coming. Oh God I am coming. Oh fucking shitting cunting Christ I am coming. I am coming . . . '

I replaced the receiver and put my wet cock away. The one annoying thing, to me, is the nonsense talked about sex. The fuss made about it is out of all proportion to its importance. When observed in the cold light of day it is absurd to suppose that the act has any meaningful relevance.

V

The problem remained: what to do with the colour transparencies? By this time Dmitri Zeilnski would be far across the sea, either with or without his Italian friend. The eeriness of the Italian still plagued me — what was one supposed to make of him? It always disturbs me when people do not fit into the pattern of things.

For the umpteenth time I looked through the transparencies; each separate batch dealt with a particular facet of the papermaking process. It was all there, ostensibly, in glowing Kodacolor, and yet it wasn't. Dmitri had caught perfectly the purpose of the plant but not its reason for being there. For example, the giant Millspaugh was shown churning out reel after reel of paper, turning it from wet sludgy 'stuff' into creamy white, neatly trimmed lengths of 'stock'. But why hadn't he photographed those rooms and galleries behind and beneath the machine wherein could be found the real life and beginnings of power that gave the plant its volition? He should have known that surface things are false. One had to climb (as I had done!) over pipes and ducting, squeeze through shattered walls and squirm along passageways thick with dust to discover the living, moving guts of the place. In this shot, for instance —

I stared hard at it and my heart started to pound. It showed a room full of slapping pulleys. The rows of leather belts were connected to spindles on the ceiling, and from these other leather belts disappeared at speed through rectangular holes set high in the walls. Why hadn't I seen this room? Had Dmitri, by some remote chance, stumbled on a hidden section of the plant of whose existence I was ignorant? Feverishly I scattered the heap of transparencies, searching for the next shot in the sequence. There it was. In through holes came the leather belts, blurred with motion, winding onto hubbed wheels whose spokes were invisible due to their rotary movement. Now this was a revelation! How on earth had Dmitri managed to trace the evolution of force from its primeval source? I studied anxiously each of the transparencies in turn. Here was one showing the dust-laden galleries, and here another with a terrifying configuration of tubes and pipework, and yet another showing a figure kneeling in front of a wall, and an entire sequence devoted to a precise and detailed study of — not the foreground incidentals — but the intangible vortices of abstract inertia which spun the very planet beneath our feet.

The thought occurred to me that perhaps the planet itself was riddled with such subterranean galleries, shafts and passageways, connecting this chamber to that, one to the other, each of them filled with tubes, ducting and pipework, slapping pulleys and humming spindles. It would explain much, if not everything. One of the most remarkable shots depicted the internal workings of something — difficult to say what exactly, except that with the clever use of light filters he had succeeded in capturing a glimpse of wetness surrounding a single central orifice. Beyond was a hint of moorland and a blue sky deep as space itself. Remarkable!

In the heavily-shadowed office I was plunged into a quandry. Dmitri had demonstrated the practicablity of recording those things which I believed to be instrinsically formless: without shape, substance or physical presence. Then why wasn't I capable of achieving the same? Was I so superficial and talentless than I could not perceive the essential reality as Dmitri had done? The question angered me, and, more than that, weighed like an insupportable burden on my spirits. I was dragged down absolutely to rock-bottom. As far as I was concerned Dmitri was my inferior; could it be that during our entire relationship I had misinterpreted his personality? Was it conceivable that this snapshotter was more *intelligent* than I? I tell you, gentlemen, the notion fairly shook me.

In such moments of despair I have a phrase, or saying, which I repeat over and over to myself, as an incantation. Its exact form I forget, but the gist of it is: 'Confident people are made hollow by their own confidence,' followed by 'The essence of my superiority over others lies in my reserved, sensitive nature.' Usually this does the trick. However, on this occasion, I must confess, the words lacked conviction, and also the comfort which I had come to expect from them.

Outside the bright circle of lamplight the office was now in total darkness. Night had dropped swiftly onto the city, the people gone home, the streets deserted. The bulks of large buildings leaned over the street lights, in shadow and in mystery. Eventually the pubs would empty. I was saddened to think of myself being alone, but that was my permanent condition. A fly would have more respect for itself.

Somebody was banging about in the corridor. Instantly I became furious and, rushing to the door, flung it open. A man of sallow complexion (a foreigner, no doubt) was mopping the floor, dragging a clattering bucket after him. He caught sight of me and nodded, or was about to nod, when I shouted hoarsely, 'Is it necessary to disturb people with your racket?'

The man paused, the mop in his hands. 'I'm sorry, sir.' He shrugged in a half-hearted, apologetic sort of way. 'I didn't know anyone was here.'

'Didn't you see the light?' I was still furious.

'The lamplight doesn't shine into the corridor.'

I checked my reply, for it was true that from the corridor the office appeared to be closed and dark. Nevertheless, the fact remained that I had been disturbed. 'Perhaps next time you will make sure before you make enough noise to wake the dead.'

The man wore a cleaner's brown smock. The cuffs were ragged and the hem had come undone, hanging down. The man's complexion was further darkened by a heavy growth of stubble. His face wore almost a smile, and his shadowed eyes were piercingly keen.

'I can only repeat that I'm sorry, sir,' the cleaner said. He leaned on his mop. 'You must admit that it's very late to be working.'

'The kind of work I do,' I responded coldly, 'requires to be done very late in the evening.'

The cleaner came near to me, holding his mop. 'The same can be said for me,' he replied. Then, 'Does your work also require you to go on long journeys?'

'What if it does?'

The cleaner lowered his eyes and smiled. His hands were clasped round the mop handle. 'I've seen you in the mornings, sir, very early, on a number of occasions.' He added, almost apologetically, 'I'm in the building myself before five.'

'Do you want my sympathy?' I said, becoming irritated with the fellow. 'Is that why you disturb me? Is that why you question me? Why don't you go about your business?'

'We have all of us a crust to earn,' the cleaner said enigmatically.

I was growing more and more vexed with him. 'Look here, if it was your intention to make a nuisance of yourself, you have succeeded. First you disturb me and then go on to ask questions about my personal life. It so happens that I *do* go on a number of long journeys, to London, Reading, Immingham and various other places. Does that satisfy your curiosity?'

Once again the cleaner seemed to smile, a half-hidden smile that he attempted to conceal. 'I'm sorry if I have in any way distressed you,' he said.

'You haven't distressed me in the slightest,' I corrected him. 'It would take far more than your meaningless questions to distress me. Now if you will excuse me – '

Without waiting for his reply I re-entered the office and closed the door. The trouble with modern life is that there is no privacy.

Beneath the bright lamp lay the heaped transparencies,

the light catching their acetate surfaces through the frosted packets. What was one to make of them? There was even a shot — indeed several shots — of a crumbling boarding house, a dank, narrow passageway, and a congealing back room. Now in what situation or circumstance had Dmitri found himself which enabled him to photograph such scenes? They constituted a blatant intrusion of private reminiscences. And here: here was another, showing, of all things, the very office in which I sat! This really was too much.

The bucket clattered distantly down the corridor and there came the sound of running water. I secretly hoped that the cleaner had upset filthy water all over his handiwork; it would teach him to respect silence more. It was quite clear (to me, at least) that he hadn't paid the slightest attention to my admonishment. So much for the modern habit of displacing service with incivility, manners with the morals of a dog, and restraint with a lackadaisical disregard for fellow humanity. It would serve him right if his bucket developed a hole.

Presently I calmed down. I reasoned to myself that it was futile to become annoyed over things one did not understand. The world was a mysterious, magical place with dark forces moving stealthily along its lower strata, and who was I to doubt the logic of this or to seek to interpret and explain it? Besides, I had enough on my plate. The worry of what to do with the colour transparencies was reaching intolerable proportions. Additionally I was at a loss as to how Dmitri had managed to accumulate the material in front of me in the first place. Certainly he had covered the paper mill assignment with exceptional thoroughness, right down to such details as the room of slapping pulleys, the dust-laden galleries, and the myriad tubes, ducting and pipework. And here was a surprise if ever there was one: an out-of-focus shot in the wrong colour register of the Italian sipping beer from a lipstick-stained glass. The exposure was so bad and the colour so muddy that the man might have been mistaken for almost anybody, Shirl's boyfriend, or even the cleaner down the corridor. It was plainly ridiculous on Dmitri's part to expect me to make anything at all of such an ambiguous effort.

Seating myself at the desk — but no; suddenly seizing my coat I ran out of the building and went directly to a bar to which I was not altogether a stranger. We mortals find solace at times like these in the company of others. This was a dilapidated place. The attempt had been made to make it a fashionable drinking spot: the usual shabby plastic seat coverings and masked fluorescent lighting, the cheap chairs and scratched formica tables; there was an air of desperate second-rate unease that gave one grubby hands even to enter the fanciful door and order a drink. I sat in a dark corner, a solitary figure, shunning the crowd making believe it was having a good time. The girls were cheap here. They carried their bra-less bodies like premium offers. Had I not been so repelled by them I could have taught them a lesson.

As the evening grew late I consumed a considerable amount of liquor and before long my head was buzzing with noise and my face felt rubbery. In the darkened booths teenage lovers sat crushed in pairs, their hands in each other's laps. The table-tops swam with beer. In and out of the crowd ran the uncouth waiters, tall, slender, with stained white jackets. So befuddled was I that I didn't notice when a young person sat down opposite me, and it was only after a certain time had elapsed that I became aware of his persistent gaze. His brown eyes stared at me out of a blank face; from the threadbare sleeves of his overcoat emerged two thin white wrists from which hands sprouted like ungainly red cabbages. Plainly he wished to converse with me. He licked his raw lips and began:

'It was necessary for me to come to Manchester this evening.'

Not knowing how I should react to this I remained silent.

'I came on the bus,' the young man continued. 'It would have been easier in a car but I came on the bus.'

There was something in his manner that was rather disquieting. My head sang with alcohol. The bar was well-known for half-wits, simpletons, liars, cheats and other assorted riff-raff: was this young person to be included amongst them?

'Why was it necessary to come?' I enquired.

'To see Kim Novak.'

Unaccountably I found myself unable to respond to this statement. The young man didn't flicker. We sat looking at one another, and at length it was I who was forced to lower my eyes. A sort of feverishness, a helpless frenzy, gripped my brain, and the heat of the room became suddenly stifling. I ventured to ask him, 'Is she in Manchester?'

'Oh yes,' he replied confidently.

'Where?'

'At the Studios.'

'Which studios?'

'Behind the Stores.'

At this we lapsed into silence. It occured to me that the young man was an odd character. He had about him an unhealthy appearance, and yet why he had sought out *me,* of all people, to confide his desires and aspirations to was a facet of our relationship I found puzzling. Why, also, should he want to see Kim Novak? What possible reason could he have? Were they acquainted, I wondered?

'Why do you want to see Kim Novak?' I found myself asking. If the truth were known it annoyed me to think that this weedy specimen of a creature should consider himself a superior personage. Physically he was degenerate, wearing shoddy clothes and old shoes. His hair stuck out of his head. Whatever Kim Novak might see in him wasn't apparent to me.

'To talk to her,' the young man said without expression. 'Just to talk to her.'

'And she's at the Studios.'

'Behind the Stores.'

'Is she expecting you?'

The young man stared at me. 'Do you want to come with me?'

That was a thought.

'You could show me where it is,' the young man said.

I didn't like the sound of this. Why should he suppose that I knew the whereabouts of the Studios? I didn't, as it happened; and if he had travelled all the way to Manchester without knowing their precise location it didn't seem to me that he was the kind of person one could put one's faith in. Altogether a peculiar fellow. The reputation the bar had acquired for harbouring such species was not undeserved — or so it seemed in my humble opinion.

I beckoned to the waiter and ordered more to drink. Even at that moment I realised that this was so foolish as to not bear examination, but I am driven to push my life to extremes when a victim of my own depressive states. Due to my acute sensitivity I find it impossible to live in permanent consciousness of what I am and the actions I envisage. (Naturally I never *do* anything; it is the pure thought of the possibilities of those actions that I am anxious to obliterate.)

At any rate we drank together and in no time at all my head was spinning. I clutched at the table to prevent myself from falling. I perceived that the young man was somewhat disgusted by my conduct.

'Why do you behave in such a fashion?' he asked me, his white unremarkable face stiffening. 'Do you suppose that it amuses people to see you like this?'

'Do you think I care for the opinions of others?' I returned sharply. My speech was becoming slurred. 'I detest charlatans, fools, and the empty fripperies of life.

Do you think,' I said, sweeping my arm over the crowded tables and at the room in general, 'that any of this impresses me? Do you think I am envious of such goings-on? Ha!' I exclaimed, my sleeve dipping in the beer, 'I would rather retire now, this instant, to my little dark hole than stay and witness all this meaninglessness.'

To this outburst the young man said nothing, apparently stunned into silence. I say 'apparently' because there was some difficulty in detecting any actual change in his demeanour; his passivity under all circumstances remained intact and under strict control.

'What do these people know of life?' I demanded, continuing my tirade. Accidentally I knocked over some bottles with my elbow, sending them tumbling unheeded to the floor. 'They seek after pleasure as though life had nothing more to offer. They are vain, foolish, hedonistic dunderheads who cannot distinguish between good and bad because such words have no meaning for them. Whereas I – I – '

Speech temporarily failed me, and in desperation I took hold of the glass in front of me and drained its contents in a single draught. The young man had begun to mutter through clenched lips, but such was the pandemonium in the hot, low room that he might have been uttering gibberish for all the sense I could get out of it. I could not decide whether he was agreeing with me or pursuing some abstracted line of thought of his own choosing, therefore I pressed on with increased determination and vigour:

'The second point I should like to make concerns the nature of the good and bad previously referred to – how are we to distinguish the reality, the essence, of these qualities if we do not experience them? These people here – ' again I swept out my arm ' – have no comprehension of "the good and the beautiful" because, *precisely* because, they are amoral creatures living their lives without purpose or motivation. Indeed, their lives are lived in the full glare of the incomprehensible, and not comprehending this they are mindless innocents to whom the dark inner core of truth is forever hidden.' My heart was beating painfully inside me. I was giddy with alcohol and semi-exhaustion, yet the blood was racing through my arteries with the exhilaration of my own rhetoric. 'Do you not see — do you *now* see — why it is imperative for us to experience all things? Why we must seek out the filth and the squalor, wallow in the dregs of life, so that our sensibilities are awakened and we become creatures of choice instead of unthinking appetite?'

The young man had stopped muttering. His brown eyes were fixed unblinkingly upon me.

'Can you direct me to the Studios?' he mouthed through pale lips. The condition of his face was apathetic.

I went on, 'In speaking of life I mean, of course, "the self". For life is nothing until we perceive it. During my various searches and nightdrives I have uncovered much that would perhaps have been better left covered — but as a man do I not have an obligation, a duty almost, to establish that which is true and meaningful, at least by my own definition of those terms?

'Take, if you will, those men of the twentieth century to whom order was the state to which we should aspire. Could they not see that in this universe two and two make three? Possibly five; perhaps even nine?'

'Two and two is a simple sum,' the young man said.

'Yes of course it is,' I agreed, 'for those who have eyes to see. But you misinterpret my point —'

'Then where are the Stores?' asked the young man with a heavy finality.

I had no idea what the idiot was babbling about. I had never heard of 'the Stores' in all my life. Did he expect me to go out into the prowling streets of Manchester, with all its inherent dangers, to help him find a place whose existence I doubted? What did he take me for? No sensible person would be seen dead off the main roads at this time of night.

'If you do not go soon you will never find them,' I found myself saying. Since he would not listen to me I would take no further interest in him. I do not suffer fools gladly.

The bar was even more crowded than before. (It might have been less crowded but in fact it was not.) The more crowded bar was filled with people to whom death meant nothing. Neither, in my opinion, were they worth saving. Anger and bitterness welled up inside be because they wore smart, expensive clothes, while mine were stained and tattered. Yet I knew that they could not hope to keep up the facade for long: once the perspiration broke through the crust of cleanliness they would revert back to the stinking human condition from which none of us can escape. I had never left it, nor wanted to leave it, because to do so was merely covering a cess-pit with a bed of roses. The humour of their predicament lay in the fact that they were apeing an electronic image behind which did not exist a basis of reality. They did not know that many hours of preparation were needed to project a figment of mass consciousness; and that by living up to a myth they were perpetuating their own unreality. Just as an impressive granite building, gleaming like a white shock in the sun, has underneath its foundations a labyrinth of sewers, so the one inescapable truth about their stainless steel lives was that, sooner or later, at one time or another, they were obliged to defecate.

Watching them now I was torn by the conflicting passions of amused hatred, rabid scorn, pity, and self-annihilating envy. Yes, I must confess it — envy. But what was there to be envious about? My one self was equal to any ten of them, and as I so despised their mean, empty lives it was all the more surprising that I should wish to emulate their kind of crude, superficial existence. So this is contact with people, I remember thinking to myself. I have ventured out of my little dark hole for this. Good God, I was worse (being wise) than they were!

Finally, being tired of my obsessive thoughts, and having drunk myself into a near stupor, I fastened my coat and went out into the night. It was black, black, and ice-cold. I walked along under the clattering stars, befuddled to the point of exhaustion. The planet spun beneath my feet. How many more nights like this before death came? I had lived vicariously through all the ages of mankind, arriving at this, the ultimate point in time, when there was nothing in the world left to experience.

VI

The days leading up to the central event around which this narrative revolves are vague in my memory, as are the exact reasons that brought about this trauma of alienation. The moment itself, however, and the subsequent happenings, are etched into my brain cells like acid into copper.

One of the primary sensory recollections is of a large blood-red sun hanging sullenly in front of my eyes, a fiery though perfectly tranquil hole in the sky. It was about six o'clock in the evening and I had just eaten a meal that had stuck fast in my gullet. The sky was clear, almost white, and the petrol fumes were tumbling sluggishly along the gutters. Somewhere, not many miles away, trees would be sending rubber shadows across oily roads.

I had it in mind to get drunk. Driving through the disconcerting sunshine my thoughts were aimless and sad. It didn't seem feasible that the breath I was at that moment expelling wouldn't be my last. Not that this perturbed me, for I knew myself to be immortal.

Stopping at a certain pub I drank a double brandy

straight down. The landlord regarded me suspiciously, detecting a tensile strain in me. He thought my face would splinter into fragments, the glass would crack in my hand, and the air would be rent in two.

Later that same evening I found myself in a strange predicament. The sun was as yet in the sky, illuminating an apartment house at which I hoped to find accommodation for the night. Having stocked up with the minimal provisions I entered the run-down building via the front door, only to find that I was in the wrong place. By some odd mischance I had stumbled into a scene from somebody else's life.

The room in which I now stood was perfectly bleak, its solitary window overlooking some shrubbery and a gravel path. Scattered about the room were items of furniture, and in an alcove behind a sagging curtain stood a filthy gas stove, spent matches embedded in its greasy surface. It struck an echo deep within my consciousness. I wondered who lived, or had lived, in the room. Could it have been me? Was this possibly the little dark hole of which I was so fond of speaking?

The floor was of particular interest: pieces of broken linoleum, green with mildew, were tastefully arranged at discreet intervals so as to convey the impression of artless congeniality. The upright bed, hinged for lowering into position, revealed its springs. There were mice-droppings in the corner. The room was so engagingly familiar that I became quite enchanted with it. For a moment I thought that it might be a film set, but as this wasn't a film the possibility seemed rather remote. Could it have been a visual reverberation from a remote past; or some other life that had slipped into a crevice of the unconscious? A mislaid cassette, perhaps? The idea had potential.

Presently I departed from the room, and in the short passageway leading to the front door happened to glance into another room where a girl was sitting comfortably by the fire. The look of her was vaguely familiar, yet I was certain I had never set eyes on her before. I knew that she would turn towards me and smile, which she did, and I knew also that I would stand and stare, wishing to project myself into the warmth and comfort of her room, a bow-windowed front room through whose lacy curtains the sun was eternally rising. Thus for a single long moment of time we gazed at one another; whether or not she too was aware that we had met in dreams I could not discern, but at any rate it was evident that she was not what I had hitherto supposed her to be, a figment of my imagination.

There is a theory that reality as we perceive it in every-day life is but the tip of the iceberg. For myself (and I can only speak for myself) I do not exist in the ordinary world but inhabit a spacetime zone in which the universe is waiting to be created. I am the pure thought of a being which might one day exist. Alternatively, the entire universe is inside my head. You do not exist except inside my head; we inhabit each other's consciousnesses, phantoms flitting about in nightmares, creatures of other people's imaginations.

Of course I had then to get into the car and locate a pub in the middle of a wilderness. It reminded me of a black dance-hall in that it too emitted smoke, heat and light from a dense, packed interior. This throwback of memory was of hot black bodies squashed together, sweat lodging in the moist creases of faded palms. Violence was there in a measured amount. Having ordered a drink I sat down on the antiquated leather and contemplated the oddness of a situation in which I was living out the fantasies of a fictional character. Were it not so ludicrous I could have perhaps persuaded myself that *I* was the fictional character, a pawn in the hands of an Almighty Author who even at this moment was chuckling quietly to Himself at the illogicality of the position in which He had placed me. The idea, having occured, quite intrigued me. It meant that my thoughts, actions, emotions and experiences were not my own — but His. I was responsible for nothing (as I had no choice in the matter), and anything that happened to me was the arbitrary whim of a Being of whose existence I was ignorant.

I went to the bar for another drink and almost got into an argument with a man standing there. We glowered momentarily at one another but such was the lethargy of the age that neither one of us could summon up an insult. Outside, the heaps of rubble circled endlessly, obvious symbols of decadence and decay. In nearby Oxford Street they were serving late-night Chinese meals.

It was now night, and cold. The littered roads were deserted. Passing beneath a concrete archway, the remnant of a once-imagined nightmare, I began to reflect on the tameness of my existence. There was, literally, nothing that interested me any more. The world was dead; dull and vapid. What had once seemed vital to me was transmuted into a slag-heap of lost hopes and futile ambitions. In reacting to this — and in desperation at having to continue an abortive, self-deluding life — I had turned my back on love, companionship, and true feeling. You might suppose that quite the opposite would happen: that having found the world wanting I should seek to lose myself in sentiment and similar nonsense. Such is not my method; rather, I take my revenge for having been slighted by storing up the venom inside me and spitting it in the face of the loved one. I compound my several failures in the affairs of men with a total disregard for others and a blind selfishness that obliterates every decent human impulse.

To give but one example: a woman who had loved me selflessly had received for her pains a kick in the face — in effect a complete rejection of her solicitous devotion. Having cared for me, despite, and because of, my faults, she had then been treated so despicably that one had to marvel at the tenacity and crass stupidity of the human

race — for she continued to offer her love in the blind hope
that I might deem it worthy of reciprocation. Naturally
this was out of the question. (I am as incapable of the act of
love as is a deaf-mute of reciting Shakespeare.) For several
years this situation deteriorated until my inhumanness had
grown to intolerable proportions and a scene ensued which
even to this day I find painful to recollect.

'Do not suppose for one second,' I had said harshly,
'that my life can be altered by anything you say or do. My
life is my life.'

Her reproach was gentle, as always. 'Why should I want
to change you when it is for yourself that I love you?'

This reply made me even more angry. Did she think she
could blunt my savagery with soft phrases and Christian
appeasement? The nerve, the gall of the woman, fairly
took my breath away. Particularly so in view of the fact
that I was very much aware which of us was in the right.
Had *I* been in this favourable position I too would have
smiled sweetly and spoken calmly. But! —

'Isn't it true at this moment — and hasn't it always been
thus — that your interference in matters which do not
concern you has been the cause of all our unhappiness?
You insist on meddling in my affairs, spying on me, and
yet you profess to having no desire to affect my life one
way or the other.' I was speaking quickly, in a mechanical
fashion, for the argument had been much repeated and had
acquired the tone of an actor rehearsing his lines.

'Could it not be that I am concerned about you?' she
said. Her eyes were open wide, without guile or malice.
Was it conceivable that in her God had concentrated the
ingredients of a good woman? Such goodness did not exist
in human form, surely.

'If concern it is,' I said brusquely, 'it is masked very well
by your incessant harping on topics that are personal and
private to me alone. I have said that I will not tolerate it,
and I will not.'

'But I do not mean to pry,' she said. 'When I inquire about your activities it is because of a deep and abiding interest in you; I want to know everything about you because of the place you have in my heart. Are you so afraid of love?'

I remember raising my eyebrows and snorting a little. The word that had passed her lips always had the effect of embarrassing me, and with the embarrassment came resentment and fear, showing itself in a weak, spiteful gesture or flippant reply. On this occasion I even followed my snort with a deprecatory laugh.

— For an instant I thought I saw tears in her eyes — at any rate a hint of wetness — but as I could not meet her gaze for more than the briefest fraction of a moment I had to turn my back as though out of patience with her foolish womanly sentimentality.

'You never allow me to come close to you,' she said in the quietest of voices. 'I want only to please you, to be a good wife to you, but if you will not permit me to approach you, what can I do?'

At this she did begin to cry: the most humble kind of sobbing I had ever heard. It was muffled by the furnishings in the room, almost to the point of inaudibility, yet it did communicate a sombre anguish the like of which I have never come across before or since. This was obviously an attempt on her part to gain my sympathy, to play for time and thus prevent me from leaving. There was no behaviour I found more tiresome.

Her sobbing went on for several minutes, during which I obstinately refused to look at her, busying myself with rearranging certain objects in the room. Displays of naked emotion are entirely repugnant to me.

'If you mean to kill me you are going the right way about it,' she said, the words interspersed with dry shuddering breaths.

'If that is a threat it is futile and misplaced,' I said to her.

'I am not so stupid that I cannot see through your shoddy efforts to coerce me into submission. Your plots and schemes have by this time lost not a little of their impact.'

'But what am I to do!' she suddenly cried out. 'Tell me how I can regain the happiness, the peace and contentment we knew not so very long ago — is it hopeless to want the things that gave my life richness and fulfilment?'

'Do not come to *me*,' I said, adopting a scathing tone of voice. '*I* am not able to promise this so-called richness and fulfilment. *I* know nothing of the virtues of human existence; only the baseness of it, the deceits, the falseness.'

'But you must see that the world is beautiful,' she protested. 'You must believe that the world is filled with hope, or how else can we advance from day to day? Why do we not kill ourselves this instant?'

I turned to look at her. Her face was pale and stained with tears. To think that all this had to do with me: that I was the cause: it was satisfaction at the deepest level. 'You are a poor, timid creature,' I said. 'And you are also simple-minded in thinking that the achievement of happiness is the sole pursuit of mankind — or even *should* be the sole pursuit. Nothing could be further from the truth. Our minds are not formed in order to seek happiness but to demonstrate the chaos and inconsistency of existence. Life itself is a mutation, a chance error, a *non sequitur*, and we have only to live it for a day to realise its implausibility. What we are seeking, in fact, is that state of inertness which is the natural condition of all things. Floundering about in confusion as we do is a stage in our evolution to perfect inertia. Having achieved this we shall then have joined the rest of the universe, and all this other nonsense will be forgotten for all time.'

During this she had been gazing at me morosely, almost fearfully. When I had finished she allowed her eyes to become downcast, no doubt the better to suit her choice of words, and murmured in the softest and tiniest of voices, 'Are we not to love one another then?'

I snorted again (as this seemed to have the effect I desired) and made a gesture of impatience. Evidently this woman had no concept of true reality. Like all her kind she was capable only of perceiving the crudest, most brutish emotions. Beneath a millimetre or two of skin she was destitute of any vision, reasoning, or intellect. Her mind was a weak, flabby mass of vague, formless generalisations.

'Are we not to love one another?' she repeated, this time with more firmness. There was a roughness and an insistence in her voice that belied her gentle appearance.

'What you speak of as love is mere self-indulgence,' I said, correcting her in a humorous, but not, I hoped, too condescending a manner. 'We are not creatures of love and never have been.'

'You are saying that I do not love you?' she asked incredulously. Was there a suspicion of tears?

'Not that you "do not", but that you cannot,' I said. 'There is a difference, but one that I do not expect you to grasp.'

In the months that followed, this conversation was to echo and re-echo in my brain. Like a sly, never-ending tape-recording it would play itself back without any consent on my part, interrupting quiet periods of reverie, persistent as nagging toothache.

It was with considerable disquiet, then, that I walked from the car to the door of the house, yet outwardly I was calm, having always possessed the power to control the quivering of my limbs and the spasdomic twitchings of my facial muscles. In the main room a fire was crackling cheerfully to itself, casting inconsequential shadows over the walls and furniture. Everything here was familiar to me, everything welcomed me by the very nature of its familiarity. For instance, the ornaments on the mantel – though I would find it difficult to describe them – were known to me in the same exact detail as the wrinkles on the back of my hand. On the window-sill stood a photograph in a silver frame whose image was lodged immovably in my subconscious like a metal post set in concrete. By the side of the hearth was placed a pair of tiny shoes, and in the hearth itself a dozen coloured glass marbles winked in the rosy fireglow.

As I entered she was sitting in the chair. Her hair was swept up, with fine delicate wisps of it stirring gently on the nape of her neck. The arch of her neck was white and slender, vulnerable. Her clear-browed lucid eyes registered neither surprise nor alarm at my unexpected return.

I stood rather self-consciously in front of the fire, looking down at her. We did not speak at once. Presently she said, 'You have come back from a drive?'

It was all I could manage to shake my head. An object caught my eye: a broken toy underneath the table; in the further corner a child's discarded cap. She must have seen the direction of my eyes, for it prompted her to say, 'They are asleep.'

I nodded dumbly.

'Will you stay?' she asked, not in the smallest degree prejudicing my reply, neither displaying eagerness or hostility.

'Yes —' This single word was all I could utter before something cracked in my head and I fell to my knees sobbing. I wept brokenly, begging her over and over to forgive me. If only she would forgive me.

VII

You will have gathered that the good woman, of whom I have made reference, was slighted in the more unbearable way by my intolerable behaviour. That she is still a good woman is a matter for some wonder: that she has not degenerated into an unfeeling savage says something for the quality of goodness which — I suppose — we must all possess to a greater or lesser degree. It is unfortunate that her goodness could not alter my character. But then if some of us were not born evil, against what standard could we measure the good people of this world? You see, there is a reason for my existence after all.

Yet it is no consolation to me to know that my life finds its justification in moral corruption. Scuttling into my little dark hole like a spider I stare out with spider's eyes at a world that is disgusting beyond the power of words to convey, and it is seen thus because my eyes are concave mirrors reflecting the inner workings of my soul. Were I a 'good' person then no doubt the world would appear good (a truism), and if that were the case there would be no need for this book of so-called 'Confessions'. The sum of which brings me to the conclusion that they have achieved nothing but your confusion and my depression. If anything, I have retreated even deeper into my shell of morbid introspection, sucking vainly on my own entrails just as Val sucked dispassionately on my most private part. It would have at least achieved something had I learned from my mistakes, or had the setting down of them generated remorse, pity, bitterness within me. But alas, gentlemen, filling these pages with words has merely tightened the band of iron around my head. And as for emotions — well, I had better tell you that such emotions as I have are laughable tricks of the imagination, in most instances self-induced to provide motives for my meaningless actions.

In my own defence I can only say that such negative persons as myself are necessary, if only to act as counterpoint to the bright world of living things. After all, seeing reality as I do is just as valid as that of a scientist observing natural phenomena. If he represents the positive outlook on the universe, surely I have just as much right to put before you the nihilistic concept of it? That you do not wish to have this presented to you is none of my affair; indeed, I might reply that if you want to dwell in daydreams instead of facing reality the loss is more yours than mine.

For during my short stay on this planet it has become increasingly clear to me that we are all playing the devil's game. At this I can imagine you thumping the table and frothing at the mouth. 'Do not be so presumptuous as to say "we are *all* playing the devil's game",' I hear you cry. '*All* indeed!' Nevertheless, gentlemen, the fact remains that none of us is engaged in God's work, and the only conclusion to be drawn from this is that the opposite applies. And again, despite your protests, I insist on the word 'all', because it usually follows that those persons who most vehemently deny the fact are the very ones engaged exclusively in playing the devil's game. But what is this game to which I refer? The term confuses you, so I will attempt to make it clearer. Firstly, it does not appertain to evil (at least not in the sense we have come to understand it); no, it relates to a game in which there are no rules. We play it as innocents, blithely unaware that the reason for our existence is the chance encounter of one molecule with another; had the two molecules never met we should not be here. Of even more significance, had two *other* molecules encountered one another − again purely due to random factors − another life-form incomprehensible to our senses would now occupy our segment of time and space. We were not destined to be created; neither are we destined to survive.

And the reason I choose to call it the 'devil's' game is that one might be led to suppose that a fiendish intelligence is responsible, such is the beautiful paradox of the system. (Nothing is more paradoxical than a game without rules.) But to suppose an intelligence, fiendish or otherwise, destroys the initial proposition that the game is without purpose or meaning, for if such an intelligence were to exist then so too would purpose and meaning, even if these were a mystery to us.

But at this my mind wearies. Had I not better, at this point, bring these 'Confessions' to an end? I cannot be expected to go on indefinitely bringing to mind the painful recollections of imaginary events and experiences . . .

We live in a dream. Our pragmatic age has produced a nation of dreamers, and none more so than those who choose to deal with the bedrock realities of practical affairs and worldly success. Their web is woven of insubstantial stuff, as light as nonsense, that would blow away at the first faint breeze of common sense. I myself am not a dreamer: I am a realist. A romantic realist maybe, but a realist all the same. Again you smile. But why? I am a realist because, quite simply, my perceptions are clearer and sharper than yours. I insulate myself from the everyday fantasy-like world that most of you inhabit – shutting out the peripheral static and dwelling quietly with only my own thoughts for company. Be assured, gentlemen, that were I to suppose for an instant that you genuinely wished to be acquainted with my secret I should not hesitate to reveal it. But you do not. You would rather have your senses befuddled by half-truths – in fact you prefer to be cheated and misled by pretty nonsense rather than have to face the bitter, unpalatable facts of our meaningless lives. You want, at bottom, to be left undisturbed in your little dark holes, snug, safe, and comfortable, encapsulated in embryonic blackness. In so choosing you have brought about your own damnation – for did I not say that the pragmatists of this world are the real dreamers? You will recall quite distinctly that I did. If you wish to be a dreamer, that is your affair, but do not forget that it places you one step removed from the apprehension of true reality. The only solution I can see is that you must leave your little dark holes and come out into the light, cast aside your comfortable shells and be re-born with new eyes. It is a painful process; I give you this advice for nothing. Neither, paradoxically, and in spite of all I have said, will it be of any great benefit to you, because with your heightened perceptions you will at last begin to appreciate the utter bleakness, the total incomprehensibility of the spacetime flux in which our molecules revolve. Naturally I will not look for your thanks, knowing that you would as soon spit in my face for having introduced to you the featureless wastes of the underlife. But at least you will not be comfortable. You will not be self-deluded. Beneath the stone that covers us all you will observe the scurryings of your fellow ants in all their unmitigated horror and desolation: the deviousness of their brains and the selfish chemical reactions which constitute their emotions. I write the word 'emotions' with a twisted smile on my lips: I fail to see how one can attribute emotions to fictional characters — such as we all are — unless, of course, the emotions themselves are fictitious. Not a single one of us knows what it is to experience a genuine emotion, for we are all conditioned to behave in a stereotyped, fictional sort of way, like puppets; yet we cling to our spurious beliefs that we are reacting truly and unconsciously, as free agents, to external stimuli. We do this for the reasons I have stated: that the bulk of us never comes into contact, *throughout all our lives,* with the true realities of the underlife, but dwell like water insects on the skin of the universe. This phrase is badly chosen. It tends to imply that the physical universe is true reality, when any fool can see that it is not. Rather, the mysterious life-force which permeates space and time, as radio waves passing through solid matter, is the base element of the stuff we call reality, and is by its very nature beyond our savage perceptions. But enough of this: I intend to bring this section, 'A Visit to a Paper Mill', to a close.

It may be added that the 'Confessions' of this dealer in paradoxes did not end here, since the writer could not forbear continuing them; but I who have been responsible for their transcription choose no longer to perform the task.

HOPE HOSPITAL

Having rid myself of burdensome thoughts, I feel that now is the time to embark on a more lucid tale, leaving behind the occasional jottings and note-takings that have hitherto served to convey my attitudes towards life. Yet it is not a tale in the accepted sense of the word, neither is it written in the form of the 'Confessions' that have gone before. However, you should know that it has taken me in excess of two months to write, and therefore I hope you will bear with me. I earnestly crave your indulgence.

No, it is not a story, nor does it have a plot, nor is it in any sense 'realistic' — so what is it? you may legitimately inquire. Well: I ask you to suppose that a man sits in a car in a place which has the powerful effect of nostalgia upon him; it is evening and the environment recalls to his mind a certain person with whom he once had an intimate and deeply-felt relationship. He recalls too the despicable way she was treated, and feels an aching sadness because time is irretrievable, their past lives are gone forever, and yet this memory, to him, remains the most real and vital aspect of his present-day existence. Naturally, his thoughts are not coherent, as he is a man like any other, but had it been possible to somehow capture his thoughts intact and transpose them to the printed page I doubt whether they would have emerged any the less coherent, and possibly a good deal more so: yet, for me, their *psychological* order would have remained unaltered. As for his being consistent or consecutive, both in thought and deed, I do not believe it matters that this is not the case; rather I would insist that his inner confusion, his hotch-potch mixture of memories, requires just such a method of transposition.

Thus he sits, sunk in retrospection, living vicariously his past life and seeking to make order of it, to wring some sense out of it, just as a child repeatedly shakes a kaleidoscope in an attempt to achieve a prettier pattern or one that pleases him the more by its comforting juxtaposition of irregularly-shaped coloured bits and pieces. By degrees he begins to understand better (this, at least, his subjective impression), and towards the close of the story thinks he has perceived the reality or truth of things — or what he conceives to be such.

These are the bare bones of my tale. It goes without saying that whereas the actual transcription of these reminiscences has taken a lengthy period of time, the human mind is so constructed that it skips lightly and artfully from thought to thought in the merest fraction of an instant. A single image generates an entire sequence of brain-pictures; a flashing wisp of thought acts as a catalyst for the simultaneous reincarnation of myriad sights, sounds and smells from the past — which is our human term for the collective backlog of experience contained within our minds. So, while the man appears to dwell to the point of wearisome self-indulgence on quite worthless topics, the topics themselves are in fact dealt with summarily and in a twinkling. The passage of time can be no more than a matter of hours, yet he spans the wave-peaks, troughs and undulations of a complete relationship, reviewing, as it were, the catalogue of an entire human personality. The same thing has been done before in Art. For example, Vladimir Nabakov employed a similar method in his novel *Glory*, in which the backward and forward shuttling of time and experience produces a dizzying effect. Of course, this re-arrangement is only made possible with hindsight, a quality absent at the moment of involvement: yet had not Vladimir Nabakov permitted himself this licence, there would never have resulted what constitutes at once the most fascinating and the most successfully achieved of all his writings.

PART I

CHAPTER I

THE NIGHTDRIVE BEGINS

The central pivot around which my thoughts dip and sway is indeed Hope Hospital (that bleak, featureless, forbidding place!), yet oddly enough none of the events which follow, and which are crammed with special significance for me, actually took place there. It is as though its existence in my memory is a key, a cypher, unlocking an entire chestful of dusty, half-shadowed reminiscences dating back to prehistory. Thinking back on it, the Hospital was instrumental in triggering off this chain of events, for it was there that Tee worked, and had I not met her none of this would have happened.

We had been lovers, Tee and I, for a period of time not exceeding two years. Or would it be more correct to say that she had been my mistress? At any rate we had been frequently physically intimate. To employ a worn cliché, Tee was the most alive person I had ever known; it did not seem feasible that any man would not be immediately and catastrophically entranced by her, nor that he — fortunate fellow — would have the power or stupidity to restrain himself from falling in love with her. It goes without saying that I was infatuated and flattered to be the chosen one. I kept looking over my shoulder to see who could be the recipient of such a dazzling, loving smile. Standing under a black stone railway bridge in the countryside, somewhere in the past, we had held each other very tightly, the entire world in our hard pressing lips as our hearts thundered in tune with the train passing overhead, and had the universe blinked out like a light at that precise moment it would have been a fulfilling climax to the whole sorry charade. The fact that we did not, could not, belong wholly to each other made our being together all the more poignantly tender; an incredible aching bitter-sweetness. One is only truly alive at such moments . . .

However, this is an old, outdated memory, a flickering movie image on the concave wall of my brain: really I should be telling you about my guilt-stricken ride to visit her, at a flat in Urmston, where I knew very well she was not to be found. How often do we make these futile journeys, just to complete a formal pattern, as though life were a jigsaw? I arrived in the courtyard of the flats, blurred cubes of pale concrete in the twilight, and went up the viciously sharp steps to the thin, warped door upon which I knocked timidly, afraid that someone might be in but knowing full well that the flat was empty, its square rooms floodlit by streetlamps through the uncurtained windows. When, having knocked again, there was no answer, I retreated to the courtyard and sat in my car smoking a reflective cigarette. At such moments I feel uniquely alone: the leading player in a tragedy of epic proportions. I recalled, painfully and with clarity, my previous visit to the flat, when those same uncurtained windows had, on that occasion, hampered and ultimately wilted my anticipated performance. Tee never took it amiss; she was generous and understanding to a fault. We sweated for a while, attempting to succeed with our eyes mentally averted; and then, pretending that the two bodies locked in heaving combat were not ours, watched disinterestedly from a distance as we sat in chairs drinking coffee and smoking. Always it seems that my finales are anti-climaxes.

In actual fact the daylight intimidated me. Tee and I were dark people (Tee especially) and to have the grey, tumbling, unwashed clouds — and perhaps the head of a windowcleaner — witness our mindless indulgence brought rushing to the surface all my latent Anglo-Saxon paranoia. Her boyfriend at the time, Desmond, whose flat this was, was again not a steadying influence; for while ostensibly on a business trip to London it seemed appropriate that he could, would, burst in at any second, eyes bulging, nostrils flared, his thick lips drawn back in snarling rage. Obviously I did not want to be present when such an entrance took place. After much groaning and cursing, and following a number of self-disgusted sighs, eventually I accomplished my side of the bargain and sank back — shrank away — from the pitiless, unyielding light.

It was this uncomfortable, not to say disturbing, experience which decided me not to visit Tee at the flat again. In the cold box-shaped living-room, with its exposed plastic-topped table and four vulnerable straight-backed chairs, we made polite, inconsequential conversation, at a loss what to do with our eyes, hands and bodies now that the rush of hot quick blood had dispersed and resumed its prosaic function of keeping us alive. Something else that I had noticed: the ever-present aliveness of her personality wore rather thin, became cheapened and threadbare, when not clothed in the richly textured tapestry of night. Her eyes were too bright, her teeth too white; like an actress who had strayed into an ordinary room wearing stage make-up and displaying the full gamut of theatrical mannerisms and emotions. It was tiresome, and not a little embarrassing.

Thus two weeks went by and here I was, sitting in my car, looking out at the dim deserted courtyard and feeling — what? Mixed up in my memory, in addition to Hope Hospital, was another hospital, this one in Hampstead, and some more flats, two square concrete towers with swiftly-rising lifts rushing one to Tee's tiny apartment on the top floor. Further back again: the loading of her belongings, suitcases, trunks, carrier-bags, and three years' accumulated paraphernalia into the car, then driving towards a westward-sinking sun marred, yet made beautiful, by rainbow-coloured streamers of smoke from the CWS Soap Works, drifting wisps held in suspension in the clear, warm, rose-tinted sky. The evening air was very still.

And as I drove I had the most peculiar feeling: that I was a dwarf. Crouched, hunched, squat behind the wheel, my chin near my knee, my entire body capable of being wrapped in a round, lumpish parcel. Tee was wearing a short skirt from which her long black legs protruded; she carried with her a musky smell — whether it was the soap she used or the natural odour of her body I do not know — and her eyes and teeth flashed brighter as the motorway merged into night. Not at any time did I touch her, or feel like touching her, as the miles sped by; and as for talking, that dreary chore of making polite conversation, Tee saw to that. She was indefatigably cheerful, always grinning, chattering incessantly (to herself) so that the narrow humming air-conditioned compartment was filled with the dark-brown drone of her husky voice. I smoked, and nodded; nodded, and smoked. The ribbon of grey asphalt disappeared under the car. We began to get hungry. Somewhere on the southern outskirts of Birmingham I stopped and we ate fish and chips out of newspaper with our fingers. The fish was hot and greasy, breaking into pieces and scorching our fingertips; it was delicious on the tongue to lick away the salt — Tee laughingly inserting my fingers into her warm mouth to cleanse them.

What I liked about Tee was her wonderful directness, her warm-hearted naiveté, and not least her unfailing good disposition. To these attributes must be added an extremely attractive appearance: wherever we went men would stop and stare, mentally straighten their shoulders and comb their hair. I would feel both proud and uneasy, yet displayed an outward nonchalance that relied on her being with me for its success. Sitting alongside her inside our little den, smelling her musky perfume, was in many ways the fulfilment of all my dreams. She had black, tightly compacted hair, inclined to frizziness, and a fine broad nose whose nostrils flattened outwards when she laughed. I remember her face as the embodiment of her personality; open, outgoing, relaxed, expansive.

Today she was leaving Hope for good, and no doubt there was an element of sadness in the departure, but her fun-loving nature refused to acknowledge its existence. Life was a never-ending series of gay introductions and sad partings, so why be upset? why not just accept the fact? her attitude seemed to imply.

After our makeshift meal we continued the drive. It was very dark now, the road a black insidious snake undulating through the rolling undergrowth of the countryside. Lights flashed, villages whizzed by, and empty crossroads, while we reclined snugly on cupped seats, safe inside behind the fascia's greenish glow. At one point the headlights picked out the squashed remains, with blood like black oil, of some creature or other.

'Do you think your mother will be surprised to see me, or will she welcome me?' I asked Tee, my left hand having recently withdrawn from her thigh, and her right one from mine.

'She won't mind; she'll be glad to see you. Don't worry about that, if that's what's bothering you. She will thank you, I'm sure, for having brought me all this way.'

'I hate imposing on people,' I said, 'especially under the circumstances. Won't she wonder who I am or where I come from or what I do?'

'She won't think of you as a ghost, if that's what you mean,' Tee said, showing all her sparkling teeth in a wide-mouthed smile that was turned like a horizontal crescent moon in my direction. How many people had been the recipient of such a smile, a beaming flash of light that envelops one in a laser ray of human love and understanding?

Doubtless she took me at face value — being the handsome spectacle that I am — and was far too simple a soul to guess at the strange metaphysical idiosyncracies lurking behind the bland convex outline of features I presented to the world. She thought of me, perhaps, as being 'mysterious'; certainly she credited me with more real depth than I possessed, and I was not so foolish as to disenchant her with a true version of my secret underlife. (That such a creature existed would, in any event, have been incomprehensible to her.)

Having parked and locked the car we carried our suitcases into the hotel via the rear entrance, finding ourselves in a narrow, unhealthily-lit passage leading to a tiny semi-circular segment — the reception desk — from behind which a somewhat austere middle-aged woman appraised our arrival with hard, colourless eyes. Many years of managing an hotel had made it childishly simple for her to recognise instantly those who were married and those who were not; a glance at Tee merely confirmed what she already knew. I signed the book, with those dead eyes upon me, and the proprietress instructed the bell-boy, a dark-skinned youth of foreign origin, to conduct us to our room.

It crossed my mind to wonder then, as now, why he, of all people, should be lying in wait at the end of a long, haphazard journey down an indistinguished road: for a suspicion entered my head that we had met before. Was he not a photographer, or a dancer, or something? You can imagine how carefully I kept him in my sights. Never once did he have the opportunity of looking at — much less communicating with — Tee when my back was turned. This stems from a nasty childhood experience, an emotional mishap which inhibited my natural development but failed to stunt my imagination.

I tipped him a shilling (this being before the introduction of profit-mongering decimalised coinage) and he backed out of the room, bending slyly forward with an obsequious yet vaguely threatening motion.

The room was an old-fashioned hotel room, nothing more; with twin beds. Exhausted after our long drive, eyelids bloated with fatigue, we nevertheless fell fully-clothed on top of the bed, clasped in each other's arms, and began immediately, and without any further thought, to make love. Tee seemed very close to me physically, warm, solid, her body and limbs substantial underneath the stuff of her blouse and skirt, yet because of the tiredness it was as if I were dreaming the episode; as if each of us was encased in a layer of transparent jelly through which we had to swim blindly.

Without quite knowing how, we were naked, her long-legged boyish body next to mine on the bed covers. As usual her head was thrown back, her eyes closed, her mouth open, white teeth, pink gums and protruding tongue, uttering unintelligible gutteral sounds. Then, at a certain point, she would raise her awkward head, open her eyes and look straight into mine, reproachful, almost in pain, almost accusing me of hurting her; and again — a sullen animal desire in her eyes that perfectly accompanied the croaking grunts issuing in rhythm from the back of her throat. Thus she would stare at me, her eyes clouded with pain, until the final long-drawn-out whine and fall of the head: creases of sweat shining on her neck.

I breakfasted alone in the dining room next morning. The proprietress nodded curtly on some professional errand or other. I heard her call out to the bell-boy, 'Brett', or something that rhymed with it, but the dark, pock-marked youth was nowhere to be seen. Perhaps he was in the kitchen; perhaps, indeed, he had just cooked the bacon, eggs and fried tomato that lay on the plate before me, and which I mopped up with soft brown bread and alacrity.

'The sun is shining, it's a brand-new day,' Tee remarked as I climbed into the car beside her. She had bathed, changed her clothes, and was as fresh and sweet as a summer flower. The muskiness of her perfume filled the car.

'Before long you will see your family,' I said rather nervously.

'You can stay with us for a few days, can't you? My mother will love to meet you.'

'I have to go to the Exhibition,' I reminded her. 'You can come too, if you like.' My hands on the wheel had the early morning quality of new pink life, the fine hairs vibrating in the slipstream from the open window. Tee was attending to her nails. They were long ovals, unpainted, and flecked here and there with white.

'Did you happen to notice anyone in the hotel?' I asked mysteriously. She flashed me her bright, brief smile. 'Anyone in particular, I mean,' I continued. 'Someone on the staff maybe.'

Tee showed no sign of having heard — or having paid the slightest attention — to my question. The words might have been simply words, without significance or meaning. Her head was bent, her eyelashes charmingly lowered, her whole attention on the task in hand. To cover my embarrassment I said:

'If the sun keeps shining we can improve our tans,' which amused her immensely; she was not without a certain sense of humour.

There is nothing quite like riding down the neat clean roads of England in the morning sunshine. Greenery throbbed on either side, a powerful fecund cheeriness and good temper which arouses a sense of what it is to be uniquely English even in the leaden-hearted. This love of my land, of loving England, is much stronger and more substantial than I could ever feel for any person. It is a palpable reality of earth, grass, trees and sky, whereas people are intangible phantoms who only exist insofar as they populate the figments of our imaginations. How can Englishmen help but have pure souls when they inherit such a beautiful country?

Tee had become silent (unusual!); could she be experiencing sadness at the end of an epoch at Hope? So many late-night meetings in draughty corridors with asthmatic radiators; so many giggling assignations in parked cars; the smell of hospital canteen food, warm and sickly sweet in the nostrils like the odour of small furry mammals herded together in winter quarters – it must have seemed to her that she had left the old dry husk of at least one life at the top of the stairs, third door along, right-hand side.

Indeed, on closer inspection, it appeared that she was crying. I asked her quietly what was the matter and tried to cheer her up by saying that, never mind, she would soon be home. Evidently this was what I should *not* have said, for she started shaking and weeping harder.

'Hey,' I said, 'hey: I though we were going to sunbathe.'

A muffled snort of laughter came in the middle of her tears, and this made her undecided as to whether she should laugh or cry; for a while she did both, drawing in deep shuddering breaths and sniggering down her nose. Then, predictably, she blurted out, 'I was thinking of the first time we met. That was going to London too. Now I shall be here for good and I shan't see you again –'

'Of course you will see me,' I interposed gently.

'But not very often!' she wailed. 'Not every week!'

The handkerchief was held to her nose, pressed between her long pale nails. The skin was creased and puckered at the knuckles; how deeply I felt it then: the heart-felt pang that signalled the end of our relationship. Pointless to delude ourselves; yet if we constantly faced up to life's realities we should have no desire to keep on living. I had a letter from her not long ago; she is married now, to a man whose first name is Richard.

CHAPTER II

BLACK DANCE

Entering the municipality of Reading down Oxford Road, who should we see but Tee's mother, a frail bent figure carrying two shopping-bags filled with groceries. Tee skipped across — her high spirits having returned (she was as irrepressible as a bobbing cork) — kissed her mother, and introduced me. The old lady smiled distantly, alone in her world of sickness and pain, weary with the thought that the sun shone so infrequently.

The house reared up, straight-faced, behind a few square feet of scrubby garden: basement, ground floor, two upper floors and attic occupied by a number of people and children, all of them related to Tee by some devious ancestry, and all of them surprisingly friendly. There was no prejudice that I could detect.

In the front room, on the mantel, on the radiogram, and on various shelves, hazy colour-retouched photographs in cheap gilt frames of the children accosted the visitor with wide-eyed innocence. Much of the bric-a-brac was second-rate, contrasting dramatically with the image that Tee herself presented: invariably she dressed in the best of taste and was meticulous in matters of grooming and personal hygiene. However, the room was clean, and it was there I waited, being visited at intervals by one or more of the children who peeped shyly round the door, stared unabashed for several moments, and then ran off squealing. Mock shrieks, whisperings and muffled laughter would ensue, followed by yet another pair of lustrous dark-brown eyes edging sideways round the woodwork, never more than three feet from the ground.

Tee brought me two fried eggs, yolk-hard, on a plate; I made an attempt to eat them, though I wasn't the least bit hungry. Shortly afterwards I was invited down to the basement where a meal awaited me consisting of chicken, rice, a type of bean with which I was not familiar, and for dessert, fried banana. The family sat round watching me eat — or pretend to eat, because of course by this time I had no appetite whatsoever, least of all for chicken, rice, a type of bean with which I was not familiar, and fried banana. If ever one could be killed by kindness, I was the one.

A male cousin (uncle? nephew?) of Tee's smiled at me with his wide mouth, a sympathetic sort of smile that for some unaccountable reason made me faintly uneasy. The presence of her family gave Tee an additional facet somehow out of keeping with the personality that had already jelled in my mind. Leaning against a car parked on the perimeter of a field in the dying days of summer, the grass waist-high, she had pressed herself to me with an absolute sensual abandon that caused white sparks to flash behind my closed eyelids; then running, slipping, stumbling through the long grass I had chased, caught her, and held her to the ground. The throat-catching smell of close-packed growth and insect-life was heavy in our nostrils. The air was like liquefied velvet. At that moment I had looked into her eyes and seen the inverted glassy dome of the sky, fringed by swaying stalks of grass with tops the shape of candle flames. And in that same instant I knew Tee as I had never known another human being; strangely, our ethnic differences seemed to aid rather than hinder my understanding. As darkness came on, the people in the room acquired the characteristics of humped, shrouded silhouettes, the chicken, rice, etc remaining virtually untouched, a centre-piece in the claustrophobic lower room.

Later it was decided that we should attend a dance, Tee and I, a regular Saturday evening event held in what amounted to little more than a nissen hut. Darkness: I parked the car on a dirt-rutted track running alongside the railway lines and, holding Tee by the hand, danced nimbly round the black pools of water to the wooden entrance steps. Men in sharp suits and pointed shoes reclined here-abouts, eyeing Tee lecherously and me contemptuously, waiting, or so it seemed, for the opportunity to slide a knife between my ribs.

The place was jammed to the door, a central clearing being used for the terpsichorean meeting of the sexes. Recalling this experience I am tempted to report that the interior of the hall was almost in complete darkness (so my memory informs me), but rationally I do not suppose this to have been the case. More likely it was the heat and sweat and sheer *density* of human bodies which fostered this impression and imprinted it on my memory cells. Tee, meanwhile, had disappeared to search out an old acquaintance, and I dawdled self-consciously by the door, ignoring the colour of my skin and lighting several cigarettes in rapid succession.

It is moments such as these which are the stuff of night-mares. For who has not dreamed of being surrounded, harrassed, encumbered by a multitude of faces ranging from the indifferent to the hostile? Is it any wonder that I hovered nervously near the door, afraid to enter the hall proper and yet too shamefaced to retreat outside to the rutted track and pools of black water with the moon in them?

We didn't stay long. When she returned I immediately took her arm and stumbled to the car: I knew what it was like to be a cowboy besieged by Indians.

'You are a funny boy,' Tee said to me when we had settled down with our drinks in the pub. Her nose and cheeks were shiny, her eyes alive and gleaming, and it hit me then that this was one of our few remaining occasions together. Within days we should see each other no more. The trouble was that I had no other means of revealing the depth of my feeling than by fornicating with her.

'Your mother seems a very nice person,' I said, enclosing her hand in mine.

'She likes you: all my family like you,' Tee replied.

We sat gazing at one another. Her neck was vulnerable, tempting a caress. She read my thoughts: her silky lips parted ever so slightly.

'At any rate you will be near her,' I said abstractedly, lost in futile wonder at the way *this thing* suddenly clamps down and shuts off forever an episode of one's life that will continue to be enacted and re-enacted over and over again, endlessly, *ad nauseam*. Tee would never advance beyond this point: my memory would trap her in a window-reflecting bubble, a creature of time and space suspended in amber.

'You have made the last two years bearable,' she said.

'But all thing must come to an end,' I said inanely.

'You can't have all your eggs . . .'

'. . . on one plate . . .'

'. . . and eat them,' Tee finished, and we burst out laughing. Her command of English had always been suspect, and – because of my profession – the subject of a private joke. That she would from now on be sharing private jokes with other, unknown persons depressed me more than I can say. (She had not, as yet, met Desmond.)

'Never mind, one day you will meet someone and marry him and you will forget the nightdrive to Reading, the hotel, the bell-boy, the dance, the pub, this conversation, me.' Would this have the calculated effect or would she misconstrue my meaning?

'I don't remember the bell-boy,' Tee said out of the blue.

'Of course you remember the bell-boy. He touched your leg, or at least tried to. There was rape in his eyes; you must have noticed.'

'At the dance?' Tee said, bewildered. Her very pale nails traced the rim of the glass. The moisture gathered under her pink fingertips and she licked it off with a pointed tongue. Her jaw line was firm, almost square from the front: her long brown cheeks were flat planes, raising her cheekbones to support slightly elliptical eyes: her long-limbed stance possessed the awkward grace of a baby gazelle. And above all, what attracted me most powerfully was her complete lack of self-consciousness. In a universe populated by script-readers she ad-libbed her way through life with remarkable facility, never forgetting a line, never missing a cue.

An old lady came into the bar balancing a hat on her head like a bowl of cherries. The cherries quivered with each faltering step. Tee held her hand in front of her face, laughing politely. However, this old woman reminded me of her own sick mother, whom Tee must have forgotten was at this moment lying in pain in the back room on the ground floor of the house at 312 Oxford Road*. Difficult to state, but in that instant I really believed that it was our destiny never to be parted; she belonged to me, and I to her, and it was a crying shame that our lives were to diverge at this point.

Hardly had this thought had time to grow stale when Tee — characteristically one would have thought — rested her head on my shoulder and put her arm around my waist, saying, 'If you think I'll ever forget you, you're mistaken. But what future is there for us? You have a wife and two children; if we had a child it would be a beautiful baby boy with big brown eyes, I would call him Edmund, and our two lives would be merged into his. Two wonky, wriggly paths creating a straight hard road. Can you imagine what he would be like, his two eyes looking out at the world, one yours, one mine, and our two brains combined into one? He would be half me, half you; in a sense we should be sharing the same skin, the two of us sitting in each others' laps and looking out through the eyes of our child.'

---

*As far as I am aware she is still alive to this day.

CHAPTER III

Press Day at Earls Court was a veritable cacophony of scraping, sawing, banging, clanging. Unusually for such a large open area the air was humid, saturating the gangs of workmen roaming the stands in search of a nail to hammer, a terminal to connect, perhaps a cleat-line to adjust. Everything was false-fronted whitewash, with the names picked out in hysterical day-glo. TV cameras on low-slung dollies rolled silently on fat rubber wheels, lenses glinting viciously in the glare of the movable lighting, earphoned lackies carrying thick writhing lengths of cable and following clipboard instructions with their miming lips. Above it all in the lifeless air hung the wrinkled satin flags emblazoned with the manufacturers' names: Norton, AJS, Honda, Triumph, BSA, Suzuki, Yamaha, etc.

The stand with which I was involved was nearly, but not quite, finished. The *aficionados* would see gleaming machines that had taken weeks to polish and bring to this state of perfection, yet the startling fact was that, unbeknown to anybody, nobody had so far ridden any such machine without it getting dirty. Moreover, the ratio of dirt to gleam was 4:1; that is to say that somewhere in an oily workshop a vast amount of filth and rubbish had accumulated — the penalty for having so many immaculate specimens on display. I must confess that this notion choked the breath out of me. The amount of slime requiring disposal in order to produce one clean, decent, respectable human being must be staggering; one wonders where they hide it all.

I was greeted by Alan Kimber, a man I liked because I respected him. He had a capable, understated manner which gave one immediate confidence in his ability and integrity. As usual he was dressed in the best of professional taste: pale green shirt with unblemished collar and cuffs, a discreet striped tie in the same shade, expertly pressed suit upon which a faint sheen gleamed, and, of course, the essential attribute, the remains of a tan acquired in Cyprus. His voice was calm and well-modulated, bearing the traces of an accent I had never been able to identify.

Alan liked women (what marketing manager doesn't?) and cocked an eyebrow as we shook hands. 'A cousin of yours?' he asked humorously.

'Distant,' I replied, playing the part of man-of-the-world-womanising-rake with all the aplomb of the confirmed neurotic.

'The machines look grand,' I said, sticking my hands in my pockets and placing one foot on the stand. The stiff satin flag hung above our heads, the Japanese word for 'Smith' spelled out in crumpled silver letters eleven feet high. 'It always seems to me,' I continued, 'that year after year we arrive here, never progressing or making any headway other than the accumulation of prosperity.'

Alan stroked his chin with his nicely-kept hand. 'There's technical innovation,' he pointed out. 'Last year we didn't have Posi-Force; this year we do. Six gears too. Not many two-strokes can boast the same.'

A shambling horde of press photographers passed by, scouting for subjects to fill tomorrow's newspapers. One of them, a slim, small, darkly complexioned man did a double-take on Tee and scuttled across. By this time I had been invited to step behind the make-believe wall of the stand to have a double whisky, but you can bet I drank the whisky with both eyes fixed on what the photographer was doing to Tee. In fact what he did was this: sat her on a machine, made her cross her legs, knelt down himself and clicked away from several different angles. Her legs looked a pasty kind of grey in the stockings she was wearing; but she conjured up the most dazzling of smiles, as though to the manner born, smiling into the black pin-prick pupils of his eyes. He then gave her a card and asked her to call him (this I surmised) at his home number, and maybe — who knows? — step out for a drink and a bite to eat one evening. Is there nothing that photographers won't stoop to?

'. . . in this industry,' Alan was saying, 'it's very difficult to keep one step ahead of public demand. All the time they want more chrome, more gleam, more gadgetry —'

'Which means more production line wastage,' I put in, keeping an eye on Tee and the photographer.

'Exactly. Do you know, in Birmingham we have several workshops in which it's impossible to move because of the filth? All that oil and muck and waste, tragic.'

'Isn't it the same with human beings?' I said, pressing home a line of thought. 'We see immaculate people in the street, sitting in restaurants, riding on buses, and we take it for granted that that's the natural human condition — but it isn't. You've only got to see a human being after a single night's sleep: hair matted, eyes congealed, mouth foul, pillow marks on their face, and needing to urinate, defecate, and so on. The amount of work it takes to bring us anywhere near perfection is quite remarkable, if not incredible.'

'You must have rather an odd idea of human beings,' Alan said, narrowing his eyes and regarding me curiously. 'Or is that how you yourself look in the morning?' This last was said gently, with a slightly mocking yet good-natured tone, and it struck me that what in the mouths of some people would be taken as an insult, from others we accept with good-humoured equanimity. Such is the strange magic of personality, or perhaps one should really say 'character'.

Enough time had now elapsed for the fact to have sufficiently impressed itself on Tee that I was a person of some importance at the Exhibition. She had had her doubts, even when I had presented my complimentary pass to the commissionaire at the door; though now, surely, the matter was beyond question. I beckoned her to me, knowing that her presence lent my image a romantic flavour. A great number of people live out their lives in the pallid glory of borrowed light, and I more so than most.

We walked, Tee and I, past the giant Honda stand on our way to the exit, and I was stalked by the old, depressing notion of the futility of all this glitter and glamour, this helter-skelter toil and frantic preparation which in the final analysis would advance civilisation no further than the depth of a micro-dot. The street outside affected me the same way, as did the hoardings on the buses; it was no good pretending any longer. If man had a purpose, and if I by fantastic good fortune had succeeded in detecting it, then my so-called existence might have soared to the sublime instead of descending to the bathetic.

CHAPTER IV

POINTING A CATFORD WALL

Catford is an outlying district of London and it was there, down a backstreet of crumbling red-brick terraced houses, that I parked the car and accompanied Tee to a door in which two elongated frosted-glass panels were separated by a strip of bubbled, pitted paintwork: the result, doubtless, of years of continual action by a sun whose rays had penetrated the ninety-three million miles of black dead space with no other purpose (presumably) than to cause this unsightly disfiguration of a door in the backstreets of Catford. One might almost suppose this to be an analogy for all life-forms. Whether or not it is I'm not qualified to say. It will come as no surprise, though, when I remark that this too echoed the purposelessness of the Exhibition to which I have just made reference.

Tee held my hand tightly as the door opened. Life was

turning into a play again. Could it be Gary Cooper opening the door, or Marilyn Monroe, or Kim Novak? I felt distinctly queasy and was aware — as at all such moments of fear or excitement — that my penis had shrunk. It had withdrawn into my belly as a snail into its shell. Liquid gurgled in the depths of my stomach and, much to my discomfort, the load in my bowels shifted, creating a hot vacuum down below. The passage along which we were led opened into a small square room in the centre of which stood a table and four chairs; there was margarine, a pot of jam, and a packet of cream crackers, fragments of them scattered round its base, others adhering to the coating of jam on the blade of a yellow-handled knife. It struck me as odd that cream crackers should be in the process of being consumed at this hour of the day. However, I never — ever — comment or make any observation that could be construed as criticism. It is not in my nature.

The girl to whom I was introduced turned out to be Tee's cousin; and indeed, there were certain physical similarities that struck one immediately the relationship was made known. She was more buxom, it is true, and generally fatter, but essentially of the same genetic strain. Chatting as they were, it brought about a situation where I was standing idly near the table, my left hand resting on the back of a chair, my right half-in, half-out of my pocket, and both legs aching from the awkward stance a man adopts whilst listening with polite if feigned interest to a conversation between two women. I used my facial muscles to smile, and I occasionally nodded, and once even raised my eyebrows at something Tee's cousin said, although it would have necessitated a Divine Forefinger crashing through the flaking plaster ceiling to have evoked an unsimulated gesture or expression of surprise from me, so certain was I that the Heavens were in chaos and God nothing more nor less than a bottomless black hole in space. On the buckled flagstones in the tiny backyard stood a ladder, at the top of which a man was pointing the corroding brick ruin. His strong, capable hands wielded the trowel, cutting a criss-cross in the mortar, patting it, taking a triangular portion, and buttering up the cracks with smooth, firm, clean strokes — like putting grey ice-cream between thick red wafers. He was friendly enough, smiling down at me, acknowledging my existence, uttering a monosyllabic greeting; and at the foot of the ladder I returned his smile and offered his compatriot a cigarette as a strangers's confirmatory token of being in the subservient position of a guest in the house of friends of a friend.

The pointing continued apace. I was anxious to show that I knew nothing of it: that I could not distinguish one end of a trowel from the other, and more, could not have pointed a single brick had my life depended on it. To this end I gazed upwards with the wide-eyed totally preoccupied fixedness of a child or simpleton, as though the pointing of a wall at the rear of a house in the backstreets of Catford was a unique and wondrous revelation that would have had the world agog had the world but known about it. My brown-irised eyes were open to their fullest extent, my head had fallen back, my jaw partly drooped, my cigarette smouldered unheeded, and I maintained this ridiculous posture until a choking sensation at the back of my throat made me swallow saliva in order to lubricate the parched membranes. (The man up the ladder, I was later to learn, was called Darwin.) Why is it that such commonplace capsulets of time become fast in one's mind, as the faded school photographs of one's youth in which a face is forever turned towards the camera, half-smiling, with the sunlight casting a perpetual shadow from the nose across the cheekbone? Is God at work then? Has Eternity frozen? Is the Universe pinned to a piece of card like a butterfly, transfixed in a gelatine coating of absolute stillness and timelessness? For who is to say that Darwin is not at this very moment pointing that self-same wall, his honest, broad-palmed hands working the mortar, slicing it, extracting soft grey wedges to insert in the cracks of decaying red brick? To the inhabitants of a planet circling in one of the great starry arms of the Galaxy of Andromeda he will be seen to be performing this task two million years from now; and so, at some point beyond our solar system, the image of a man on a ladder and two men at the foot of it is proceeding this instant in accordance with Einsteins's Theory of Relativity: timeless, eternal, infinite.

Shadows lengthened in the yard; the crippled flagstones assumed an even drunker aspect, and I went through the kitchen to where Tee and her cousin were still in earnest discussion. The cream cracker crumbs remained on the table, their significance unnoticed, and there they lay throughout the meal that followed, which consisted of sausages, bacon, and beans. As will be assumed, quite rightly, the jammy yellow-handled knife too was left to its own devices.

It was suggested later in the evening that I take a bath, and forgetting to lock the door was surprised to see Tee's smiling head observing my splashing and scrubbing. Uninvited she entered the bathroom and dried me with a large, soft, white, fluffy towel, doing this carefully and professionally as befits a psychiatric nurse. Arousal was not long overdue, on both our parts, and my penis lifted its weary head and took a look at the same stale world it thought had expired once and for all following its last appearance; naturally the terrain was familiar to its greedy gaze. Tee was a devotee of male anatomy, in awe and fear of the consequences of her actions, fascinated as a child with a new, terrifying plaything. Matters were progressing as planned when the buxom cousin came in, another grinner, it transpired, who stared with unabashed curiosity at my now much-enlarged penis protruding in the air, the focal point of all our neuroses, standing there like a superior fourth personage who accepts as a matter of course his privileged position in an oligarchic society populated in the main by idiots, imbeciles and half-wits.

The cousin placed her hand on my buttocks, holding one of them very firmly, and looked with downcast eyes, savouring both the visual and the tactile sensations that my hard and soft flesh made available to her. Meanwhile, Tee, whose breathing had become slack, was slowly lifting the hem of her quilted house-coat to facilitate the introduction of my erect penis — not into her, but against her, so that its blind probing head would feel the bristle of hair growing at the front and curling between her legs. She closed her eyes luxuriously and a slight sigh escaped her lips. Very shortly we were all three naked, I cushioned between their black bodies, their black bodies cushioning me. The cousin had fine ample breasts which she manoeuvred against my back, her two arms underneath mine, her fingertips skimming over my belly to touch, test, and finally to take hold of my swollen penis, at the same time licking the sensitive spot where my neck merged into my shoulder.

Tee was kneeling before me, her nostrils dilated, loathing the thought of what she was about to do and yet withholding the dreadful moment as if to extract from it the greatest possible amount of ecstatic terror. In such a nano-second do we perceive the true state of all things. Urged on by her cousin — who during this had manipulated the taut flesh to majestic proportions — Tee accepted the globular, moist end and, her mouth open to its widest extent, felt its increasing pressure at the back of her throat. Her breathing was nearly stopped; her eyes started to bulge; the skin of her face was tight and shiny as, being obliged to stretch to its utmost, it had far exceeded the accustomed facial pressure loading.

A goodly portion remained unmouthed, so it came as no surprise when the cousin knelt at the side and wrapped her lips round the barrel. Thus they hung on to me: two terriers jaw-locked to a rat until the death of one or all three should intervene.

I stood with my hands on my hips, lord-like, and felt the ripple of a thrill shudder into their mouths; at once there was a mute protest, and the cousin looked up at me beseechingly, afraid that I was about to expend everything without due consideration of her needs and desires. She stood up quickly, straddling Tee, and lifted her breasts for my inspection, hoping, possibly, that the sight of their fullness, the size and state of her nipples, and her general brazen attitude would induce me to withdraw my jerking penis and slide its full-grown length up her cunt. The proposition was tempting; I narrowed my eyes so that the eyelashes interlocked at the outermost corners and contemplated her lazily, deliberately lingering over the decision, Tee sucking on me, the cousin offering herself, the image of the three of us on its way to the Galaxy of Andromeda — and eventually came to the conclusion that, due to the size of her breasts, the cousin merited that which Tee was in the process of receiving. Whereupon I laid myself down on the floor, in a supine position, and had the cousin squat over me, thereby offering her most vulnerable parts to my tongue, lips, and mouth. Thus immersed in the hot blackness, and with Tee fighting for breath, struggling to contain me, I realised that my fantasy world was far more substantial than the material universe.

The cousin was, in fact, very quick to come, and almost in the self-same instant I felt my bursting, pulsing penis discharge itself into Tee's mouth, and to afford myself the optimum pleasure I reached up and grasped the cousin's heavy breasts, fondling them, playing with them, squeezing them, vibrating my fingertips over the stiff nipples, manipulating them in every way until they had been exploited beyond the point of having any physical relationship with a human being, had ceased to be objects of sensual desire, and were merely non-associative appendages hanging in a black void. That the experience was real there was no doubt; and with the passage of time would become the subject of masturbatory release and, after that, would coil inwards, feeding on its own entrails. It is in this way that the masturbator masturbates on the memory of previous masturbations.

CHAPTER V

CONVERSATION IN A DARKENED ROOM

Tee and I maintained a very beautiful relationship. There was nothing strained about it, or awkward, or in the slightest way uncomfortable. Occasionally, of course, we fell silent in each other's company, wishing, for the moment, to stay locked inside our own minds. But these were far outnumbered by the times when I was glad to be with her, joyous in her presence and content to let life unroll before me like a series of unrehearsed scenes in a film. It was just as though someone had slackened the reins on my shoulders, released the strait-jacket, and I was free to drift through minutes, hours, days with no conscious destination, without a fixed point of reference to which I must always align myself.

That evening, for example, we took a leisurely stroll in the warm, caressing air and Tee gently recalled some of the incidents that formed part of our lives — that is, our lives with one another. She held my hand strongly as we strolled along. People glanced askance but we were not to be deterred. They could think whatever they wished: we were living out our singular, unique lives and we knew that — supposing no new moments were being minted — these could be our last together, and therefore very precious. If everyone lived as if it were their last day the world would be a finer place. (The nightdrive from Reading was yet to come.)

There were few people about, and soon a chill pierced the air, making us grin through our clenched teeth despite our hunched shoulders and quivering stomachs. Her hand was hard in mine and not at all feminine. Again, as so often in the past, I saw myself from the outside, as a complex, dithering mass of uncoordinated impulses shooting in all directions like the electrons in a nuclear reactor when the rods are withdrawn. That people should see a complete, fully-formed man when they looked at me was a source of wonder, practically endless. Tee ran laughingly, oblivious of the rule which says that everything, including life, is finite.

That night we slept together in a narrow bed in the back room, the cousin at the last moment before lights out popping her head round the door, her face split in a brilliant crescent: an image that stayed with me till the following evening when Tee and I were in the front room of the house in Reading, waiting for the appointed hour when I would climb into my car and drive through the night to the North. The smudged colour photographs of the little girls stood looking at one another, eyes wide and staring but winking slyly when our backs were turned. The room gathered up the darkness and stored it in corners; the amber street lighting sent slanting trapeziums across the walls, and the deep mournful moan of a scratched 78 record entered one ear, while the silence entered the other. The singer was Percy Sledge.

Tee said, 'How old is your little boy now?' I answered her, asking in the same breath why she wanted to know. Questions can be so irritating; I dislike questions intensely. She had never met him (it would have been out of the question anyway) and it was approaching the point of futility to expend breath asking or answering.

'I saw a photograph of him once,' she remarked, and

indeed she had, for some campaign or other.

The darkness of the room was pressing heavily so that her face lost its features one by one. They dissolved into an amorphous black blob framed by hair on which the yellow light had gilded a vertical halo. We were sitting close together on the sofa under the window. The record scratched. She wasn't laughing, or smiling even, any more.

'Will you never leave her?' she said in a low voice. An articulated lorry filled the pause.

'What would we do if I did?'

'We could live together,' again in a low voice. 'I will soon have a job and we could get a flat in London.' She was simply making words with her low voice. The needle reached the centre groove and hissed round the label.

'You've never been so blunt about it before,' I said. Did I say that? Does one ever say that? Another lorry rumbled past and the trapeziums on the wall trembled. We sat with our arms holding the other, hugging tight, our hip-bones pressing hard. 'You will have a good life,' I hazarded to say. The road North, with its squashed animals, was beckoning me. The heat of her thigh had communicated itself to the full length of mine. The record continued to hiss.

Tee held my left hand in hers, working the fingers as if they contained malleable rubber bones. The coarse muskiness of her perfume titillated the hairs in my nostrils; and with her next words came a slight catch in the voice:

'If my mother dies I shall think of going back home.'

'Is she going to die?' I inquired politely. Was Tee's mother, at this instant, labouring for breath in the next room? Was she indeed lying in the middle of the rumpled double-bed, gasping, her blind eyelids upturned to the ceiling? It is sobering, saddening, to reflect that some people live their lives in constant pain. It must be like having a great iron spike encased in one's chest, belly and bowels, the cold malignant metal pressing against the warm vital organs. You cannot escape it, no matter what you do.

The world revolves around an iron spike: the peoples of the earth are parasites spinning about an axis of cold metallic malignancy.

The room had assumed complete anonymity; it could have been anywhere, and probably was. The silver frames of the photographs glinted in the murky depths like little, bright-eyed, malicious winks. The likenesses of the children were gleefully eavesdropping. And still we pressed close, Tee and I, drowsily warm with the pain of leave-taking. A number of memories plagued me: the bell-boy at the hotel — Brett (?) something-or-other — and the similar-looking photographer at the Exhibition. Had she made a secret pact with them? Were they even now waiting, two gigglers, in the passageway outside, gasping soundlessly and digging each other in the ribs, biding their time?

'Had we never met do you know that I might have married Darwin?' Tee's voice said in the gloom.

'So the pattern would have been changed yet again,' I said.

'If I had met you before — before . . . Do you think we would have got married? Would you have asked me to marry you?'

'I don't know; probably; yes; I might have; I don't know.'

Tee's breath shuddered in her chest. 'I am going to miss you. Will you come and see me? You can come down, can't you, once a month at least?'

'Not every month; I'll come and see you when I can. But I expect you'll have plenty of friends, photographers and people.'

Outside, the first pang of black night air had touched the metal door-knockers and bell-push surrounds. The traffic lumbered by, tail-lights flashing. The redness of these flicked like lighthouse beams across Tee's face in the dimness of the room, and her large eyes appeared to be bathed in shining transparent oil, so deep and magical in their opalescence that her reality as another human existence, breathing, palpitating, became apparent to me. Conversely it made me aware of my own real existence, such as it was — an unusual occurence, for I do not, as a rule, believe in the existence of the material universe.

'Would you like something to eat before you go?'

'No,' I replied, remembering the hard fried eggs. Her smell was very strong now. Her harsh hair rustled against my cheek. Her invisible eyes stared sightlessly into the anonymous room. When I kissed her and threaded my tongue between her lips I felt her suppress a dry choking sob at the back of her throat: she held it intact with her stomach muscles, entering into the kiss with her head thrown back — silently screaming as it were. 'Oh,' Tee said, speaking my name. Again I kissed her, her lips flattening against my teeth; then her mouth was fully open and eager to accept whatever silky explorations I might devise. Nothing tastes so sweet as the saliva of a nubile girl.

'Oh,' Tee said again, her mouth half smothered. Sparks were presumably flashing behind her shut eyelids; she was experiencing the wet probing of my tongue everywhere throughout her mouth; the dull hot growth was spreading between her thighs and inching its way up inside her belly; her limbs were uncontrollable; her backbone might at any second dissolve, leaving an open, inviting, defenceless receptacle, shapeless, yielding, ready. 'Oh,' she said.

A sombre groan intercepted my next ploy: it was the old lady turning in troubled sleep. Our huddled shapes sat motionless, silhouetted against the night window through which the anaemic lamplight cascaded as in a dream. Tee uncoiled her limbs gracefully and set the needle in a new groove. Percy Sledge began to sing 'When A Man Loves A Woman', a sound that to this day recreates Tee, that room, the house on Oxford Road, the smudged smiling children in their silver frames, the old lady amidst crumpled sheets, and the smooth tarmac snake outside upon which the

lights looked down like yellow eyes on arching concrete
stalks.

'I love you,' Tee said softly, back in my arms. Or perhaps
it was my imagination that had uttered the sacred words.
Perhaps it was the sly winking children. Perhaps, even, it
was the giggling gasping eavesdroppers in the passageway,
convulsing soundlessly over a joke at my expense. But one
thing for certain: it couldn't have been the sick old lady
muttering and twisting in pain-filled sleep. Or could it?
Everything is possible: nothing can be proven, only falsified.

In any event it was time to leave. I had difficulty in
tearing myself away from her grasp, which was only to be
expected. It is always a wrench at the best of times. Tee
clasped me lovingly, and then, in the depths of the
darkened room, disappeared like a puff of smoke. I sat on
apprehensively, the hissing record scribing a scar on the
delicate tissue of my brain. It was almost feasible to
believe that I was a ghost inhabiting an alien time zone and
that it was not Tee who had vanished, but me, and the
room I now perceived was a trick, an illusion, a blurry
error left behind like the residue in an empty wine bottle.
But no, I *was* here; the sofa was solid and substantial
beneath my fingers, the record was crackling, the
articulated lorries were lumbering past, the silver frames
were glinting viciously. Then where was Tee, and by what
magic had she removed her physical presence from the
darkened room? Could it be that certain people had
received instruction in the art of molecular displacement
while my briefing had been woefully inadequate? Had I
missed a vital parade? Had my number been called when
I was absent offstage?

Later it was to seem to my scrambled memory circuits
that the scene had been snatched intact from a novel. The
Exhibition, Catford, and the coming nightdrive were too
fantastic to have taken place as a random series of events,
experiences, happenings. Of course Tee wasn't a real

person; of course her mother was not dying in fitful agonised sleep. And as for the watchers in the passageway I did not believe in them for the simple reason that two gasping laughers such as they could not have remained so silent during the preceding conversation. (Besides, they would have wakened the mother, and Tee would have created an awful fuss.)

Straightening my limbs and feeling the tingle of fresh blood in my buttocks I set the playing arm to one side and slowed the record with the tips of my fingers. The machine emitted a mechanical protesting whirr.

'I'll see you to the door,' Tee said. In fact she came and sat next to me in the car, crying, leaving my face wet and smarting. I was never going to see her again. No more. Never again. Driving along Oxford Road I tried to purse my lips into the shape of a whistle.

CHAPTER VI

M6/EXIT 21/A57

The car hummed along, the needles quivering in their little green portholes, and soon illuminated Oxford Road gave way to twin pools of light fanning across the shiny black A34. Through villages I sped, the houses like scenic flats without substance, supported from behind by slats of soft yellow pine, criss-crossed and battened to make them stable. Two-dimensional people slept inside, stacked like flattened cardboard boxes in airless storerooms. Stratford-upon-Avon was grey and ethereal in the moonlight, the old stone bridge over the river made of papier mâché; and the river too contained a perfect simulacrum of the moon on the placid oily skin of its surface. Not a creature stirred in the dead town, and in vain I tried to hush the engine noise which thoughtlessly echoed and re-echoed, boomed and reverberated over the flat water.

Midnight ticked by: the planet swung like a blue-green pendulum in the starry void. England slept; I drove; the old lady moaned; the moon sank to meet its rising image in the slack waters of the Avon. On the smooth ebony-like wheel my hands performed exquisitely expressive gestures as they guided the heavy car across the bridge and through the slumbering town. In its ball-and-pinion socket the gear lever clucked with precision-engineered smugness, the cogs gliding into mutually-acceptable grooves as between the hedgerows the lone car with its single occupant followed the wavering line North on a memorable nightdrive!

Birmingham, in the early hours of the morning, had about it that quality of an unfinished pencil drawing whose outlines have not been shaded in with varying tones. The place left a taste of unreality in the mouth — a bitter taste reminiscent of aluminium saucepans containing zinc. The first light of dawn was drab and dead, washing all vitality away and draining the air of life: and the air itself was so still and calm that gossamer would have hung in it, transfixed as between two panes of glass. I will confess it: I was deathly tired. My eyelids kept drooping over my parched eyeballs, two leaden weights against which all my willpower was pitted. Goodness, what a struggle.

In a motorway self-service cafeteria on the M6 I ate bread and cheese and drank two cups of coffee. Other night travellers wandered about with eyes freshly hatched and wearing their clothes like pyjamas; at the moment I felt secure within myself, safe with the inner knowledge that I could come and go as I pleased, stand or sit, walk or run. The place was laid bare with flourescent lighting, as clinical and white as an operating theatre, yet so filthy that one's hands became soiled from merely handling the cutlery. Under the table my feet shuffled in rubbish. A girl opposite me smiled as she poured sugar onto a spoon; it piled up in a small conical hill.

'Aren't these places awful?' she said, and on 'awful' her nose ruckled up into several corrugations; yet she was smiling all the while. Her hands were rather chubby. The flesh hung underneath her fingers like furled sails. I noticed too that the lipstick had faded away from the corners of her mouth, and just below her left ear the grain of the fine fair down was most discernible, moving up the neck and then turning ninety degrees to follow the line of the jaw. Notwithstanding, she was extremely attractive: buxom, two slightly protruding front teeth giving her mouth a moist, provocative, faintly gasping look that was three-tenths on the way to a smile. (Some people cannot display their teeth, no matter how hard they try.) This was without doubt the reason why her lipstick had worn thin at the edges. It wasn't every night one sat opposite an attractive girl in a motorway cafeteria. She picked up the cup in one hand, holding a paper handkerchief clawlike in the other — as such women do — and took tentative sips with pouting lips, then dabbed away the residue behind which hovered the glimmerings of a smile. She was the kind of woman upon whose body can be found a preponderance of moles. Her ankles would be slim, and she would tan easily, and in due course would discover that short hair suited her best. At this point in my assumptions a man came up and said brusquely, 'Ruth,' and stood looking down at the two of us, shifting his gaze from one to the other. 'Ruth?' the girl said, shaking her head. She looked at me. I looked at the man. The man looked at the girl. The process reversed itself, like alternating current. 'I'm Ryl,' the girl said. She had very full lips. 'Oh,' the man said. 'Didn't you teach primary schoolchildren in Oldham?' 'No,' the girl (Ryl) said. 'I'm not a teacher.' 'You're not?' 'No.' 'You're not from Oldham?' 'No.' 'Sorry,' the man said, going. 'Where are you from?' I discovered I had asked. 'Rusholme.' The circle was tightening all right.

Ahead the early light was shining through the mist, and

the air became colder as the motorway screamed North: a concrete stripe obeying the contours of soft green velvet. At Exit 21 I followed the full circular sweep leading to the A57, the road Tee and I had driven along not many days before. Now the passenger seat was empty, her luggage gone, and the nightdrive with its squashed animals a segment of instant nostalgia. I looked at my watch; at this pace the Corn Exchange would be open – just – to admit the cleaning staff. It was a vast, ornate building with dank corridors and antiquated lifts. Wrought ironwork protected the greasy litter-strewn lift shafts – although few suicides had been recorded of late. I had it on reliable authority that the building was good for another ten years.

In the clear sky of morning it seemed that the world had reassembled itself into some semblance of order; perhaps it was the lack of people, or maybe the quiet beauty of a new sky, or the disquieting knowledge that despite all setbacks and doubts and horrifying premonitions I was, incredibly, still alive . . . and the fact that I could think of myself as being alive was the most incredible self-knowledge of all. I had come through to a new world, surfaced in a fresh day, and the dark, mysterious, unreal events of night had ceased to exist. The girl in the motorway cafeteria was a blur of hieroglyphics on the opposite page. Catford was a dying sunset. The Exhibition a laughable paranoiac exercise. Tee's cousin, Tee's mother, Tee herself, and all the other invented characters safely behind me on numbered pages. And, even more of a jolt to the imagination, had but one atom been displaced at the beginning of time none of this would have happened; nor, more than likely, would any of us have inhabited the planet. We are but a single possibility in a universe of accidents, a freak draw in any one of ten trillion permutations. There was no plan – unless it could be conceived that a random, haphazard scheme was predictable in its very unpredictability. But after the next cataclysm when the exploding fragments of matter have ceased to be expelled and begin to fall inwards to the central molten core . . . when time has run backwards and we are born old and age to embryos . . . when elements are created anew and gravity becomes a racial memory . . . after this — what? Some might suppose that 312 Oxford Road was destined to exist (and some might even doubt its present existence), as though time possesses its own irrefutability; they might also be inclined to believe that the lives we inhabit like pips inside a grape are nothing more than line-learning dress rehearsals preparing us for the Oxford Road of our dreams. The fact that Tee and her entourage were, are, real to me is no guarantee of their reality. This is not to say that I have imagined them, but rather that memory has the irritating trick of turning into fiction, just as experience becomes transmuted into myth even at the point of being experienced. Would it be nearer the truth, or further from it, to regard an imagined future as having more substance than the remembered past? Is it at all *possible* that, as I sit here in the courtyard at dusk looking out at the cubed concrete shapes and recalling all that has supposedly gone before . . . is it within the bounds of human credibility that, unknown to the narrator, I inadvertantly swapped places with another persona and am not now who I think I am?

PART II

CHAPTER I

Hope Hospital must once again be the focal point of my memories, even though nothing happened there that is worth recounting. But how many evenings have I sat alone in the car watching the cloaked nurses hurrying back from duty, waiting to catch a glimpse of those flashing eyes and teeth!

When I returned from abroad Tee had been in London several months, living and working in Hampstead. On the train I wrote a shaky letter to Jay, posted it in London, and went in search of Tee: at length I found her in charge of a small psychiatric ward; we kissed furtively in the office and she gave me the key to her flat which was at the top of a tower block guarded by a decrepit commissionaire. The flat was small, modern, delightfully compact, and clean; the communal kitchen was along the hallway, and I saw not another soul (except the commissionaire) as I took the lift to the fourteenth floor and let myself in to the one room in which everything was thoughtfully provided. Everything I saw and touched reminded me of the Urmston experience. The rooms and hallways were the same box-like cavities and the light was merciless, unfeeling, drab. Even the plain cream walls, with an eggshell sheen on them, were featureless monstrosities upon whose surface a fly would not have dared to leave its droppings.

So I waited in yet another darkened room, waited for Tee to arrive, and imagined what I would do to her when she did. The radio was tuned to a popular station and music was playing. Lying on the bed, afloat at the peak of a concrete tower, I looked at the unblemished ceiling and visualised myself as the only man on earth thinking these certain thoughts. The visualisation exhilarated and frightened me, because from it followed the hypothesis that I was unique, and to be A Unique Man and yet a speck in infinitesimal time was a concept too overwhelming for my mind to encompass. Even the thought of the thought of it had to be kept at arm's length, glimpsed out of the corner of my eye, so to speak, which is why I busy myself with inconsequential doings, fill my head with plans of action, in order to delay the fatal moment when I must reverse my eyeballs and stare into the murky contents of my brain.

Traffic noises faintly from below: subdued whine of the lift rising up the shaft: disturbed shadows on the ceiling: radio singing inanely to itself — audible and visual impressions of being alive in the latter half of the twentieth century. The fact that I was alive was confirmed by the beating of my heart. It thumped inside my chest causing the material of my shirt to vibrate in tiny spasms, and when I held my breath and raised my head to witness this miracle it thumped all the harder. The little pearl buttons trembled with each reverberation. It was terrifying to imagine what would happen if the blood ceased to flow: the skin becoming cold and clammy, the eyes fixed like dead marbles, and the stiffness creeping through the trunk and limbs until a statue lay on the bed like an effigy on a tomb. Desperately I sought to keep this from happening, urging the hot body flow, encouraging the heart muscle to clench and release, willing the liver, pancreas, bladder, bowels and other organs to continue their functions unabated — all this to little avail, because the machine went its own sweet way unheedful of my frantic attentions; it might not have belonged to me. Gradually, imperceptibly, my heart returned to its accustomed rhythm and I relaxed inside myself (as it were), lay down at ease within my own body, a small timid creature trapped inside a mechanical husk.

At several minutes before eleven Tee returned from duty, moving briskly about the tiny flat as though unaware of my presence, ignoring the supine figure in the corner underneath the window. She made coffee and brought it to the bed. There was something different about her. I had detected it in the office adjoining the psychiatric ward, and now the feeling came over even more strongly. She was not the Tee of previous times, not the girl who had pressed her hard body against mine and whispered sexy innuendos, not the girl beneath the stone railway bridge who had almost crushed the air out of my lungs with the fierceness of her long-armed embrace. And her hairstyle too was changed: encircling her head in a black frizzy mop. She sat down and, in characteristic fashion, rested her hand on my palpitating shirt. This was in the nature of a friendly reassurance, though it was obviously nothing more or less than a token gesture. The spark had gone out of our relationship, that much was clear. What had happened? Was she married to Desmond? Had Darwin recaptured her love? Was her mother deceased? Had she become acquainted with the photographer? Had my charm lost its magic appeal? When a girl loses interest nothing in the world can revitalise it. Her opening remark confirmed my doubts and suspicions.

'I never expected to see you again.' Yes, even the tone of her voice was altered. She had lost her laughing manner and was now hard-eyed and utterly business-like. Nothing remained of the tender girl of sweet temperament with whom I had been intimate on at least six hundred occasions.

Tee took up the cup in both hands and lost her face in it, either deep in her own thoughts or perhaps wishing to avoid my gaze. Possibly she was finding my unexpected visit inopportune — at any rate she had firmly set her mind against any welcome. Of course, I realised belatedly, the girl was not entirelv to blame: an appointment I had promised faithfully to keep (at the Urmston flat) several months before I had wilfully let slip, being concerned at the time with another person who, still a virgin, held more promise of spicy adventure. To make amends I apologised for my nonappearance.

'When was that?' Tee asked, lowering the cup. 'I had forgotten. And anyway —' she shrugged '— it doesn't matter,' and the old grin came back for a bare instant. I propped myself up to drink the warm, sticky coffee. A muskiness from the hot folds of her neck hit me below the belt like a sledgehammer whiff of nostalgia. I leaned forward and kissed her cheek, the side of her jaw, and the soft part of her neck, in shadow, from whence the wonderful hot fragrance emanated. There was a new tensity about her whole being, a finely concealed reluctance which disappointed, saddened, and finally angered me. When a man is thwarted his spirit wilts as well.

'You are welcome to sleep here,' Tee said, placing no particular emphasis on the word 'sleep', which emphasised it all the more. Did she expect a docile acquiescence to this remark? Was I merely a body to be accommodated for the night? Would she, in her heart of hearts, have preferred to see me walking the gutter — cold, hungry, roofless, without a friend in the whole of Hampstead? Such is the transience of sexual attraction, which, when the juices have ceased to stew and curdle, becomes an empty echo of itself, souring the heart and leaving the flesh in a state of repugnant flaccidity.

Yet still I pressed forward, nuzzling the arch of her neck, almost in a fury of desperation, eagerly, foolishly, inveigling her torpid co-operation in an act which, at best, could only be described as perfunctory; for immediately afterwards I would dispose of her existence in a hidden pocket in my mind and turn over into a dreamless sleep.

'You mustn't do it; it's perfectly all right for you to stay the night but other than that I can't promise anything.'

Why was lovely Tee saying these words? Had she forgotten so quickly the long sordid history of back rooms, hotel rooms, bathrooms? Why, we had even made love (inexpertly it is true) in the rear of a green van converted into a mobile touring home. Did none of this mean anything to her? Was she so spitefully heartless that she could deny our devious and intricately-woven association stretching back over two years and seven months?

By degrees my nerveless fingers crept round the starched apron of her uniform: exploring imploring hands that were eloquent in their dumbness. The breath was solidifying in my throat, my pulse was tick-tocking madly, the blood was beginning to clot in the bulging arteries of my neck — soon the suffocating blanket of sexual heat would blot out the world of sane, civilised creatures, of sweetness and light, of intellect and reason, and I would be transformed into a rabid thing with a blood-red mist in front of its eyes. Tee's cool dark hands held the sides of my face, yet it was a restraining gesture and not an endearment. 'I don't want to do it,' she said quietly.

Oh what was this? What was this? What was happening? What was going on?

'You can stay here,' she repeated. 'I couldn't be so unkind as to turn you out on a night like this. Besides,' she added, 'the commissionaire would almost certainly have his suspicions aroused if he saw you leaving at this hour.'

This triggered something off in me. 'He has a fairly common face,' I ventured to say.

'What do you mean, "a fairly common face"?' Tee said,

cradling my head in her two hands. The pads of her fingers supported the receptacle that contained a million possible universes.

'I mean,' I said, 'that his face strikes a chord; it's a face I've seen before. A familiar face.'

'Possible,' Tee conceded. 'He hasn't been here very long.'

'Do you intend staying at this hospital yourself?'

'What has that got to do with the commissionaire?'

I said, 'Nothing. Nothing. The one thought simply led to the other, that's all. I didn't mean to imply a connexion between the two.'

'You are a silly boy,' she said, and suddenly it was the old Tee, the laughing Tee, the sexy Tee, coming out from behind her mask of frigid indifference. Her great mouth split wide-open in a tremendous grin, her beautiful sparkling teeth flashing behind the stretched fleshy curvature of her lips. What had passed between those lips since last we met? Who had stood before her and inserted himself into that gaping maw?

I pressed my forehead to her breastless chest and the thuds of her heart jarred my skull. I was alive, and Tee was with me, and of what consequence were all my other problems alongside these two statements of fact? If only we could die at such moments of lucidity perhaps we might be granted a brief insight into the true nature of all things.

'Your body is brown,' Tee said.

'I've been to Spain.'

'Look at this white mark round your waist!' She was tracing its undulations with her fingers.

'I thought you were going to throw me out,' I said like a little lost puppy.

'Silly boy,' said Tee, slipping naked under the covers beside me. 'But you realise that we can only sleep?'

'Only sleep?'

'Only sleep.' Tee was quite definite: absolutely adamant.

'But you were laughing; you were grinning all over your face. I thought it was a joke when you laughed, as though —'

'What has grinning and laughing to do with anything?' Tee said, puzzled in her turn.

'Well, doesn't it mean —?'

'What?'

'I thought it meant —'

'Since when did grinning and laughing mean *any*thing?'

Obviously it would be wise for me to desist, otherwise her perturbations might increase out of all proportion. I lay down, pulled the covers over me, shut my eyes, felt Tee's bony knees against the backs of my legs, and pretended to sleep. But in a little while, having edged and wriggled and squirmed under the covers to the foot of the bed, I found myself between her legs, my mouth against her furry pubis, my tongue inserting itself between the several soft layers of lips, flicking, darting, trilling, so that Tee muttered in her sleep and came drowsily, deliciously awake with a sensation that was balanced between ecstasy and agony, on the verge of a scream, a long-drawn-out whine of endurance as though someone or something had touched the raw nerve-endings of the tender root that was the central growth from which the whole of her being sprang; and to my ears came the familiar, welcome gutteral sounds of pleasure, while of their own accord her legs stiffened outwards, quivering like a water-diviner's rods, her toes curling and flexing as the hot quick thrill rose up inside her belly and set her thighs a-tingling.

In the morning I rode down, haggard but proud, in the lift, emerging to face the seated commissionaire, and with a flash of instantaneous recognition knew him to be a cleaner who had once worked at the Corn Exchange.

CHAPTER II

THE REPETITIVE NIGHTMARE

I never saw Tee again, and haven't seen her to this day — to this moment, if the truth be known.

But now we must hasten backwards in time to the scene of rather a remarkable coincidence: bowling along the motorway in a green van converted into a four-berth camper, my spirits were as heavy as lead weights, unremittingly oppressive, because no matter how hard I pressed the accelerator to the floor the vehicle refused to exceed twenty-eight miles per hour. This was so tiring that I took to using alternate feet, crossing my left over my right and sitting side-saddle on the seat facing the open window. The other three occupants, in the rear, suspected nothing. We proceeded in this ridiculous, exhausting fashion as far as the northern outskirts of Birmingham where total reluctance overcame the beast and it slumped sullenly at the side of the road, spitting and hissing with ugly spite. I was very near suicide at this point, or if not suicide, tears. Would we ever reach Spain in this condition? Would we ever reach Southampton? Would we ever reach Abingdon? The beast thrutched forward a couple of miles and failed again. It repeated this magnanimous gesture several times until — the engine smouldering in hot black rage — I decided to let it subside peacefully in a convenient layby while the four of us ate fish and chips with our fingers. The two children were tired but excited, and grimy from doing nothing. Sitting at the formica table propped on its single strut I happened to look out at the lighted shops bordering the main road; I happened casually, disinterestedly, to assimilate the streaking metal shapes of cars with their cruel, fiery, vanishing tail-lights: and by pure chance I came to recognise this as the very place where Tee and I had sat eating hot crumbly fish and she had sensuously licked my fingers one by one. I found it difficult to believe; it was verging on the unbelievable.

My life was a vicious circle. The atoms were circular, the molecules were circular, the planet was circular, the solar system was circular, the galaxy was circular, our local cluster was circular, the universe was circular, life itself was circular, time was circular . . . which explained, in part, why wherever I went I met mirror-images of myself going to or returning from Somewhere. At will, it seemed, I could walk out of one scene and step into another; life was a circular stage divided into sets like the segments of a cake, and there stood I, watching them twirl by, each brightly-lit fully-contained fragment a separate, independent and yet integral part of my life. Some of them had inter-connecting doors, while others (on opposite sides of the circle) were inverted replicas: exact inside-out-upside-down-back-to-front mirror-images of past or future existences.

Thus the flashing black road with its shrieking imbeciles was in direct communion with the winding midnight snake (and its squashed animals) of several months previous. The two were the same and I would not have been unduly surprised, or disturbed even, to find Tee's laughing eyes twinkling mischievously up at me, the hot grease shining on her lips and fingertips and running down her wrist. Had I turned to my left, there she would have been: had I turned to my right – as I did– there would sit Wife and Children. Yes, there they were: travel-tired, a little upset at these enforced halts, a little frightened too by the violent, unfamiliar environment into which they had been thrust. The sand-coloured hills of Spain wreathed in distorting layers of light were far away in time and space, as yet unexperienced and therefore unreal, fictitious. The reality of the moment was confined to the cold interior of a van, a piece of suicidal road, the oncoming night, and a fluttering fear that left the thick batter and fish part-digested.

Sitting and thinking about this – in addition to several

million other thoughts at any given nano-second of time —
and staring out at the aforementioned roadway, I was
struck by the absurd repetition of circumstances that so
far had been the outstanding characteristic of the trip.
First, we had ridden singing past the entrance to Hope
Hospital, that repository of all my phobias and fetishes;
then the Soap Works and its attendant rainbows had jolted
into view, illustrating the thesis that pollution can be
beautiful; then followed the countrified A57 curving
finally into a concrete arc which slid into the motorway
like a tributary joining a great river; and now, would you
believe, hot greasy fish at the side of a road that had
become part of the folk-lore of my head. This chain of
coincidences was dizzying: no doubt a bell-boy with a
pock-marked face was at this instant preparing a meal or
making a bed in an as-yet-unspecified hotel. How far could
one's credulity be stretched? To what degree was I willing
to suspend my sanity and abandon myself to these
fantastic delusions? Was life *in actuality* a spool of film, so
many frames per second that could be run, re-run,
rewound, stopped, run backwards, run upside down,
inverted, projected in negative, made blurred, sharpened
into focus, slowed down, speeded up, edited, spliced,
dubbed, colour-heightened, tone-eliminated, and then
re-re-re-run till the actors wearied of parodying a pastiche
of a parody of a shadow of an image, etc? It was
conceivable that such interminable convolutions were the
very stuff of living matter, that the humdrum, everyday
world was gloss, static, the spume of a wave, while in
nightmares was to be found — not truth! — but the
wonderful total meaninglessness and horror which is the
interpretation of the human brain — the reaction of the
primitive human mind — to events, happenings and
experiences in a particular stratum of the space time
continuum.

After putting out a tractor fire with our extinguisher we

arrived in Abingdon and sought an hotel. We sat in the lounge eating sandwiches and watching late-night news. Strange, but these mass media events too, without the framework of a familiar environment, were make-believe fairytales cooked up moments before to make us feel at home: a semblance, if you like, of comfortable disasters and reassuring catastrophes which told us all was well with the tired old planet.

The children were falling asleep with their mouths full. They were tucked up in bed between strange white sheets stiff with too much laundering; and we too fell soundlessly asleep, our limbs entwined in embryonic knots of self-defence. We breakfasted together, the four of us, our nerves on tip-toe because a) it was a bright, glorious, late-spring day, b) would the van start and c) once started keep going? d) would we reach Southampton in time to catch the boat? e) what lay ahead of us in that vast foreign country with nothing between us and unimaginable terrors but a sheet of steel and four worn tyres?

'Would you like porridge or cereal?' the Wife asked, her slate-grey eyes preoccupied with the minutiae of motherly concern.

'Porridge,' the Boy replied, resting his jaw on the table and feeling the texture of the white cloth with his chin. The orbs of his eyes had been washed perfectly clean by sleep; those eyes sucked in the vivid images of morning: the sunlit dining-room, the black-clad ghosting waiters, the reflections of the marmalade dish on the ceiling — accepted them all with marvellous incomprehension. It was to him a day like any other: ordinary, unexceptional, a positive miracle.

The Girl, being older, had erected a barrier of composure which was a prelude to becoming an adult. With an ultra-delicate air she surveyed the world (and her parents) as from a great distance, peering at life long-sightedly, as it were. Her beautiful slim hands conveyed toast to her mouth by means of suggestion rather than actual physical movement. Everything was just so: had to be . . . just so. Bodily functions were a matter of extreme indelicacy and were not to be spoken of, referred to, or in any way hinted at. We were all of us gross creatures, her look implied, so better not to harp on the unpleasant albeit unavoidable fact.

The Wife busied herself with trivialities in order to displace the fear that was nibbling at the edges of her heart. She had been torn out of her environment and forced to participate in a nerve-racking nomadic life-style that had begun disastrously and looked like getting worse. Not to have a house, with walls, doors and windows; not to have a fixed point of reference but to be an aimless wanderer; not even to have a bed or lavatory one could call one's own: these were terrifying alien concepts which transformed peaceful, humdrum normality into a weirdly wild and uncontrollable landscape. Demons lurked everywhere and in the most unexpected places; even the faces of people (all of them strangers) took on grotesque aspects which suggested hitherto unguessed-at depths of alienness.

As for me I was, as usual, myself.

'Would you like some more coffee?' the Wife asked me, wielding the silver-spouted pot like a talisman.

The Boy was scooping toast crumbs off his plate and into his mouth, his eyes swivelling from plate to ceiling to waiters to coffee-pot to parents to plate. Nothing was spared; everything was devoured, toast crumbs and all.

'We should be moving,' I said, the clichéd man-of-action. At such moments I was fond of my wife. Together we were the dual poles that gave a framework of sorts to an unimaginable nightmare.

'Can I have some more toast?' the Girl said.

'How far have we to go?' the Wife said.

'Can *I* have some more toast?' the Boy said.

Waiters came and went. Toast appeared on the table and

stood like triangular records in racks. The sunlight shifted imperceptibly across the white cloth, and the miniature contents of the table were twice reflected in the Boy's round shining eyes, complete with tiny crucifixes – the window-frame.

'If only they could see us now,' the Wife said, attempting bravado. 'You know, we should be all right: we put out that fire.'

'Why should putting out that fire make us, or see us, all right?'

'Well . . . it's one favour owing, surely?'

'From who to whom?'

'If there's any *justice* we should be all right.' This was said fiercely, which were you to know her is quite out of character. It must have been fear or perhaps a residue of naive belief in Christian ethics. And I thought I had knocked it out of her head.

'How do you feel this morning?' I felt it incumbent upon me to ask this, as a monk mumbling an ancient liturgy; and besides, the Wife believed and found comfort in the balm of tame words.

'I feel better this morning than I did last night' – again the soothing familiarity of the bland reply. Had it been raining we should have remarked on the weather, but it was disconcertingly sunny.

'I want to go now,' the Boy said, or 'announced' as novelists say.

I beckoned to the waiter who stood motionless near the door, like a black lizard sunning itself, oblivious yet at the same time attentive to its surroundings. He swept away the tray containing the money and returned with a few coins glued to their silver images. Afterwards the four of us walked across the sunlit car park and positioned ourselves in the van. I was experiencing a mixture of elation and despair: I was glad we were together, a unit, a joyous family, and yet the dark side (everything has a dark side) would not relinquish my thoughts and let them fly up like seagulls. Why is it, I asked myself, that my nature will not allow the undiluted pleasure of the senses, of the moment in which I am living? Why should it be that I live life holding my breath? Who or what is pulling me back, its claws taking up all the slack so that my life has the texture, consistency, volatility and vulnerability of a taut balloon?

It is as stupid to expect answers to these questions as it is to ask them. Surely I worry unduly; undoubtedly I panic at nonsensical notions which lesser men rise above because they do not entertain morbid reflections on the nature of things. The sulking black engine burped and farted into reciprocating motion, diverting my attention from the ridiculous to the expedient.

CHAPTER III

THE PRINCIPLE OF INDETERMINACY

Having spent the night driving, with only one short rest midway between the M1 and M6, I was eager for sleep and hungry for food. It would be too early to gain access to the Corn Exchange — the cleaners not yet on the premises — and so I drove about the city's quiet antiseptic streets, grey in the encroaching dawn, and came upon an all-night café where a woman in a dirty apron put fresh bacon and egg between two slabs of bread. The coffee was the first to go, scalding the fur off my tongue and burning the tubes in my chest right down to my belly, and then I opened my mouth wide and bit cleanly and ravenously through the bread, the bacon, the egg, clamping my teeth hard and shuffling the delicious stuff round and round my palate. A man rescued from drowning could not have sucked his first gulp of air more gratefully. The second mouthful was, if anything, even better: the hot molten egg-yolk mingling

with the salty tooth-clogging strips of bacon, counter-
pointed by the soft bread into which the butter had seeped,
melted by those contents only recently scooped from the
sizzling frying-pan. A further cup of coffee, the sandwich
having vanished, constituted the ultimate pinnacle of
perfection, and I subsided blissfully into a warm-bellied
doze, a cigarette held lightly between my fingers.

The occupants of the café were scavengers of the night.
They had wandered in from the Friday night streets to this
Saturday morning oasis of warmth, food, music and
friendly yellow fluorescent light. I sat luxuriously happy in
my wellbeing, surveying these dregs of misfortune with a
semi-fearful and not unsympathetic eye. Their feet were
tied up in bundles of discoloured rags. Their eyes were
bloodshot, befuddled, and caked in the inner corners with
dirt. They inclined themselves over the tables, bent from
the hips, under the impression they were upright and
behaving with absolute decorum: the studied impossible
equilibrium of the habitual drunkard who maintains a
position of untenable imbalance in blithe disregard of the
law of gravity. What would, could, they do till nightfall?
This was the end of their day, the beginning of mine; the
the daylight must have stretched ahead like an innumerable
number of elastic hours, leaving them mercilessly exposed
as a man stranded in the middle of a desert under the
white disc of a noon sun. This living evidence of the
nearness of the abyss clamped my mind in freezing fear —
it was reminiscent of back rooms from which one could
view sinking blood-red suns through dust-laden venetian
blinds; it brought cascading into the mind unruly images of
isolated pubs in wastelands of rubble and leaning, leaking
gaslamps. It shattered in an instant the sensible façade of
clean, well-adjusted, odourless living behind which we
shelter in cowering timidity. (Does it disturb you to know
that this café exists? That at this moment it is open for
business? Is it like reading smugly about a fictional murder,

only to realise afterwards with a sickening shock that the murderer is real, exists, is living and breathing at this moment in time?)

In any event, the denizens of the café speckled my mind with uncertainty: made me conscious of the dreadful pit forever waiting with a black gape, eager to suck me in and swallow me down. A relatively untainted body and moderately clean clothes were all that kept me from sinking into the foul depths — my mind was no saving grace. And what, should it happen, would await me in that twilit half-world of perpetual dampness and decay? Would it, for example, assume the hellish landscape of silver towers and spheres with slim metal chimneys sending forth pluming jets of flame? Or a maze-like series of corridors, passageways and tunnels leading to galleries of slapping pulleys on whose walls indecipherable hieroglyphics had been scrawled by long-forgotten hands? Conceivably it could be a darkened room in which tinted photographs grinned and grimaced in silver frames, party to a private joke shared only by the silent laughers in the corridor outside. Any of these imagined hells was real, existed as valid alternatives in a stratum normally excluded from my sight. Just as the neutrinos inhabit a different kind of space, ungoverned by the mundane rules of Newtonian physics, so there lurk impulses of subterranean mindpower which can conjure up the most beastly visions foreign to the everyday functioning of our brains; yet just as real for all that. The fact that none of us exist — except as tiny spurts of energy — makes everything possible and impossible at one and the same time. Just as entire galaxies of anti-matter are adrift in space, a complete reversal of known and accepted physical laws, so in fiction we have the anti-hero, a negation of positive values, whose very being is diametrically placed in relation to the time-honoured concepts of empirical and materialistic man. Thus the anti-hero has the properties of anti-particles:

negative mass, negative energy, and the facility to move backwards and forwards in time.

The road home (the Corn Exchange behind me) lay cleanly and hygienically before me like a path towards sanity, respectability and order. I had departed on so many previous occasions, driving headlong into a westward-sinking sun, and returned just as often to seek and dwell in comfort and warmth. She had been left alone, unmourned, for a considerable time now, and I was undecided as to whether joy or humble humility should strut or wander despondently across my face (the age of spontaneous emotion being long gone). It was a political decision. Receding freshly from my mind were the cornfield and the green train in the green distance, the harsh indentations on soft warm flesh, and not least the odd evening of drunkenness in the Islington pub, surrounded by respectable-looking men and lecherous women. All the while this loving woman had been going about her business as a simple, unsuspecting soul, full to the brim with brave good cheer and a stoical sense of duty. I resolved to generate a feeling of genuine abashment, of contrition even; I would go down on my knees and beg her forgiveness, plead to have my sins forgiven (that is, supposing her to be aware of them).

At the door, a suitcase in either hand, I paused, debating between joy, humility, abashment and contrition. A mixture of all four perhaps? She came directly down from the bedroom, dressed in a house-coat, her hair pinned up and creases of sleep on her face like crumpled paper. Her large round eyes, recently opened on a new day, asked beseechingly if my return was permanent or a transitory practical joke. Yet it was not she who should have abased herself, but I! This sick irony was the first proper intimation of what I now conceive to be the true horror of my debased personality. To knowingly and deliberately wreck an honest human heart — to wring the final drop of blood from it as though it were no more than a dishrag, used and done with, having served its purpose . . .

She said, 'You must be tired, not having slept.' We were drinking coffee in the living-room, holding the cups between our crescent hands and staring at the dead bits of coal in the grate.

'I don't feel tired.' The two young ones were still asleep.

'Was it a very long drive?' she asked, seeming to ask the question out of interest rather than prying curiosity.

'Yes.'

Surely our words should not be at this low-level intensity? We were discussing our lives and futures — or would have been had the world contained a single grain of sense. As it was we exchanged platitudes and sipped the cooling liquid. The sun described a lazy parabola, its morning rays striking into the room and glancing off the corners of hard objects. I noticed a toy underneath a chair.

'I've painted the bathroom,' she said. Her bare knees protruded fron the house-coat.

'What colour?'

'Purple. But I mixed white with it' — defensively. 'To occupy my mind.'

'You mixed white with it to occupy your mind?' Had I missed an inference somewhere or perhaps a qualification?

'I painted the *bathroom*.'

'Yes?'

'To occupy my mind.'

'That makes more sense. Yes, I'm with you now. You occupied your mind —'

'— by painting the bathroom.'

'Purple.'

'With white mixed in with it. Did you stop for a meal on the motorway? You must be hungry too.'

'No, I had a sandwich in a café. Horrible place.'

'You spend a lot of your life driving from here to there.'

She really was gentle and I detested myself. The figure I had dreamed up to bear the brunt of my detestation was not at all strong enough to maintain the pose of scapegoat throughout the long history of my insufferable behaviour. He had been made to do things I myself had done, as if I might expiate my guilt in fictional comings and goings. But none of it was, or is, fiction. That is the trouble! If only I could invent terrible visions instead of having to live them, the possibility could exist of my being a real person writing about a world of make-believe — but, as I have said, I am an imaginary being writing about the pragmatic world of surface realities. If I exist at all it is in these symbols you see before you; my name, as you will have guessed, is not even Creely. I hid behind it, held a mask in front of my face to pretend that behind this despicable rogue of a character lay a wise and benevolent Narrator, full of insights and sympathies which, in truth, I do not possess. And if I am being totally honest I should at the same time confess that the Narrator does not exist, or, to be precise, I am not he. (That he could exist — as he might — in some nebulous cloud of mind-stuff or 'wave of readiness' is a matter of futile conjecture.) And behind him too — yes, yet another trapdoor — lies the shadowy, mysterious, omnipresence of the Author, who, one presumes, is penning these words crouched in his little dark hole. But neither is he real. Thus you see the merry dance I have led myself: the innumerable charades, illusions, deceptions and graven images perpetuated in the name of seeking a glimpse of the truth. As made clear by Heisenberg's Principle of Indeterminacy, however — that bane of science — my feeble efforts were destined from the start to result in failure; that we are fated to know less and less about more and more is the only lesson of any worth to have emerged. Ah, but in very truth, why were we given minds at all, and by whom, and what will become of me?

THE IMMINGHAM DRIVE

PART I

THE MYTHICAL FUTURE

I

At long last Gorsey Dene found himself on the way to Immingham, a drive he had been keen on undertaking ever since he had received Jay's letter informing him that she was to return from Sweden during the winter months, and suggesting — or rather hinting — that he might travel across the country to meet her at the dock and bring her home. As the young man was anxious to see her, for sexually hedonistic reasons, he immediately wrote back pledging his part of the rendezvous at the specified time and date. It was a brilliant, cold and endlessly blue day, the sort of day when the air is described as 'crystal clear': a perfect fusion of hard pure light and cold crisp fields lying open and bare with their worn green cheeks turned heavenwards. It was possible to imagine the sky as clean empty space, which was how Gorsey Dene thought of it as he drove the small blue car up the curving road rising from the valley to the moor. The close-cropped greenness turned to brown and purple patches of coarse, brackenish growth at a certain exact point — a topographical oddity he had noted before. On the tops the air was rushing coldly — he knew this from the slanting stalks of grass and buffeting brambles — but inside the metal/glass casing he was snug, smug and beautifully content. He was going to meet Jay; and yet, as usual, within his flesh/bone head abided the worm of

disquiet, of trepidation, as if a giant from above were
scrutinising his puny progress, allowing him to go so far
and no further: until the dreadful moment when a
monstrous hand would reach down and pluck him off the
road, wrench him out of the dream, and toss him in his
metal/glass/flesh/bone environment into the pit. It was the
turmoil of a deluded mind but nonetheless terrifying for
all that. Supposing, for example, that Jay had developed a
growth on her face? It was entirely possible. Or, if not a
facial disfigurement, had been party to a cancerous breast,
having had the offending portion removed, so that now she
lurched lop-sidedly along with but one breast to call her
own? Her hair could have fallen out: head hair, underarm
hair, pubis. What would that imply — some dreadful
Swedish disease? But, Gorsey Dene realised, he was just
being silly. As a child he had suffered from hallucinations
and ever since had been especially wary of those occasions
when it seems that life is wearing thin — when, in fact, the
canvas backing begins to show through the decorative
embroidery. Of course she would be all right; of course.
But, then again, he had often suspected her of being
unfaithful. There had never been any proof of this —
rather, he had had the nasty idea that secretly she thought
him a fool, a dupe, a weak and worthless charlatan, and at
the first opportunity would not hesitate to 'make eyes' at
friends, acquaintances, strangers, entering with them into a
privileged and covert understanding, establishing a rapport
which he, Gorsey Dene, and she, Jay, had never managed
to achieve. The fault, perhaps, was his, for her image in his
eyes had always been of a pair of large breasts and a
desirable cunt. Never had he seen her as a person. And in
truth he had never once understood or even faintly grasped
the nature of that *thing* which is said to constitute a
relationshop between a man and a woman. The fault
resided in him: it was, to put it simply, an inability to look
into her, or any woman's, eyes. Young lovers gazed one

into the other, locked eye-to-eye, and delivered up 'the secrets of the soul'; stupid brooding youths and ductile empty-headed girls possessed this quality, this innocence and sterling worth, while in his own depths — as deep as the reflection in a mirror — all that could be seen was what the reflection in any mirror yields up to the onlooker: their own frightened eyes and palsied complexion in mirrored reverse. With Jay he had had intercourse in cars, in beds, in armchairs, on living-room carpets, and had fucked her well and properly as a substitute for feeling. He was now driving desperately towards her, across the country from west to east, with just the singular hot intention of lying on top of her and inserting his rod and being made to feel, if only for the transient ejaculatory moment, that he was more substance than shadow.

It had not always been so. On first meeting, when his quite-normal-looking exterior had sufficiently camouflaged his actor's inner vacuum, Gorsey Dene had fixed her with a steely-eyed stare, slitted and sexy, to which she had (almost) immediately responded. Being a man full of tricks, surfeited with trickery, a trickster, he had bedevilled, bewitched and bedazzled her with his steadfast gaze until the fluid had gurgled in her belly and her bowels had creaked — undergone that discomforting shift which signifies abrupt emotional excitement. On that occasion he had been with a friend — the mutual intruder — who had gabbled with such innanity as to deceive Jay into mistaking Gorsey Dene's introspective silence for depth of character, durable spirit, and an intelligence worthy of respect. (It is a fact that all Negroes' teeth appear exceptionally white against their contrastingly darker skin tone.) Later she had confirmed this impression — an admission he had exultantly chortled over — remarking that in all the din and bustle he alone, in his self-contained quietude and isolation, had possessed a distinctive presence, an aura that was almost tangible and which set him apart from the rowdy company. This first meeting had been in the small back room of a public house, a room with varnished wooden benches fixed to the walls and a floor of ragged linoleum. Young men, his own age, had swaggered about belching and farting with masculine disdain while his own bodily excrescences had been neither seen or heard, discreetly emitted behind a raised hand or beneath muffling clothing. The human race was a collection of mindless brutes, and as he had no desire to join it he would go out of his way to remain alien to it, separated by as great a gap as possible. The truth was it revolted him. That he too from time to time was obliged to belch and fart was a distasteful biological prank.

(1) The girl Jay had long hark hair; her face was a pale oval with exaggerated eyes, big and dark, and with finely delineated full lips which now and then formed themselves into a softly cynical shape — a habit indicating unease and a lack of assurance. She had good teeth, a nicely proportioned nose, and her fingernails were clean, trimmed, and unpainted. Her figure was pleasantly rounded and she had not outworn the antiquated convention of lowering her eyes mutely as maidens were once instructed to do. She was strikingly beautiful; and the more he stared at her the faster Gorsey Dene's heart started to beat.

(2) The face of the girl Jay shone palely, reflecting the room's crude, dim lighting. Her forehead was shadowed by the long dark-brown hair which fell straight on either side, separated by the tracery of a fine white parting; her eyes were large and round, thickly made-up, and her lips were full, sensuous, yet occasionally unsure. With the certainty that she was looking at him Gorsey Dene kept his eyes studiously averted, projecting a wearied indifference that was the antithesis of his inwardly churning processes and deranged bodily functions. That she was deceived by this paltry subterfuge is indicative of her own insecurity and world-innocence generally.

Looking down on her — his feet wide apart — with a pleasant drunken torpor weighing on his eyelids, Gorsey Dene next came into contact with her as Jay lay with several others on the studio couch in the flat of a German student, and, not yet familiar enough to engage her in direct conversation, had taken to observing the proceedings from a distance and on a slightly higher plane, as if this self-imposed objectivity and elegant aloofness were sufficient in themselves to mark him off from the common herd and even conceivably suggest a depth of character which did not exist. Later that evening (or it might have been the early hours of the morning) Gorsey Dene found himself lying alongside her on that same studio couch, in the company of others, and discovering to his delight and relief that they had at least one interest in common. And when she castigated the poor German student for his meekness and gullibility Gorsey Dene was only too ready to agree: it united them in a shared dislike (which on his part was created instantaneously for just that purpose).

The student's rooms were mean and shabby: bare walls to which were affixed tattered posters: but his few possessions were precious in their shabbiness, and for once Gorsey Dene felt a cheap pang of guilt and, very nearly, contrition. But after all, he reminded himself, Jay merited first consideration, above any misguided sympathy for a poor foreign student. And what the hell, the guy was a kraut.

'I left school last year,' Jay said in answer to a question. 'For a while I took drugs but not any more. They were little blue cylindrically-shaped tablets which, when taken with alcohol, were supposed to induce an hallucinatory effect. Once I stood on the balcony of a high flat and thought seriously of jumping.'

'To your death,' Gorsey Dene interjected, thrilled — indeed quivering inside — to be engaged in natural conversation with this fantastic person: she had said something and he had responded, both of them perfectly at ease. Could it be that she considered him worthy of such attentive respect? Could she not see the hollowness behind the eyes? Apparently not!

'To my death; possibly.'

'Probably.'

Her eyes flicked across his face, and instantly Gorsey Dene manufactured a white, widening smile of good-natured self-assurance which checked any reproof she might have considered necessary. Nevertheless he had committed an error and it was as well to remember that white, widening smiles were not in endless supply; or, if they were, could not be expected to retain their potency indefinitely. 'You were saying,' said Gorsey Dene.

'Yes,' said Jay with unnecessary emphasis, altering her position so as to lie more favourably amongst the several cluttered bodies on the couch. (What would be her reaction, he wondered, were he to . . .) Smoke filled the air and incessant chatter mounted in waves to lap against the ceiling. (Now: what if he were to put his hand *there* . . .) Jay laid the desirable object of her head on the cover and looked at him from beneath silken eyelashes.

'There are not all that many genuine people about these days,' Gorsey Dene said, surprising them both with the thought.

'Even fewer in this room,' Jay responded, making them both smile into each other's face in sudden delight at a shared private joke. They were going to get on well together; it was on the cards or in the stars or wherever it was written. Thereupon they started talking about people and about the common experience of being born in a Northern industrial town and of their lives (GD revealing at the correct psychological moment that he was ten years her senior) up to this point — all of which lifted Gorsey Dene to rare heights of volubility until he became quite drunk with the intoxicating splendour of his own wit, charm, astuteness of insight and powers of didactic reasoning. She was dazzled, flushed, and silent.

'Then after the juvenile drug scene I started going to the Coach with Viv, which is where —'

'We met.'

' — I first saw you.'

'Yes.' A grin.

'You didn't say much that night.'

'The bloke you were with put me off.'

'Alan.'

'He kept lifting his leg and farting.'

'You get used to Alan.'

'But not to the smell.'

Now Jay grinned. 'He's all right.'

'He wasn't — or isn't — a boyfriend or anything?'

'No.' A tiny frown. It puckered the smooth texture of her forehead. Had he strayed over the boundary? If so it might mean a swift return to wit, charm, astute insight and didactic reasoning. 'Why did you ask that?'

'Why did you frown?'

Jay's slate-blue eyes, downcast (for she would not meet his look) and pensive, were adorable to him. He wanted to see them tightening with pain as he —

'Do you think that someone like that would be attractive to me?'

'I fail to see what is attractive in any man to any woman; no — I mean I do not know what it is women find attractive in men. I was once told that it was the set of the buttocks but I refuse to believe that women notice such things; if they do it is out of pure detached scientific interest. Their minds do not conform to the masculine pattern.'

'A woman — if it's any consolation — doesn't know what it is she finds attractive in a man.'

'I know,' Gorsey Dene replied. 'That is the entire trouble.'

'Why is it the entire trouble?' Jay asked, faithfully making up the other half of the dialogue.

'The entire trouble is that women do not *know*,' Gorsey Dene said heatedly. He was lying beside her, cramped and hampered by other bodies. Little, if any, room for manoeuvre. 'If they did know, then by hook or by crook I should find out what it is about men that attracts them.'

'It is an indefinable something.'

'I know that.' He was leaning on one elbow, his face overlooking hers. Her dark hair was spread out on the cover. Her eyes were avoiding his. 'The trouble is that it's indefinable. Supposing that it were not, then I should be able to ask a woman and she would be able to tell me. But as it is no woman can define the indefinable.'

'What she finds attractive in a man.'

'Yes.'

'That is the entire trouble.'

Still she would not look at him, but he was nearer now, the sides of their bodies in contact along most of their lengths. In fact all that was required of him was to –

Since childhood Gorsey Dene had had a number of strange feelings, eg: there were times when he felt himself not to be inhabiting his own body; that by merely wishing he could make a growth appear on his face; he felt too that beneath the real world there existed another out-of-sight unacknowledged place – but this one non-spurious; he knew almost for a certainty that the whole of his mind was not contained within the bone construction of his head; when talking to people he would sometimes stand aside and observe what kind of a botch-up his husk was making of the job, or perhaps wander away across the room and leave the husk to get on with it; he had recurrent premonitions and was subject to hallucinatory coincidences that could not be explained in terms of the accepted rational sciences; there were times when he felt the whole of the world to be a vast, complex, incomprehensible dream through which he was floating, lost, alone, a single speck of consciousness in a medium of dark drifting shadows; on occasion he supposed himself to be inhabiting a small gloomy hole, huddled inside like a shivering, furry, frightened animal at bay, crouched with its back pressing against the soft moist earth; he was also prone to attacks of suicidal depression when it seemed that everything he turned his hand to was a wasted nihilistic emptiness; of late he had begun to receive visions of ravaged landscapes: desolate skylines upon whose hellish surfaces spurted gaseous jets of purple flame; and now — yes even now — his heart was bludgeoning the breath from his body, crashing like a mad trip-hammer until it was feasible that his rib-cage would splinter and shatter and the pulsing fist of his heart would punch gobs of blood directly into the face of Jay, who lay, innocent and lecherous, between the crushed bodies on the couch. The room was smokier than ever.

Jay said, 'Some people think that because you go in the Coach on Friday nights you're loose and easy. They think that your virginity must have departed long ago.'

'During the juvenile drug scene days perhaps,' interjected Gorsey Dene. His eyes were ill-focused due to the smoke and the heat and the proximity of bodies. It came to him that the room was a hot white hollow cube, noisy and laughter-filled, surrounded on all sides by depressed industrial chaos. That his life should have arrived in this geographical location at this point in historical time was a quirk of fate requiring a certain amount of cogitation; it intrigued him; but it would have to wait for a spare bit of solitude.

'For example,' said Jay, turning her face sideways towards him yet still lowering her eyelashes so that they threw fringe-shadows down her cheeks, 'you would expect me not to be one, wouldn't you?'

'Not to be one what?' asked Gorsey Dene. He was being

compressed, overpowered, intimated.

'Not to be a virgin. Wouldn't you? You would have expected me perhaps to have had relations with a man. Isn't that so?'

'Yeeees —' The heat. The smoke. The noise. The light.

'And not being a virgin — so *you* think — would automatically classify me as loose and easy. Yes?'

There was a dead tingling in Gorsey Dene's right arm and shoulder: caused by the unremitting pressure of leaning at just such an angle for so long a period. He adjusted the triangle formed by his forearm, upper arm and torso, and a shock ripped from his shoulder to his fingertips.

'Not necessarily.'

'How not so?' And this time her blue slate eyes did look at him, unflinchingly. What wouldn't he have given to put his —

'Because I think you are.'

'Are what?'

'A virgin.'

She smiled (or was about to smile) just as a number of additional bodies were crammed onto the heap, and it really was becoming quite intolerable; though, in its favour, he now found himself forced to lie half on top of her, one leg — the left — astride both of hers. A thump between his shoulder blades was followed by a voice complaining of inadequate space.

'Al*an*,' Jay said, her cheeks flushing in annoyance.

The head of the boy turned: a big, red, beer-dazed face with startled fair eyebrows. A gangrenous grin appeared, gap-toothed, accompanied by a forced, squealing, flesh-rippling emission of wind. It infiltrated softly, the dull heavy odour, rising sluggishly in contoured streamers of varying strengths, pressing its sweetish fetid breath to their faces and wrapping the heads in smell. Gorsey Dene had circumspectly allowed his hand to rest on Jay's stomach, feeling the swell and fall of her diaphragm, the tensing and releasing of her abdominal muscles. He could hardly believe his own good fortune.

'Jay — mean as hell with her touches,' Alan said. 'Mean as fuck.'

The eyes of the girl Jay flashed momentarily; she was about to retort, but now Gorsey Dene was close, above her, bearing down on her, his heart thumping madly, with an inside chance of dipping his wick.

'Al*an*,' Jay said again, as once more the offending party released a fart whose sound and smell disrupted the several erotic overtures taking place on the couch. (I see, Gorsey Dene realised immediately, his insight compounded by anger, you're one of those who because he can't get it seeks to spoil everyone else's fun.)

Alan said, 'She pretends to be a real goer, yet she's a virgin.' He jammed his elbow into the back of Gorsey Dene. 'Hear that, matey? Didn't know it, eh? A real goer who's a fucking virgin.'

Gorsey Dene half turned, smiling conspiratorially as one male to another. His look implied: We all know what women are like, don't we, matey? They're only there to be got stuck into. We both know that, you and me. Eh, matey? Not that I would stick it into her — not if she's yours, that is. If she's yours I'm just chatting, aren't I? If she's yours she's yours. Say no more. If she's not yours, though, I'd just as soon stick it into her as go for a quick crap. What else is she there for? What other use has she except to be got stuck into? And don't worry, I will, leave it to me. If, that is, she isn't yours, in which case I'll stick it right up her, way up, as far as it will go, till she coughs; get her crying for mercy, eh? Matey. Unless you want to stick her, do her, exercise the old ferret, in which case again, matey, you can have her and welcome. You can step right in and stick her, stick it up her, hard; I'll not interfere; she's all yours. Just chatting, that's all. Close to her because I can't help it, what with the overcrowding and everything. All right? Matey. No offence. Never come between a bloke and his bird. Eh? Matey. Too fucking true.

'He's a foul pig,' Jay said, hard-eyed and stiff-lipped.

Christ, Gorsey Dene thought tremulously, keep your voice low.

'I don't care if he does hear me,' Jay said. 'He's no right to call me that.'

'That what?'

'A virgin.'

The very word made bells clang inside the head of Gorsey Dene. Virgin. Jesus. What a wick-dipping thought. Just looking at her you could tell she was the type who would open her —

Their heads were close, his shadowing hers, and eye-locked-to-eye he lowered his lips swiftly onto hers, their coming together so perfect that it was the first time the first time the first time without doubt — with all the associations of new kissing flesh. Bubbles burst in his eyeballs and he held a deep-drawn breath, his lips urging, moulding, shaping themselves in ways he knew would please and impress her. The room went. His hand rummaged between packed bodies to slide underneath her spine. The bulk — the actual warm solid bulk of her was under him, responding to his lips. Envious others (Alan included) were all around, but Jay and he were divorced from their surroundings, oblivious to everything except squashing pink ridges of yielding muscle. When later his sweeping right hand grappled — as if by accident — with her left breast, passed on above and below, and then returned to grasp and knead the provocative self-supporting mound, there was a minimum of adverse reaction . . . save that she slid bottom-forward in the passenger seat and gurgled the air in her throat; by this time the windows were clouded and they were safe from parents' and neighbours' eyes behind their rectangles of council house glass. Then, because he had inserted his longest finger into her vagina, she swung her fist and hit him on the ear. She did this several more times in the weeks, and evenutally the months, that followed; always after he had stuck his vicarious wick into her and brought her to the point of orgasm. Gorsey Dene came to the conclusion, painfully arrived at, that this was not because she did not enjoy being digitized (far from it) but, rather, that she was being led along a path of emotional heat until, as a virgin, she could do one of two things: either submit to further digitizing and ultimately wick-dipping, or, to release and displace her natural sexual propensity, hit him on the ear with her coiled fist. Usually she burst into tears after the blow, the second part of the catharsis, upon which Gorsey Dene would slump back in his seat and smoke a crumpled cigarette. Once he went too far and her hymen came away in his hand. As was their custom, he complained:

'If you don't want me to do it you don't want me to do it. And if you don't want me to do it you shouldn't allow me to continue doing it.' He put the cigarette to his mouth but it remained stuck to his fingers.

Still sobbing, Jay banged her head on the window. The tangled impression of her hair was printed in the condensation. 'I know, I know, I *know*. Is it my fault? Can I help it? Do you blame me? What can I do? Do you think I want to do it? Do you think I can help myself? Don't you know that if I could I would?'

'I understand very well,' said Gorsey Dene. He revelled in the apologetic whine of her voice. It was a novelty for him to receive the weeping excuses of a virgin who was contrite because she would not allow herself to be taken. Were he not so magnanimous he might never have forgiven Jay for her inconsiderateness.

'I want to,' Jay said. 'I do want to, you know I want to, I desperately want to –'

'Yet you can't.' There was a sufficient strain of *ennui* in his voice to promote the idea that he was growing tired of her continual reluctance; she sensed it and became even more distraught, rocking sideways in the seat, her head buffeting the window, her fists clutched impotently on her thighs.

From this they progressed in fits and starts to a blanket in the damp grass on a hill overlooking the bus depot. Underneath his bare knees, through the rough weave of the blanket, he could feel the crackly brush and squelchy earth, like kneeling in the middle of the Sargasso Sea. Below them, beyond the precarious trees overhanging the rim, the steep valley was a bowl of yellow light with the miniscule buses to-ing and fro-ing through the zig-zagged black-and-yellow corrugated doors. Condition perfect: green and all set to go; but the operation was not a success. The raw night air set him shivering feverishly; clammy dew coated his drooping flanks, and Jay, a vague white lump of gooseflesh in the darkness, seemed not to possess that desirability which had obsessed his daylight fantasies.

Gorsey Dene squatted again, guilt-ridden. Though he could not, incomprehensibly, dip his long-awaiting wick, there were other compensations, namely two: the fine breasts of Jay. Leaning towards him, avoiding the steering-wheel, she presented their palpable opulence over which he jerked himself, the oily spittle splattering hotly and draining away from the reddish, puckered, nippled areas. At such moments they were swollen with temptation — her breasts and nipples — the skin strained and tight — until it seemed they might explode with a dull, ponderous, slow-motion roar. Undeniably it was enjoyable; neither Gorsey Dene nor Jay could deny it, and yet their consummation was delayed as if a process of contra-momentum had been set up against which they were powerless — indeed, their struggles served only to strengthen the intangible force of resistance confronting them:

A law was operating somewhere in the universe.

Gorsey Dene began to fall in love with her; though perhaps not as much as Jay had begun to fall in love with him. Nothing was revealed overtly, only hinted at. They would sit in the Coach amidst tables to whose surfaces beer-soaked cigarette packets clung, empty crisp bags crumpled in glittering cellophane fist-sized balls in the ashtrays, and speak politely and distantly to each other, the lust hidden in their eyes, awaiting with a thrilling rush of dark-blooded anticipation the car-borne finale of jerking spittle over palpable opulence.

'Mean as fuck with her touches.' Alan said, swaying back on his heels as he up-ended the glass of beer into his throat. The girl Jay jerked her head away and her breasts shook. Gorsey Dene smiled pleasantly, partly in appeasement and partly because his thoughts were several miles distant: he should not have been here.

'Virgin kidder,' Alan said, exchanging his empty glass for a full one. 'She's a frigid prick-teaser, GD.'

'Al*an*,' said Jay. Her colour rose. The door to the lavatory banged. The floor trembled. Somebody fought to reach the bar. The saloon, as big, or as small, as a railway compartment, reverberated with grunted snarls, snorted laughter, coughing gasps and choking sniggers. Gorsey Dene knew that he should not have been here.

'What is she?' Alan said. 'What is she, What is she, What is she?' He was bent at the waist, swivelling his startled face like the hook of a crane back and forth round the seated semi-circle. A glass smashed; a bottle spilled.

Yet Gorsey Dene kept his eye on the clock. The day before, during the afternoon, he had arranged an assignation, intending full well to keep it, but it was quite a drive and here was Jay, large with promise, her downcast maidenly eyes suggesting that the night was ripe for wick-dipping. She said:

'There have been numerous rumours about you.'

Gorsey Dene looked askance into her slate-blue stare.

Her chest heaved and fell. Flattering, he reckoned, to have been the subject of numerous rumours; it proved too that he existed in the minds of others. Why, he could be dead and still they would perpetuate him *in memoriam.* 'You go away a good deal, driving. Mostly you drive overnight the story goes.'

'Doesn't everyone drive in this day and age?' said Gorsey Dene. 'It is an era of drivers. I don't see much of a rumour in that.'

'Depends,' Jay said, for something to say.

'Everything depends,' Gorsey Dene promulgated, noticing how the slight bone structure of her shoulders supported the massive weight below. He bet that, were he to ask her, she would lick —

. 'I might; yes, I might,' Gorsey Dene said defensively, fractionally unhappy that she supposed him to be such a coward — for she had protested that if Alan went too far — as he frequently did — he (Gorsey Dene) would not be bold enough to take her (Jay's) part; and in reply Gorsey Dene had ruminatively tapped the steering-wheel with his knuckles and cautiously made the addendum that 'I might; yes, I might.'

Jay was sceptical and scornful. Like most of her species, particularly the intelligent ones, she made the mistaken assumption that equality as a human being necessitated a streak of harsh and unyielding obduracy: as though the soft, subtle, feminine aspects of personality were not to be countenanced at any price. To this end she adopted a wilful cynicism and a deliberate — albeit childish — hardening of the gentler traits of an essentially sweet nature. (So Gorsey Dene reasoned to himself.)

'And why,' Jay interrupted, 'were you continually looking at the clock? Isn't it the height of rudeness to be forever checking the time?'

'Depends,' said Gorsey Dene.

'On what?'

'Well, why *should* it be considered rude to look at a clock?'

'It isn't rude to *look* at a clock,' the girl Jay said; 'it's the implication of what looking at a clock is. In other words you're suggesting that the present company isn't fit to be with.'

(He couldn't bring himself to tell her that he oughtn't to have been there — 'there' being the crowded smoky room of the Coach earlier that evening. By rights he should have been meeting the black girl at the Urmston flat, as planned and promised, but now the moment had fled, the opportunity lapsed, the contract negated.)

Even now — driving through Yorkshire — Gorsey Dene couldn't repress a pang of conscience at the recollection. Though, as it happened, Tee hadn't reproved him when they had eventually met (several months later): almost seeming to imply that the incident, ie: his non-arrival, had been of little, if any, consequence. Knowing her as he did, however, Gorsey Dene suspected that this was a cover-up — for the sheer unbearable tensity of her life was such that she disguised any threadbare patch of existence with a devastating peal of laughter, dazzling herself and her onlookers with the vibrant immediacy of response. When the mouth is wide open with laughter the eyes cannot see very well.

— Having said this, at the same time it should be admitted that he had never thought her to be unintelligent. If anything she had amazed him with the list of achievements to her name; she read thick volumes in the course of her work which to him were meaningless tracts of vague mental disorders, abstruse in the extreme. Yet when questioned systematically she went quiet for a brief space of time and then out popped the answer, usually correct or very nearly so. No, she was not without brainpower — or, at any rate, a mechanically-sound retentive memory.

In addition, her relatives were nice to Gorsey Dene.

They fed him, bathed him, gave him cigarettes, fed him again, introduced their children to him, inquired after his health, allowed him to sleep in their homes, packed him (and her) off to dances, and all without bitterness, antagonism or prejudice. They were, the top and bottom of it, kindly people to whom he appeared as a pleasant, civil English boy, able and only too willing to observe the decent niceties of social etiquette, colour apart.

'Well were you or weren't you?'

'Was I or wasn't I what?'

'Suggesting it by implication.'

'No. I was looking to see what time it was.'

This answer stumped her, and she sat slumped in a position of resentful indolence, desiring him and at the same time sick with jealousy. Jay's character was like this: guarded, eager, and open to hurt. Her face adopted a stubborn, obtuse expression as she realised that his past contained an infinitely greater number of people than her own — just as when we enter a room wherein a party has been a long time in progress and, as a stranger amongst drunken friends, feel that an entire intimate history has gone before from which we are excluded, mistaking unfamiliar speech patterns and private idiosyncratic references for erudition. So Jay felt alienated from the wondrous events of Gorsey Dene's mysterious past. His long-standing affair with a black girl had been made known to her, and it was the fact of the blackness that knocked her askew . . . that he should have lived such a magical life as to have been ensnared by the broad-nosed, thick-lipped wiles of an Afro-Caribbean culture!

Thus: while she felt to have him in secure possession as he ejaculated over her, the rest of the time she was — as stated — guarded, eager, and open to hurt.

The car was parked near some garages. They were made of white concrete and reminded Gorsey Dene of flats which from time to time he had cause to visit. In fact everything he looked at reminded him of something.

Jay suddenly leaned right over to his side of the car and thrust her mouth against his. (This happened not infrequently.) She had come far enough along the road of sexual emancipation to enable her to do this. Gorsey Dene acted surprised, though wasn't, and they fell to smearing their wet lips through which their tongues worked, and his hands pulled and pawed at her top-heaviness while hers rummaged between his legs. Jay had been initiated into the secrets of male anatomy, regarding the ultimate symbol of sensual pleasure as a deadly plaything which, to her surprise, she was allowed to control and manipulate. Her incipient fear and thrilling terror had been replaced by a childlike sense of power and accomplishment.

The moon rode hugely through the branches of the trees, its anaemic light falling softly like snow. The garages, the trees, the grass plane of the golf-course were silent under the weight of the hard white light. Everything was clearly visible; but to Gorsey Dene came again the wearisome sickness of guilt, as though his bowels were made of lead, that he had further betrayed those things called love, trust and human consideration. And so he resolved, opening the buttons on Jay's blouse, the very next week to visit the cold box flat at Urmston and present his apology in person.

II

A violent horizon greeted Gorsey Dene on his arrival in Immingham, casting his mind back to corridors, alleyways, chambers and to the rooms of slapping pulleys. He had never before seen a landscape like it: shining aluminium towers and spheres circumnavigated by spiral stairways, score upon score, separated by wire-netted perimeter fences into which slim concrete posts intruded at intervals. The entire layout was most bizarre. The road went

through, not curving but turning abruptly at right-angles
to skirt this towered complex, or that. And – along the
further horizon – a number of ragged sheets of purple
flame spurting fiercely against the sky over the North Sea,
its grey-green bleakness compounded by the fall of evening
and the gathering of a storm. The light was unearthly: as
artificial as a stage-set, so that the shiny towers and spheres,
the flame and the fences, were illuminated from below as
it were; from the footlights. The daylight colours were
now gone, replaced in this sameness and evenness of drab
light by mysterious sombre blues, browns and reds, the
former the reflection of Gorsey Dene's car as it scuttled
between the monsters. Still the flames leapt, evaporating
into curling black smoke which lost itself in the dark
stormy air.

In the forecourt on the edge of the dock he left the car
and drank several cups of coffee in the reception building,
until eventually the moving iron side of the ship filled the
window-frame and it seemed that he was moving and the
ship was stationary. Running lightly down the steps and
through the doors into the forecourt he ran into the arms
of Jay, her big solid body buffeting the air from his lungs,
her arms crushing the excitement out of him. She was real,
she was here, she was his! Their lips were pressed together
but it was as yet token affection, a mere greeting kiss. The
slow blood-pulse had not yet begun to beat; but were he
to think ahead he could feel its slow quivering throb in his
throat and deep in his chest. Jay too was out of breath
with anticipation. On first impact Gorsey Dene had noticed
a new smell about her, a different kind of bulk in his arms.
They sat in the car not looking at each other, overcome
with shyness and a strangeness that in itself was strange:
after all, he had been the first to penetrate her.

Jay's luggage filled the small car so that they were
hemmed in on all sides, two bodies in a cubby-hole. She
was expansive with the newness of arrival, scattering

cigarettes everywhere, rings and bracelets jangling, flouncy
arms fluttering like enormous butterflies, her unpredictable
smell and foreign perfume making his senses dense. Now
with the night-time the car was a tiny speck, shooting light
ahead. The storm just waited, unexpended; on the main
roads the leaping headlights of oncoming vehicles — not
many — lit up their white faces in a quick rushing glare.
Gorsey Dene glimpsed her black lips. She was smoking
and talking together, gusts of smoke and words hitting the
windscreen. Gorsey Dene listened, nodded, smiled, shook
his head, widened his eyes, compressed his lips,
occasionally smirked. He was wondering whether they
ought to accomplish the greater part of the journey or stop
soon for a drink. The drink would speed the inevitable.

'I'm really back with you.'

'You are,' Gorsey Dene agreed, 'really back with me.'

The shyness hadn't altogether departed: this was also
why they needed to drink. But he was very happy; it was a
time when he knew himself to be happy. He smiled with
happiness.

'Why are you smiling?' asked Jay.

'You're always asking me why I'm doing things,' Gorsey
Dene said good-humouredly.

'I want to know everything in your head. If I know
everything in your head I know I have you.'

This made Gorsey Dene laugh. The drive continued into
the night. Not very far along the road he pulled off and
parked the car with the bonnet butting up to a pub wall:
the engine ticked for a moment, then fell silent. The room
in which they found themselves was semi-deserted, it being
early. The landlord had upon his wall a coloured cutaway
section in isometric projection of a Posi-Force lubrication
system (which Gorsey Dene immediately noticed) and he
commented on the fact to Jay, who did not know what he
was talking about. Whereupon he explained to her his
theory: that by inadvertant mischance he had inherited a

whole series of coincidences belonging to someone else. Jay asked him who this someone else was, but he did not know.

They sat thigh to thigh on the supposedly comfortable seat taking deep draughts of their first drink together for many months. It didn't take long for her to kiss his neck, burrowing her cold nose into the warm crevice beneath his collar. Gorsey Dene shivered at the tactile contact.

'Are you earning any money?'

'A bit,' he admitted.

'Have you undertaken any assignments recently?'

'There's one coming up in January.'

'What's that?'

'A paper mill.'

'What do you know about paper mills?' Jay said good-naturedly.

'Nothing as yet.'

'It could be interesting —'

'— if the photographs come out,' Gorsey Dene finished off for her, and they laughed together. He looked into her mouth and supposed that she might be persuaded to suck —

'Do you think if you hadn't met me —'

'But I did.'

'Yes, I know; but if you hadn't do you think you would have ever gone away?'

'You went away too.'

'I *know*,' said Gorsey Dene. 'But would you?'

'I don't know.'

'Is it likely you wouldn't have?'

'Possible.'

'If not probable.'

Jay sighed. She quickly wearied of his attempts at coercion. Gorsey Dene needed all the time to feel that he affected the way in which people lived their lives: it gave him a sense of importance. Also (though this had no direct connexion), he was experimenting with a method of making a growth appear on his face by means of thought control. The area he had selected was just below his left cheekbone, and in time, with luck, might gradually extend to envelop his entire head . . . but as yet there was nothing to show for his concentrated efforts. It would prove (should he succeed) that a separate underlying reality was abroad in the universe, unbeknown to men: he was forever searching for the ultramundane. Just as when, taking Jay to the train, he had deliberately opted for a route unfamiliar to him in order to avoid any repetition of scenes from a previous life. Then, if such scenes did occur, it would prove once and for all that he was an actor in a screenplay, obeying the directions and repeating the lines as per printed script.

They had taken the moor road, hitting the motorway north of Sheffield, and swept down to London through the heat of a July day. Her luggage filled the car, heavy suitcases presenting a formidable bulk on the back seat. As usual she was smoking ten to the dozen, shaky puffs whiling away the minutes as though this life was in preparation for another, squeezing out the slow hours like toothpaste from a tube. In a motorway cafeteria — bright slats of sunlight slanting through the broad windows — they had dunked toast in oxtail soup. Music oozed along the ceiling and dripped onto their heads. There was the hushed expectant bustle of people going somewhere; of people actually with a purpose. And to know that the car was loaded and waiting for them outside was the greatest thrill of all.

'You will write to me, won't you?' This was said with a hardness that concealed a soft underbelly of trepidation.

'Yes.' (He was much more an uncomplicated person then.)

'I'll send you my address.'

'Good idea.'

'Do you think I'm leaving because of you?'

'Do you mean am I instrumental in your leaving?'

'Yes.'

'No.'

'That's to say I should have left anyway.'

'Possibly.'

It was rare for her to look directly at him, into his eyes; and if he happened to glance momentarily into hers a shadow of embarrassment or inadequacy dropped quickly over them: a lurking heaviness in the eyelids. At other times they became glazed with feigned *ennui*, accompanied invariably by a slick remark or deadpan statement. But Gorsey Dene was not deceived. The main compensation for his repellent appearance was a hyper-sensitivity to the reactions generated in others by his presence. Being himself a manipulative magician he could detect the waverings and shifts of social emphasis by a hair's breadth of anyone with whose mind he came into contact. Jay was easy meat; he met stiffer opposition every day of the week.

Heat shivered up from the motorway, the perspective converging in a broken haze of black tarmac and coloured dots of cars. Wind rushed in through a quarter-inch gap above the window; insects flattened themselves selflessly against the windscreen; the radio was playing 'When A Man Loves A Woman'; Jay was blowing smoke out, aiming her nostrils in such a way that the slipstream sucked it in blue-grey shafts through the long rectangular slit.

'When you return,' Gorsey Dene said, 'we'll go to Cyprus. Think of the white sand beaches, the olive trees, the cicadas, the ancient ruins, the bubbling surf . . .'

'I haven't gone yet,' Jay said.

'I realise that; I'm talking about when you come back.'

'But I haven't *gone*,' Jay said, her cheeks deepening in colour. 'I'm going to a cold country and you're talking about white beaches.'

'There's nothing to prevent me talking about them; talking about something never did anyone any harm.'

'It isn't very tactful all the same.'

Gorsey Dene despaired of women.

He was talking to speed the waning miles.

His hands were getting hot on the wheel. He moved them around, seeking a cool spot. The sun was keeping pace with them, rushing through the leaf-filled trees. Other cars went past, torn polythene crackling on their roof-racks. Jay said:

'Will you go with anyone else while I'm away?'

'Who else would have me?' Gorsey Dene responded egotistically.

'People come to your office.'

'Cleaners,' Gorsey Dene replied enigmatically.

'And you go to Oldham. Don't tell me that cleaners go to Oldham.'

'They must do, otherwise the place would remain dirty.'

'It's a dirty place to start with.'

'Then possibly cleaners don't go.'

'Probably.'

'Anyway,' he said, 'who's to say what you'll be up to.'

Jay released a brief, sharp laugh. A ball of smoke hit the windscreen. Gorsey Dene turned inwards on himself for a moment to examine introspectively his feelings towards Jay since her sexual enlightenment: the pre- and post-virginal Jay. Now that she had, and liked it, she probably would again. Did this churn him up inside? Wouldn't this affect him, having fallen (so he said) in love with her? He fixed his eyes directly on the road ahead and felt the thumping in his chest: his blood should have told him what to feel but it didn't. With women Gorsey Dene never knew whether he was on his head or his arse. Their first proper attempt had been in the back of a car, awkwardly perspiring amongst tangled aspirations. Then in bed at the house of a friend — the chill night air misting the corners of the window-panes; a husk around the moon. Since then she had been his, replete with young womanly confidences, intimacies, and tentative experiments. But how would he feel to have her lying under somebody else? The thought was just beginning to nag when Gorsey Dene snapped his mind shut.

The temperature had risen with the afternoon. Jay worked the louvred discs to direct cooling air into her face. She hummed along with Percy Sledge, dissipating the nervousness of forthcoming departure with gum-chewing/cigarette-smoking/nail-polishing/song-humming activity.

At the sign which read *Luton & Dunstable* the car came off the motorway and plunged into the English countryside. On a rutted track in the shadow of some trees it stopped. Gorsey Dene got out, the tingle of renewed circulation prickling his buttocks, and stretched in the sunshine; Jay jumped up and down, grateful to be released, her long hair swirling and undulating in glossy rivers of reflected light. They walked through a tunnel of arching trees, the ground moist with carpeted leaves, holding hands at arm's length to savour their freedom and independence. Mossy logs slumbered in the undergrowth, shaded by vivid green ferns whose tracery of patterns stirred with their passing. Gorsey Dene had heard of such dells but never seen one: in the near distance the tunnel's exit was confronted by a blazing field of ripening corn bearing the full brunt of the sun. They walked carefully along the perimeter, then struck inwards, the dry stalks squeaking and groaning underfoot, their feathered heads clashing back in successive layers with the passage of trousered and nyloned limbs.

When far enough, deep enough, *in* enough, they lay down and had sexual intercourse. It was, to Gorsey Dene, like lying in a golden bowl on the top of which was a blue lid. Jay straddled him, working diligently at a uniquely meaningful experience, the drops of perspiration under her eyes and the wet ends of her hair licking his shoulders. She was enjoying his penetration into her, gasping on the inward stroke and shuddering on withdrawal, her eyes half-closed and clouded with pleasureful pain, generating the sensation to the point where she wanted the full length of him to pass through her belly and into her chest, legs split wide apart and gaping orifice vulnerable to the greatest thrust-power in the world. It occurred to Gorsey Dene that her energy, transmitted through him to the earth below, was sufficient to alter, if only fractionally, the orbit of the planet in the context of the solar system. And, being thus altered, the solar system itself would deviate in relation to its galaxy; and of course the galaxy would transmit this shift from the norm to the universe at large. So it was conceivable (at least to Gorsey Dene) that the energy Jay was expending was instrumental in the development of the whole of creation. The mechanical consequences of this simple act reverberated to the far ends of existing time and space: she had made a contribution to the entire grand work, and, far from being worthless, her life had served its purpose and been given meaning.

Gorsey Dene ejected his product into her, the tremors of climax expanding him so that she knew what had happened and, replying to his question, repeated incessantly, 'Yes.'

Rising slowly off him, the flaccid tender hurt now removed from inside her, Jay lay down on the crushed corn and allowed the sun to stroke her; the imperturbable light stared at her inquisitively, blameless and amoral. In the green distance a train tooted a double note. Gorsey Dene knew that he would remember this field of corn for ever. Already he had scanned and stored the available data, holding it for instant retrieval at some past or future date. The high blue sky curved over him, its faultless weight pressing him to the ground, and in the stalks of corn near at hand invisible insects frittered and whirred, pursuing their lives in selfish and oblivious blindness. Birds chattered insatiably.

'Do you suppose that your life — our lives — were so engineered as to culminate here and now at this time and in this place?' Gorsey Dene asked.

'Fuck knows,' Jay said. She was like a languorous white slug, fat with appeasement. 'You only pose these questions to imbue with significance what is essentially a common-place event. Who cares what other inferences one might draw from two people lying in a cornfield? Just because you think you have a so-called intellect, untapped and unexploited, you feel it necessary — I might almost say obliged — to spout pseudo-philosophical gibberish —'

'Contradiction in terms,' said Gorsey Dene.

'Balls. You stick your dick in me and think it a symbolic act with far-reaching, deep-rooted implications pertinent to the whole of mankind.'

(What had happened to her maidenly blushes? Gorsey Dene wondered.)

'All I said was —'

'Your trouble,' Jay said fiercely, 'is that you have a personality defect; you feed off imagined slights. You bend double eating your own pitiful entrails. As some disgusting furry vermin, tiny-eyed and with sharp pointed teeth, gnawing at its own anus, burrowing upwards with self-destroying greed and pity.'

The sun was blinding hot.

'Self-pitying greed and destruction,' said Gorsey Dene correctively. 'And would that certain furry vermin be a mole by any chance?'

'Possibly. Why?'

'A mole is a facial growth.'

'Yes?'

'That makes the coincidence complete.'

'You haven't lain in this field with anyone else?'

Gorsey Dene shook his head. 'Not this field.'

'Isn't it hot?'

'It is hot. Did you hear what I said? The mole is yet one

more link in the chain.'

'What fucking chain is that?'

A green creature with legs hopped across Jay's stomach. The earth swooned in the heat. It really was hot. Gorsey Dene was waiting for a farmer to loom over them at any moment, a deep-burnished blue-barrelled shotgun in the crook of his arm, and leer down at Jay's white sluggish body with the black pubic vee. To obviate the possibility of this he stood up and found himself waist-high in a lake of rippling corn: and far away a thin green train slid silently through the lush countryside, a straight dark worm creeping in the undergrowth. Jay's breasts were spread spongily on her chest, lapping her armpits, nipples floating on top like candle wicks on pools of oil. Gazing down at her he began to feel the tug of a returning erection, and knelt down beside her; she opened her eyes lazily and smiled. If only she would open her mouth wide he could –

And yet still the sun beat down, right to the end of the day, when, in the early evening, they sat outdoors drinking beer beneath circular multicoloured canvas in the gravelled forecourt of a pub on the outskirts of London. There were cubes of melting ice in the glasses. Never before had Gorsey Dene drunk beer with ice. (He was to in Spain, however, the following year.) Expensive sports cars were parked a little distance away.

They were to have a few drinks, a meal, and then Jay was to catch the boat train at Paddington. Life seemed very simple to Gorsey Dene; but as yet – as ever – there was the nightdrive ahead of him. This contrast between summer days and cold shrieking nights disturbed him, hinting as it did that he was on the trapdoor of insanity. Who would guess it to look at him! However, had he been certain that it *was* insanity (which he was not), it might have put his mind at rest, for the explainable is comforting. What so discomforted him was the fear that it might not be insanity, in which case he was living two lives: the positive and the negative, and under such conditions terms like sanity and insanity were meaningless. For example, insanity in the positive world might very well turn out to be sanity in the negative world, and the converse would be true. Now, at this moment, he felt self-contained and safe within himself, but he was not such a fool as to believe that this well-being might not splinter and disintegrate, and he would be drawn willy-nilly into those shadows of nostalgia which plagued and taunted him at odd, bleak, spiritless moments of his life. It occurred to him quite at once — as he was sipping the cold beer from the beaded glass — that he was on a steady downhill path towards unhappiness: that broken promises and fragmented dreams were littered behind him like smashed china, each one in its time a mortal blow, so that cynicism, disillusionment, and above all, fear, were now his major constituents. This fails to explain it. The more he had achieved, the less the satisfaction: yes, that was it. Starting off with the vision of a series of golden futures ahead of him . . . each, upon its fulfilment, had shown itself to be a hollow sham, a despairing void. When very young he had known the power of these visions while not yet attaining them — and now that he had, found the promise more substantial than the achievement. The brilliant spheres of light glittering in the sky had seemed very desirable, but now those same spheres were dun-coloured leaden balls, some of them lodged in his belly and others at the base of his brain. He had achieved more and yet was more unhappy than at any time previously. The cracking-up of his personality made the situation worse, and the worsening of the situation expedited the cracking-up of his personality. Day by day he sank lower, floundered more, was less sure of his character (or indeed whether or not he possessed such a thing). As an ironical black joke the past had become golden and the future leaden, featureless, fearful.

They ate a meal together at the dead hour of early

evening, scooping tepid soup out of shallow metal bowls, and inflicted upon themselves a watery omelette that neither really wanted. It was a token last supper prior to departure, and when he stood with her outside the railway carriage the solemnity of the occasion weighed like iron on their shoulders and slowed the world to a series of jerking tableaux. Jay was dabbing her eyes in a parody of weeping; Gorsey Dene was thinking of the nightdrive.

'You will write long letters to me, won't you?' She looked at him from behind the handkerchief. Had he not known better it was conceivable that she could have been laughing.

'Long letters about what?'

'About the cornfield. About what you did to me there.'

'I noticed the corn left marks on your back.'

'I was on top.'

'You lay down afterwards. When you got up there were marks on your back.'

'You should have turned me over, face downwards, so that I was pressed right into the corn.'

'It would have left marks on your breasts.'

'Yes.'

'Cuts and weals.'

'You would have liked that, knowing you.'

'Anyone would think I was a sadist.'

'There were marks on your back too.'

'You were on top, pressing me into the ground.'

'I liked that : I really enjoyed that : sitting astride you. Write me a long letter about it. Tell me what it was like with me on top and the corn against your back.'

'Did you feel you were split?'

'I wish you had split me, clean in two. Right up the middle.'

Perhaps when she returned she would lean over his loins and —

'It seems incredible that you were once a virgin.'

'Will you be taking girls in that van of yours while I'm away?'

'No,' Gorsey Dene replied truthfully. (She thought him better than he was.)

'And no parties at the German student's.'

'No.'

'And no black stuff.'

'No' — laughing.

Jay's pale, anxious, oval face hovered in his subconscious, haunting him, when, later, he sat at the bar of the Islington pub and relived those final moments of parting. She had boarded the train with a mournful expression, close to tears, and her sensuous mouth had trembled a little (that mouth!), the lower lip in a pout of stoical self-denial. Gorsey Dene, having misplaced his emotions at least a decade earlier, composed his features into a facsimile of responsible gloom; a fine intelligence sober, withdrawn, and harrowed. Settling herself into a corner of the compartment next to the window Jay had shrunk to a white blob as the train silently curved along the platform, its oiled wheels hauling the whole smooth bulk from beneath the overhanging iron lattice-work and into the gentle light of warm mid-evening.

Jay had stood at the open window — Gorsey Dene having slammed the door shut — and leaned out to embrace him, stifled convulsions in her neck shuddering through the kiss, female guttural sounds issuing from her. He had felt flattered — indeed honoured — that someone should think him worthy of these deep, genuine responses; she must have been overly fond of him, he reasoned, staring at the creamy head of the Guinness and wondering at the viability of spontaneous human feeling. At his elbow a youth with thin pathetic wrists and watery brown eyes must have caught a nuance of the reflection in Gorsey Dene's face, for he smiled wanly in the instant comradeship of lone drinkers, raising sparse eyebrows in a gesture of inquiry.

'What would you say is the trouble with this day and age?' the young man began. 'Pollution, over-population, or sex?'

Clearly the young man had a morbid preoccupation with sex, which Gorsey Dene wasn't at all surprised to surmise, taking into account the other's white, ravaged face and unbecoming appearance. He almost smiled at the ridiculous vision of this paltry specimen engaged in any kind of sexual interaction with a female, however desperate or decrepit she might be. But did he really expect an answer to the question? Gorsey Dene drank his Guinness and mentally groomed himself: his confidence and feeling of superiority had returned with the chance meeting. Poor deluded imbecile — alongside him the youth must have looked a wreck. Already certain women in the bar were turning and comparing the two.

'Myself I would say it was sex,' the youth said predictably, and Gorsey Dene nodded tolerantly, quite prepared to humour the pathetic fixations and long-felt yearnings of this deprived misfit.

'Too little of it about, no doubt.'

'Too much; far too much.'

Gorsey Dene smiled easily, vastly amused by the apparent sincerity of this human disaster; he was pleased at his own ability to exercise broad-minded sympathy in the face of such blatant subterfuge.

'I bet you knew a girl,' Gorsey Dene said.

'I knew many girls.'

'Of course; of course you did.'

'This one girl in particular I grew up with. We went to the same school together as tiny children.'

'I bet you played with her,' Gorsey Dene said with meaningful emphasis.

'I played with her,' the youth said innocently, 'all right. We grew up together in the same town, as neighbours, and when we got older went for long walks. Anyway, later on the word got around — I heard it from several people — that she was handing it out. You know — you know —' he stammered.

'I know,' Gorsey Dene said patiently.

'Well, we hadn't seen each other for a long time ... a few years at least, when I happened to meet her in the street one day and she told me she shared a flat with a friend.'

'Oh yes,' Gorsey Dene said, midly interested.

The youth's eyes had become abstracted and his hand slipped on his glass, almost spilling it. 'She invited me to go and see her, telling me when she was most likely to be in. Evenutally I did go to see her, not straight away, but several weeks later. I knocked on the door of her flat,' the youth said, 'but there was no answer. At first I thought of going away, the flat being empty, but just then I thought I heard a sound — or sounds. I tried the door and it was open.'

'Yes?' said Gorsey Dene.

'As I opened the door I heard the sound of splashing water and almost immediately Shirley called out, "Who's there?" and I said, "It's me," and she said, "I'm in the bath, come through." I walked through the living-room into the bathroom and there she was, in the bath, lying back in the water. When she saw me she said, "Oh it's you."'

'Could you see anything in the water?'

'Could I see anything in the water?' the young man said, his stricken eyes staring out of a paper-white face.

'You know: any thing . . .'

'Do you mean — ?'

Gorsey Dene nodded.

'The water was soapy; the surface was covered in opaque bubbles.' He caught Gorsey Dene's questioning look. 'But she was a big girl, all right. I knew that from before.'

'You hadn't mentioned it.'

'No, but she was.'

He was lying through his teeth. Gorsey Dene didn't believe a word of it. There was nothing whatsoever about the youth that would attract a girl, much less a big one. But there could be no harm in listening to the rest of the story, ludicrously fanciful as it was.

'And then what?'

'Well . . . nothing much happened after that,' the young man said. 'She lay in the bath under the water and I talked to her for a while. Later the water started to get cold and she asked me to reach her a towel. I stood up with the towel, holding it in front of me, and she rose up out of the water, big, wet, glistening, the water running off her. She stepped out of the bath and put her arms round my neck and, clinging on, wrapped her legs around my waist. You can imagine what I was feeling.'

'Yes indeed,' Gorsey Dene said sceptically. 'Then what?'

'I couldn't believe it was happening, of course, but it was. Well, I mean, what would you have done? So I began to kiss her, my hands under her buttocks to support her in this awkward position —'

'What about the towel?' asked Gorsey Dene, a stickler for detail.

'The towel had dropped to the floor,' the young man said. 'She was wet and naked against my clothing.'

Gorsey Dene nodded, satisfied.

'— but no sooner had we begun in earnest, and we were both becoming rather excited, than she suddenly, all at once, for no apparent reason, without warning, burst into tears.'

'Still hanging —?'

'Still hanging on me, burst into tears,' the youth affirmed.

A pack of lies, obviously. Delusions of a tormented mind. Who did he think he was trying to kid? Gorsey Dene felt sick at the sham of it all but reasoned that as he was here he might as well hear the end.

'I thought at first that she was getting worked-up —
other women I've had have behaved in a similar way —'

(Other women!)

'— but she wasn't, just very upset. She clung to me, this
big girl, her arms and legs round me, sobbing her heart out.
I asked her what was the matter, thinking that she was
contrite about being so forward and throwing herself at me
in so shameful a manner. Her face was pressed into my
shoulder, her weight was getting heavier and heavier, and I
had to ask her again why she was crying. She mumbled
something into my collar and I had to ask her to repeat it,
and when she did it was, "I'm three months pregnant." My
desire vanished instantly. You've probably been in that
kind of situation yourself, so you'll know. Anyway, I just
wanted to go away and leave her but it seems that I was
the only person she could confide in: she had to unburden
herself to someone and it happened to be me. And then it
all flooded out, about how afraid she was, how her mother
was sure to have fits, what her father would say, whether
she could get enough money together for an abortion,
what she was going to do about her job, how she could
afford to keep the flat, what had happened to Creely in
recent weeks, whether or not she should commit suicide —'

'And all this time,' Gorsey Dene interjected, 'she was
hanging onto you, wet, naked, getting heavier and heavier?'
His voice became nasal with disbelief. The wretched figure
seemed incapable of holding her for seconds, much less a
prolonged period of time. He glanced about: several people
in the bar were regarding them curiously — rather, were
regarding the youth thus. What an odd specimen he was; a
real jackanapes. His hair stuck out at tangents, stiff and
spiky, and the malformed planes of his face were sharply
divided into areas of light and shade.

The young man said, 'The girl on the moor was
altogether a different kettle of fish.'

'*The girl on the moor*,' Gorsey Dene said, almost

knocking his drink over. 'What girl on the moor is that?'

'Someone I'd known when I was a youngster. She went away for several years, returning with her boyfriend, and the three of us went up on the moor. He tramped off, intrigued by the "round hills" as he called them, and when he was out of sight she looked at me and said, "You haven't given me a welcoming kiss yet," and as she said it started unbuttoning her blouse and moving towards me. The next thing I knew she had pulled her skirt up to her waist and was straddling me, her blouse fully open, and before I was aware of what was happening we were doing it and she was groaning and whispering, saying how long she had waited for this to happen.'

'And the boyfriend —'

'Out of sight over the moor. By the time he got back we had finished and were sitting talking quite naturally. He never suspected a thing.'

This was becoming preposterous. There were gaping holes in the story, yards wide. For example, there were no moors in Islington. And who would be foolish enough to leave his girlfriend and another man (youth!) alone together on a deserted moor? And again, what on earth could possibly motivate a young lovely girl to brazenly expose herself to an emaciated runt of a fellow like this, a hollow-chested, narrow-faced, spineless individual without a single saving grace?

'Soon afterwards, of course, I moved down here,' the young man said.

'Away from — ?'

'Yes, away from the North.'

'What happened to the girl?'

'How do you mean, what happened to her?'

'Where is she now?'

'Probably still in Oldham, where she comes from, waiting-on behind a bar I shouldn't wonder.'

At the bar itself, freshly-washed plastic, Gorsey Dene

fiddled with change, squaring his shoulders manfully so that Jay should not tire of him within the first few hours following disembarkation. He had again experienced the difficulty of knowing who he was: when he behaved artificially people tended to see through the sham, yet when he acted naturally (or what he assumed to be so) they disliked him intensely. It was a dilemma. Thus with Jay it was a constant struggle to strike the norm of acceptable behaviour. Either she would regard him as a fake, her beautiful face hardening grotesquely with scorn, or else she would read his true character and find it wanting. What could he do? he wondered miserably, setting the drinks down on the table and falling nonchalantly into place beside her, the sick parody of masculine insouciance.

'I had to burn all your letters,' she told him. 'They really were too naughty. I blushed when I read them.'

Life at arm's length, Gorsey Dene reflected grimly. A resounding success one stage removed. It would be better were he to live his life in a book.

'But you didn't write about the cornfield! Instead you rambled on and on about white beaches and warm blue seas, which in a cold country have no real relevance. Why was that?'

'I was trying to imagine the kinds of things we could do in the future rather than set down merely a drab remembrance of the past.'

'Did you imagine too all those things you did to me on the beach with the tide coming in — the water washing over us?'

'Of course. And next year, after the winter, we could go abroad together and actually carry out all those things to the letter. Italy, Greece or Cyprus; one of those places.'

'I'm not sure I would fancy it.'

'Yes you would.'

'I'm not sure.'

Just then a dark-skinned foreign-looking man with a bad complexion — Indian or Pakistani perhaps — came into the bar and asked for a lift to the nearest large town.

III

His name was Rhet Karachi, and they managed somehow to squeeze him in amongst the suitcases, carrier-bags and clothing on the back seat. He was a dancer by profession, or so he told them, saying he was on his way to an overnight party in Blackpool. Gorsey Dene said that he could only take him a certain distance, and from the corner of his eye saw Jay glance towards him (Gorsey Dene), a conspiratorial smile lurking around her full dark lips. Evidently she considered him (Rhet Karachi) something of a joke — at any rate someone not to be taken seriously. Gorsey Dene smiled above the dashboard glow, acknowledging the covert intimacy between them, pleased beyond words to be taken so exclusively into her confidence.

'Tell me,' said Gorsey Dene, 'how is it you come to be in this part of the country?'

'I disembarked an hour or so ago,' replied Rhet Karachi. 'I have been travelling on the Continent for several months.'

'Really.'

'Yes. I am a dancer, as I told you, returning to this country in the hope that I can get work.' There was an arrogance about him, subdued as yet, but nevertheless there, lying like strands of sinuous metal just beneath the surface of his personality.

'So you have been to this country before?' Gorsey Dene said.

There was a pause. 'I am from this country; did you think I was foreign?'

'No, no,' said Gorsey Dene quickly, ignoring Jay's

smothered snort of amusement. 'No, with you saying you were returning it somehow seemed . . . you gave the impression . . . well, it intimated that . . .' He stubbed out his cigarette in the ashtray and fiddled with the headlight switch.

'What sort of dancing do you do?' Jay asked.

'Modern. Improvisation mostly. The kind popularised by Robert Cohan.'

Jay had half-turned to hear him say this, noting that one of his eyes twitched involuntarily, the muscular membrane surrounding it galvanised by some spasmodic nervous irritant. She reached across in the darkness of the car and clutched Gorsey Dene's hand.

'I have appeared on television. You may have seen me perhaps, unknowingly.'

'We may indeed,' Gorsey Dene said. 'You've travelled a good deal on the Continent have you?'

'On the Continent and in this country. Of course the girls abroad are much better at love-making. Their attitude is much more free. I've lived off a number of them during my travels. I have one now, in London, who keeps me and buys me expensive presents. Women seem to like doing that for me.'

'But yet not a car.'

'No, not a car,' Rhet Karachi said. Could there have been a smile in his voice, or a sneer? Gorsey Dene chose to ignore it. He had made his point and was well-satisfied. He pressed Jay's hand and she responded; they were as one on many things.

'This girl in Blackpool is expecting me to stay for a few days; I don't know if I shall.'

'Another one?' Jay said, squeezing his hand. Gorsey Dene caught a glimpse of the curvature of her lips.

'I told you there were several,' Rhet Karachi said. There was the almost undetectable smell of something musky in the car whenever he spoke — an odour of foreign food and cigarettes. 'One woman of near middle-age practically begged me to live with her. I thought about it for quite some time but then decided that I wouldn't. She bought me lots of things: shirts, suits, clothing in general, a gold watch, rings.' He had leaned forward between their two heads. Gorsey Dene controlled his breathing.

'Why did you reject her offer?' he asked.

'I couldn't waste myself on that old slag. What, with all the girls there are in the world? It wouldn't be fair.'

'On the woman?' Jay said.

'On the girls,' Rhet Karachi said, smiling. 'I could never stay with one girl for any length of time. They become too possessive, they want to own you. I stay with them just long enough, then I go away.'

'Where?' Jay said, a slight catch in her voice.

'From this country abroad; from abroad back here. There is always somewhere new to go. And wherever I go there are girls.'

The car swerved violently round a dark bend, slipping on the shiny road. Jay's grip slackened in Gorsey Dene's grasp; her hand hesitated, then withdrew. But it was all right: she was lighting a cigarette, or powdering her nose, or applying fresh lipstick, or something. The car proceeded through the encroaching night, the spheres of Immingham now far behind.

'I've done many diverse jobs too, and not only as a dancer,' Rhet Karachi went on. 'I've worked in offices, bars, exhibitions, and in hotels. It isn't an easy life doing what I do. In one place I had to cook all the meals, breakfasts as well, but I must say it had its compensations. For instance, there were always plenty of girls: the guests were very careless with their wives and sweethearts. At all hours of the night and day I used to creep up and down, keeping an eye open for the likely ones. (There are always likely ones, even in an hotel of intermediate size.) On a night such as this I remember a young couple coming into the hotel, exhausted after a long day's drive, and almost right away she tipped me the wink behind the back of her friend who was signing their names in the register. Well, I carried their bags up to their room, knowing full well that sooner or later I would get the chance even though they were staying only overnight. He was absolutely dumb, this guy, and she was a real looker, a gorgeous black chick. Once or twice we just glanced at each other, not saying anything, and I couldn't help grinning . . . so not to give the game away I kept my head bowed and he must have thought I was good at my job — crawling and so on — because he gave me a shilling, poor jerk. Next morning the old slag who kept the hotel was on my back as usual, chasing after me to get this done, get that done, make the breakfast, etcetera. She had this cutting voice that carried everywhere, screaming out my name: "Rhet! Rhet! *Rhet*!!!" Would you believe I had to make the jerk's breakfast? But as it turned out this was to my advantage because the girl, for some reason or other, stayed in the bedroom while he came down to the dining-room. So I dished up the bacon and eggs and whatnot, and scooted out of the way, avoiding the old slag who was charging about, her bosom heaving. Up the stairs two at a time to the room I went, quiet as a black cat, and knocked on the door. She opened it and just stood there staring at me with her big brown eyes; then she smiled, a big, warm, real friendly-looking smile, an open invitation if ever I saw one.

'"Is your husband here?" I asked.

'"My *husband* is not here," she replied as she opened the door even wider.

'"I guessed as much."

'Suddenly she moved away from the door and I saw the state the bed was in. It was a gift, in a sense, because I started tidying it, smoothing the ruckled sheets and plumping up the pillows. She watched me through the dressing-table mirror, applying scent to her neck and wrists, a half-smile playing across her generous features. She was a looker, all right, and different from anything else I'd ever had.

'"Are you travelling on business or pleasure?" I said to her.

'"Partly both. We set off late yesterday afternoon, intending to break our journey and stay somewhere overnight. He's on business; I'm on pleasure."

'It was a bright morning, I remember it distinctly. All night long I had thought about her, getting worked up and jerking off. (You know what it's like when you can't get a chick out of your mind; drives you crazy.) So anyway, I carried on with the bed, shaking the mattress and straightening the covers. She kept grinning at me through the mirror and I thought, "Any minute now, baby. Just let me put this where it'll do us both some good." She knew what I wanted all right, and she was the kind of broad who keeps teasing and tantalising a guy. Jeez!'

At this point Rhet Karachi drew back from between their two heads and fixed his body in a semi-crouch while he lit a cigarette. The glow illuminated the sallow pock-marked cheeks tapering hollowly to the strong prominent jaw. He inhaled sharply and the smoke gushed from his finely-delineated nostrils. Then he resumed his position and continued with the story.

'She began to talk about her family, her mother and cousins — about whom, it seemed, she was pretty concerned. None of this affected me except in the sense that the longer she talked the better chance I had. Of course there was the sap downstairs eating his breakfast, but I figured there was time enough. The old slag would keep him plenty occupied. When I'd finished the bed I sat down on the end of it listening to her. By now she was doing things to her hair, brushing it up off the nape of her neck, and smiling into the mirror as she talked. I got the

whole bit: about her job and why she had decided to move
south, and her relatives, and the creep she was with, and
the places she's stayed in, etcetera. Well, anyway, this
wasn't getting me very far and I really fancied her — you
know? She had these long slim legs right up to her arse
and I was going nuts (you can imagine) just thinking what
this creep must have been experiencing during the
preceding night, having that piece of tail tucked between
his sheets; and her hot for it, that was obvious. I mean, can
you see me — or anybody come to that — passing up an
opportunity like this one? She was practically begging me
to jump her, yet all the while playing it oh so cool and
calm and dignified, like some genteel lady, just now and
then throwing me this cheeky grin through the mirror as if
to say, "We both know what you want, don't we, but I'm
going to keep you dangling just a bit longer till you're
sagging at the knees, weak at the thought of lusting after
me — unless, of course, you're man enough to come and
grab a piece right now, this minute, and lay me good,
strong and hard while the blood's hot in your veins." Yeah
that's what her look implied all right.'

To this rather incoherent narrative Gorsey Dene listened
absorbedly. Gradually Rhet Karachi's voice had increased
in excitement, and at the same time diminished in tempo,
so that his tone had become thick and low, charged with
emotional intensity. Jay sat rock-still, a disapproving look
on her face which, from the swift glances Gorsey Dene had
cast towards her from the corner of his eye, made her
appear almost ugly. Her throat seemed to be constricted
with — not loathing, exactly — but distaste. Or no, it might
not even have been distaste; too dark to tell.

'Her hair finished at last she turned round and gave me
both those big laughing eyes and that dazzling smile. It was
time to make a move: now or never as they say.

'"Where are you going from here?" I asked her.

'"Home, and then on into town."

"'If I followed you would you object?"

"'I couldn't do anything about it, could I? This is a free country, so they told me."

"'If you happened to leave the name of your destination written down lying around somewhere . . . ' "

"' – Or written on the mirror in lipstick."

"'Why not?"

"'Only he might see it."

"'What the hell?'"

'Just a minute, do you mean she actually wrote it in lipstick on the mirror so that everyone could see?' Gorsey Dene said. 'I would call that the height of stupidity.'

'I'm getting to that; as a matter of fact she didn't, but you're jumping ahead of the story.'

'Sorry.'

"'It matters to me," she replied, "because like it or not he's got all my stuff in his car. I've got to play up to him, otherwise – " and she drew her hand across her throat.

'A typical woman's thinking,' Gorsey Dene interjected. He was morbidly afraid of women and it pleased him when his suspicions were justified. At the same time he was somewhat uneasy: the story, though far-fetched, had the ring of truth about it.

"'I can deal with *him*," I said. "Just tell me where you're going to be and we'll meet up. I was leaving this place anyway."

'She came towards me, treading lightly on her feet like a gazelle, and stood a few inches away. I'd learnt a couple of tricks with dames, one of them being to press your forehead onto their pubes, clench your teeth, and moan.'

'Did you do it?' Jay asked.

'I did it all right. Jeez, it flipped her. She went berserk, writhing up against me, thrusting her pelvis forward. I could have taken her immediately, no sweat, but just then the fucking old slag yelled, "Rhet, Rhet, *Rhet!*" at the top of her gingy voice.'

'What was it like?'

'Like I told you, a real yelling, screaming, cutting tone of a gingy voice.'

'I meant pressing your forehead . . .'

'Oh that.' Rhet Karachi grinned, the cigarette smoke curling across his heavy, amused eyes. 'It's freaky. No, I mean really.'

'Which town did you want?' Gorsey Dene said.

'Just keep driving. No sweat.'

'I'd like to know, because we cross the motorway soon. If you want to go north or south, better to get out.'

'Which direction are you heading?'

'West. We're travelling from east to west, crossing the motorway, which if you want to go north or south will be the best place for you to get out.'

'West is fine,' Rhet Karachi said, nodding in the darkened rear. Jay felt the faint foreign smell of his breath on the back of her neck. 'Don't you want to know what happened next?'

'No.'

'Yes.'

'She told me exactly where she'd be, the exact location and time.'

'And the poor sap?' Gorsey Dene inquired.

'Still eating his gingy breakfast. Would you credit such a jerk? Well anyway, I knew this photographer and he loaned me a camera. It was a neat idea to gain admission into this place where she was, some kind of big transportation shindig with lots happening. I pretended I was with the press. Me, a dancer!'

Gorsey Dene rummaged for Jay's hand but couldn't find it.

'I mooched around for a while taking shots (or pretending to) and then, all of a sudden, there she was: this beautiful, long-legged, incredibly sexy broad. The sap was with her — as usual — but he was talking to another guy and pretty soon they disappeared –'

'Where?'

'Does it matter? They went who-knows-where. So I sidled up to her and started taking pictures. Long shots, medium shots, close-ups, the whole bit, getting closer and closer till we were very near. I was about to talk to her when she said:

'"Don't stop taking photographs, he's watching."

'"So what?"

'"It's all right for you but I rely on him. Write down your name and address or something and I'll get in touch with you."

'"But I thought we were going for a drink? You don't expect me to follow you all over London, hanging about with a camera in the hope that he might leave you alone for a couple of minutes. Jeez!"

'"Write it down, write it down," she said. "I'll keep smiling and you keep taking photographs, then he won't suspect."

'Some dames!' Rhet Karachi complained. 'Jesus fucking Christ. They want it every which way.'

'"Does it matter?" I put it to her. "Tell the sap where he gets off and have done." But she wouldn't.'

'I suppose you never saw her again,' Gorsey Dene said, manipulating the wheel. The car was speeding over a deserted piece of landscape.

'Yeah, at a dance. She turned up with him again but he wouldn't come past the door, the jerk. She came over to me and said, "I can't stay," and I blew my top. I said, "If you think you can give me the run-around you're mistaken. The hotel, the show, and now here, the dance."

'"It isn't my fault," she said, going all soft-eyed. "He drove me down here, he paid for the hotel, and my mother likes him. Do you like people who aren't grateful?"

'"Sure I like people who aren't grateful; I'm not grateful myself. And what's gratitude got to do with you and me?

We could make it in a big way together."

'She looked right into my eyes — wow! — and I could have taken her on the spot. You know, that's the trouble with this day and age, we don't react any more.'

This was the first thing he'd said with which Gorsey Dene agreed. The man seemed to be obsessed with his own exploits; and what most annoyed Gorsey Dene was he knew precisely how to behave, even in circumstances that might very well have been described as raw-nerved. In other words, these were so close to the ugly core of reality — so much a matter of hair's-breadth decisions — that to come through them with one's faculties intact and not shattered irrevocably into a thousand pieces was truly remarkable. That pock-marked skin must have been as thick as an elephant's hide, while he himself was transparent. Rhet Karachi knew instinctively what to say, how to say it and when to say it. Gorsey Dene on the other hand was in paroxysms of doubt over the breaths he ought to take: their frequency, duration, and volume. He had never responded humanly to anyone or anything in his life.

'Did you ever get together with this girl?' Jay asked. 'I mean sexually?'

'Sure,' Rhet Karachi said confidentially. 'Name me a girl I couldn't make if I put my mind to it.'

'You'd had three attempts and failed each time,' Gorsey Dene pointed out. (The fellow couldn't expect to have a free lift *and* have it all his own way. There was such a' thing in this miserable, cringing world as justice.) He noticed Rhet Karachi's hand resting on the back of Jay's seat, and pretended not to notice it. Jay could never become fascinated by such a creature. She couldn't.

'Are you telling me, with all my experience with women, that I couldn't have had her?' Rhet Karachi said. He laughed, and Jay hesitantly chuckled with him. She was leaning back against his hand, that much Gorsey Dene did notice.

'All I'm saying is,' Gorsey Dene said, 'how do we know there's a grain of truth in all this? I could say the same thing, that I'd had wide experience with women —'

Rhet Karachi and Jay both laughed out loud. She could feel the ridge of his knuckles in her back. Her body began to seep fluid. Gorsey Dene, in his fury, nearly drove the car off the road. Had he been in full and proper possession of his faculties he might have done so.

'You sound like somebody I once met in a pub,' Rhet Karachi said. 'I was with that photograper-friend of mine I mentioned earlier. He (this certain somebody) was always making rash pronouncements about what he'd done, was about to do, and was capable of doing. Talking of going abroad or some such nonsense.'

'He's the same,' Jay said, half-turning her smiling head to the rear.

'I'm not the same as *any*body else.'

'Yes you are.'

'No I'm not.'

'Yes — you — *are*.'

'This photographer-friend of mine was sceptical. You see, he had been abroad and intended going again on a commission from UNICEF. He planned to travel through Europe as far as Greece or Turkey and get the boat across to Cyprus.'

Jay laughed. 'The idea.'

'And he hit on what I thought was a terrific wheeze advertising for somebody to go with him. Well, he did, and got four replies.'

Gorsey Dene was more irritated than he could say. If this was going to be another rambling anecdote then the fellow would have to get out. And for a start Jay could stop leaning on his hand.

'Tell us about him, he sounds interesting,' Jay said.

'Well,' Rhet Karachi began, '——'

Gorsey Dene put the car into second gear and the

suitcases fell on Rhet Karachi's head. Jay giggled and snorted, and Gorsey Dene felt a smirk enter his soul. Dancers had always generated fury in him. They were so assured, so smug, so implacable. Physical violence was the answer.

'Well,' Rhet Karachi began, 'this photographer-friend of mine advertised for a travelling companion — for the second trip I should add — and received, as I said, four replies. The idea behind it all was to get away from his shrewish wife. Hell, what a woman. I met her a coupla times. Anyway, this other guy — the certain somebody I told you about — and my photographer-friend and me met up in a pub one time. He was going away, so he said, but neither of us believed him. He was the kind of guy who said things like that — you know? Jeez. So anyway, we met him.

'"I'm going abroad on a commission from UNICEF," says my photographer-friend, giving me the wink.

'"Oh yes?" says the other guy, a real prick. "Where to?"

'"France, Switzerland, Italy, Yugoslavia, Greece, Turkey, then by boat to Cyprus. I've advertised for a girl and got four replies."

'"Have you chosen the lucky broad?" I ask him.

'"Not yet," he tells me. "Oh by the way," he says straight-faced to the other guy, "this is an Italian friend of mine with no visible means of support."

'"How do you do?" says the other guy, to which I just nod and give him the once-over. He was a small guy; you could almost say he was a dwarf. I've seen some odd guys in my time but he was the oddest. He kept staring past my head at the patterns on the window — you know the type.

'"What about your wife?" the other guy asks, obviously trying to be smart.

'"Yeah, how about my wife?" says my photographer-friend. "I mean, if you want her you can have her."

'"But isn't she going with you?"

'"Haven't I just told you that I've advertised?"

'"Yes – "

'"Well that means I've advertised. What did you think it meant: that I was going abroad with a fucking harem?"

'"You could stay with me when you go, on my farm overlooking the Adriatic," I say in my best Italian accent. The other person looks at me as though *I* must be crazy. Can you beat that?'

'Did he ever go?' Jay said.

'No. What do you think?'

'He had the commission from UNICEF, he'd advertised for a girl,' (she said this hungrily) 'and he decided in the end not to go?'

'My photographer-friend went all right, but not the other guy. He couldn't get a commission from Fray Bentos. It was cheap talk, that's all. Just trying to impress us with his worldly ambitions. The schmuck.'

'I don't see that at all,' said Gorsey Dene, puzzled and hurt. The other two laughed conspiratorially. In truth he didn't see very much, if anything. His grasp of human situations had been weak at the best of times and was now defunct. Why (he asked himself) scoff at a man's aspirations? The fellow was obviously deadly serious about going – even though he might never go – and in that case why berate and deride him? Rhet Karachi, no doubt, struck a fine figure, him and his 'Italian' accent, but only because he was safe and snug within the confines of his own inadequate personality.

'But the best giggle of all,' Rhet Karachi said, smiling, 'was when my photographer-friend returned from his travels and we met once again, the three of us.'

'What happened, what happened?' Jay said. Gorsey Dene thought about putting the car into *first* gear.

'Listen: this'll slay you.' Rhet Karachi's strange odour wafted over their shoulders.

At about this time Gorsey Dene went for some food.

They had just passed through a set of traffic-lights and the car was parked in a lay-by. Jay and the Pakistani-looking man were left to their own devices while Gorsey Dene ran through the shiny stream of cars to the Golden Andalucia Fish Snack Bar. He returned sucking hot fish batter off his fingers. The drive resumed. What had transpired during his absence he was not yet to learn about. However, it came to his notice that both were smoking a certain brand of foreign cigarette.

'As it happens he'd had a fabulous time, but fabulous. They'd driven clear across Europe, through France, Switzerland, Italy — stopping off at Venice to take a peek — Yugoslavia, Greece, Turkey, then grabbing the boat to Cyprus.

'"And what was the girl like?" this other guy asks, eyes bulging, lips wet with saliva.

'"I'll tell you," says Dmitri. "We checked into this hotel overlooking the bay at Kyrenia. It had a balcony, a shower, maid service, the works. The girl herself was out of this world: long dark hair parted in the centre, big eyes, and a full generous month."'

'Oh yes?' Gorsey Dene said.

'"During the day we skipped along the beach, shuffling our feet through the fine white sand and splashing in the deep blue sea. Paradise. I had this work to do for UNICEF but that was a breeze. We had it in the surf, the sea washing over us, and she loved every minute of it."'

'She would too,' Jay said.

'Now just one second,' Gorsey Dene said, wrestling with the wheel. 'When *I* suggested going abroad it was a different kettle of fish. "I wouldn't fancy it," you said.'

'Woman's privilege to change her mind,' Rhet Karachi said.

'Why the hell should it be? Just because some fancy prick of a photographer — '

'Easy, man, he's my friend. Easy now.'

Gorsey Dene subdued his anger and simmered. He had a blinding headache and a pain in his stomach. There was a prickling sensation on his left cheekbone. The sooner all this was over and done with, the better. Life was more and more becoming too much to bear. Jay had been a fixed point of reference but now this insidious dancer had changed everything. He would have to get out; no alternative.

'By this time the guy's tongue is hanging out — can you imagine? He's uptight as hell. "Tell me what happened at night," he says.

'"Which night?"

'"Any night; none in particular."

'"Well," says my photographer-friend, pulling a face behind his hand and tipping me the wink — '

'One moment,' Gorsey Dene interrupted. 'Are we to understand that he was telling the truth about his experiences abroad? Because were he to be telling the truth, why the need to wink and pull a face?'

'"Are we to understand,"' Rhet Karachi said, punching Jay on the shoulder. 'What kind of expression is that? Who says "Are we to understand" outside of books?'

'You understand what it means?'

'Yes I do, friend. I understand lots of words I don't use in everyday conversation. Are you some kind of artistic nut? Is he?' — the latter to Jay.

'He thinks words count a lot more than many people.'

'Now that's wrong,' Gorsey Dene said; his head was aching quite terribly. 'I don't think words count more than people. I am singularly alone amongst many people in believing that words count. That's to say we should be careful how we use them. They have meanings; no, implications rather.'

'"That's to say,"' mimicked Rhet Karachi, his grinning mouth close to Jay's ear. His mouth was very close to Jay's ear: she could feel the foreign exhalations of his breath.

'Does he always talk like this?'

'But you don't believe that,' Jay said in reply to Gorsey Dene's assertion. 'If anything you believe quite the reverse.'

'"Quite the reverse,"' Rhet Karachi said. 'Well, well.'

'Be quiet. You believe, *if anything*, that words have no meanings at all.'

'I amended that to implications.'

'Or implications either. When people say things to you you're deeply, sensitively hurt by them; yet words to you are empty vessels, puffs of air, and consequently you use them inadvertently.'

(The truth of the matter was that he lacked sensibility.)

'I believe that a sufficient number of words can evoke an atmosphere,' Gorsey Dene said.

'"Evoke" — Jesus,' said Rhet Karachi.

'Equally, too many words can kill it,' said Jay. 'You never know when enough's enough. You keep hammering away, driving the meaning home until it's meaningless. All this leads back to the premise that words are worthless. They aren't, but you believe so.'

'Don't you want to hear what my photographer-friend said to this other guy after tipping me the wink?' asked Rhet Karachi.

'If that's so, how is it I understand perfectly all you're saying?'

'Because we're talking about concepts — things of the mind — which are real to you, while emotions aren't. You don't understand your own emotional processes and even less other people's, which leads you to say thoughtless things to them. But when they say things to you, that's different.'

'Now it's you who's repeating the same argument,' Gorsey Dene said. He could feel something growing on his face. 'I'm not the only one at fault.'

Rhet Karachi pushed his head between them. The dashboard light made the craters in his skin deep and black.

His dark eyes sparkled romantically, the quizzical brows knit together in amiable perplexity. 'Do you or don't you want to hear about my photographer-friend?'

'Since words are apparently worthless to me, no,' Gorsey Dene said rudely.

'Yes,' Jay said defiantly. 'I'd rather hear something worth hearing than your empty chatter.'

'Okay,' Rhet Karachi said confidently. (Gorsey Dene hated him; *hated* him.) ' " She was great, man, just great," says my photographer-friend, really laying it on – you know? "These great big tits, pap-white, being shaken in my face. Still a virgin, or so she made out, till I plonked it," and this other guy is green around the gills, picturing it all, living it all.

' "Course," says my photographer-friend, "now and then she hit out at me – had to – to relieve her feelings, but that made it all the better, a real rambling, scrambling fight with a big hunk o' hot red sex at the end of it. Boy, what a banana!"

' "Do you think if I advertised –" this punk was about to say, but the idea was so ludicrous that we just laughed. He was so pathetic it wasn't true.'

'Why did she hit out at him?' Gorsey Dene asked curiously.

'I guess some broads like to relieve their feelings that way.'

'Yes don't they.'

'What makes you ask, friend?'

'Oh nothing. A hunch.' But he was thinking very hard. It was exactly the kind of trick she would get up to. He could see her lolling in the surf with some prick of a photographer, all the time writing simple, sincere letters swearing undying love, unceasing devotion and eternal fidelity. Was there no end to human deceit? (His head appeared to be approaching the point of implosion.) Jay, he noticed, had gone rather quiet. She too had been a virgin. Also she had been abroad — ostensibly to Sweden, but once on foreign soil could have gone anywhere. One question demanded an answer: was her body brown? Had the Cyprus sun etched her skin golden, leaving pale strips of bikinied flesh that to an astute intelligence would constitute incontravertible proof? A burning question, Gorsey Dene thought humorously.

'Go on with the story,' Jay said, feeling knuckles in her back.

'Shall I?' Rhet Karachi said.

'Why not?' said Gorsey Dene, slamming into a new gear.

'There isn't much more to tell. They spent several months on the island, leading a perfect existence, swimming, sunbathing, skindiving, drinking cheap vino during the short hot evenings until, eventually, it was time to leave.'

'Did this other guy ever go abroad?' Gorsey Dene asked.

'Not to my knowledge.'

'But you don't know for certain?'

'Not for a definite fact, no.'

'There you are then.'

'Sounds idyllic to me,' Jay said dreamily. 'The sun and the beach and the sea.'

'Rubbish,' Gorsey Dene said. 'He hasn't told you about the flies and mosquitoes and ants. Nasty creepy-crawly creatures in your food and coming down the tap.'

Jay turned on him, 'How would you know, you've never been. You've never been anywhere.'

'I have,' Gorsey Dene said, but quietly.

Rhet Karachi said, 'I knew you reminded me of him; you actually do, you know.'

'Oh piss off you,' Gorsey Dene replied, this time becoming genuinely annoyed. 'But for you prattling on none of this would have happened. She was perfectly content till you came along. And another thing: how any one person could have had so many sexual exploits is beyond me. I don't believe half of them.'

'I do,' Jay said. 'Just because you've led a dull life.'

'I suppose you think he hasn't.'

'Not by the sound of it. The number of different jobs he's had for a start.'

'Whose side are you on? *I'm* giving *him* the lift in *my* car.'

'Does he always get like this?' Rhet Karachi asked.

'More often than not.'

'And what does that mean, "More often than not"? It's a stupid, senseless phrase. I suppose you'd rather be alone with him − me out of the way so as not to disturb you. Then he could tickle your neck to his heart's content.' Jay and the foreign-looking man spoke up together, protesting their innocence. 'I can damn well see you!' Gorsey Dene exploded. 'Do you think I haven't got eyes? Why do you suppose I keep glancing in the rear-view mirror? I can see his expression, shifty, guilty, full of secrets. Nobody looks like that who isn't on the make.'

'He can be real mean and gingy, can't he, when he wants?' Rhet Karachi said. His marked face in the back of the car was a mask of ambiguity. Gorsey Dene felt vulnerable and threatened.

'Don't say that!' he screamed, on the point of moral collapse. He was terrified, principally because he was better than Rhet Karachi at everything but couldn't prove it; neither had Jay the sense to distinguish the gold from the dross. She would − as would all women − opt for the surface show, the easy alternative. His hands were clammily cold on the wheel. His forehead was hot. As for Jay, her body was tight as a claw, wincing in anticipation of the warm foreign breath and soft fingers on the back of her neck. Rhet Karachi had white, perfect teeth which he used to good effect. Nothing could phase him: the reward of obtuseness and cerebral palsy. And Gorsey Dene couldn't rid his feverish thoughts of visions of Jay's body stretched out on the sand, at the point where the surf heaped itself up and then collapsed in a frothy hiss. *That* was another score which had yet to be settled.

'If you're so unsure of your girl you can't be very sure of yourself,' Rhet Karachi said.

'What's that supposed to mean?' Gorsey Dene said, though he knew very well. What he couldn't fathom was the change in Jay. She hadn't liked the fellow initially, even sniggering at his apparent discomfiture. Now all was different. Throughout his life he had been slighted and this was one more to add to the list. Who was to say when it would end?

'You're being very silly,' Jay said, which was the wrong thing to say to him in his present condition. The knuckles in her back, the fingers on her neck, and the breath in her ear were hypnotic phenomena, their combined influence making her senses swim. Gorsey Dene was aware of all this — or at any rate, reckoned he was.

'I suppose you thought it silly when I wrote you those letters. You were galivanting round the Continent, in France, Turkey, Cyprus or wherever, and there was I, prize chump, scribbling day after day, week after week, month after month.'

'Nobody paid you,' Jay said indifferently, screwing up her face against the glare of an advancing lorry.

Gorsey Dene said. 'If that's all the thanks I get.'

'What thanks do you want?'

'Some appreciation at least for everything I've done.'

'Get him,' said Jay.

'Gingy,' Rhet Karachi said.

Gorsey Dene touched the globular hairy protuberance below his left cheekbone: a hard, shiny, painful object about the size of a marble, the tip sprouting oddish-coloured hair. His head was aching; and the lights wouldn't stop flashing in his eyes. He thought: if I close them, and rest, just for a little while, perhaps when I wake up the people of the world will strike me as human beings.

Rhet Karachi said something to Jay, who laughed. She said in a cold and callous tone to Gorsey Dene, 'Why do you think I didn't want to go to Cyprus anyway?'

PART II

THE COLLECTIVE UNCONSCIOUS

I

'You did like him, didn't you?' Gorsey Dene said, Rhet Karachi having gone his own sweet way.

'Not very.'

'I saw the look in your eye.'

They were driving; but soon would have to stop to find an hotel for the night. On the outskirts of a city (Bradford, he suspected) they decided to look for one. But this was the strange thing: although Gorsey Dene knew for certain that such a place existed he knew too that he was doomed never to find it. The odds were stacked against him. It was futile even to begin looking for such a place, because with his luck — ! But, well, look they did, drawing a blank each time. The trouble was that the logistics of life were too complex for him to unravel. He marvelled, on his numerous train journeys, that identical portions of food could be (and actually were) prepared and served to countless passengers. This was Teutonic efficiency of a high order, for surely it was in the nature of things that something should go wrong. Indeed, it usually did: he was left without soup, or the last of the cutlet was cold, or his order for beer was mislaid — or failing these, and supposing the meal to be satisfactory — the train usually crashed. So on arrival in this city he had known *in his bones* the utter impossibility of finding, booking and securing a room for himself and Jay. Other folk would have sauntered into the first hotel they came to and registered in the twinkling of an eye, being shown to a warm, cosy bedroom, dimly-lit, in which a tray of fresh sandwiches and a jug of piping hot creamy coffee awaited them, before showering in tiled and fluffy-towelled luxury prior to creeping laughing, smacking and tickling into the huge downy bed into which they sank with contented sighs. While all that Gorsey Dene and Jay could achieve was a parked car in the forecourt of a fully-booked hotel. Not that it *was* fully-booked, Gorsey Dene reminded himself, only that the clerk behind the desk, on catching sight of them, had consigned them to that category of minor importance normally reserved for fools, dupes, morons and cretinous goons. In other words, people of no account. Others in the city on this dark autumn night were enjoying themselves in crowded bars, restaurants and clubs – an entire city involved in merry-making – but for Gorsey Dene and Jay it was, as usual, the cold outer periphery of recorded experience: an alternative stratum of fearful dreams, premonitions and forebodings.

'Did you truly miss me?' Jay said, the flouncy sleeves of her dress fluttering in the gloomy interior. Her arms went round his neck. He felt the material scrape his chin. It was the signal for his organ to grow hard, which it did. But at the same time he was wondering if her body was brown.

'You didn't go with that photographer, did you?'

'What do you think?' Jay said softly, not asking a question but dismissing the suggestion by her tone.

'But you did imply –'

'It's what your silly mind thought I implied.'

'It is silly, isn't it?' Gorsey Dene had not yet fully recovered from the shock to his nervous system brought about by Jay's supposed dalliance with Rhet Karachi. He was very susceptible to imagined slights. But, he consoled himself, her body would prove it once and for all. 'I did miss you, as it happens.'

'I missed it,' Jay moaned, putting her hand on the hard bulge in his trousers. She inserted her pink tongue in his ear. Gorsey Dene clutched at her breasts. Swiftly she unzipped his trousers and rummaged for the slit in his underpants through which she might extract the stiff member, disentangling it from the folds of material and caressing its full-grown length into an erection that was the focus of her desire. Gorsey Dene released a long-held sigh of pleasureful anticipation, feeling the hard bulk of it rising up before him: free, mindless, but with deadly intent. Jay worked the covering foreskin back and forth, gently, causing him to lay back in the seat, weak and strong at the same time, the swollen protuberance enclosed in her firm yet understanding grip. 'Nice,' Jay said. 'Big,' to which Gorsey Dene could only swallow his saliva and touch the ends of her breasts with his fingertips. She shuddered with dreadful ecstasy at the intense hotness contained within her hand. It fascinated her. It terrified her. She could feel its hot, quick, living property through her fingers, an insistent, insatiable urging that was the true life force . . . and the nearest one could ever come in physical proximity to it. 'Beautiful,' Jay breathed. Its moist head was thrust temptingly near her own. She had never before dared to approach it thus; and now, inches away from her eyes, she smelled the sweet pungent scent of ammonia that repulsed and obsessed all her senses. Nothing on earth could have induced her to open her mouth and accept it — just as no power in heaven or hell could have prevented her from so doing. Gorsey Dene felt the loose swishing fringe of her hair stroke his thighs as she bent forward, and then the delicious sensation of her lips sliding full soft circle over the tip and encasing it in hot suck. Her tongue trilled dumbly over the end, tautening Gorsey Dene's calves and arching his back until his throat ached with an unutterable scream. Could this be, he wondered in his exquisite agony, the first time she had performed this operation? How could she have possibly known what to do? and how with such expertise done it? It was less than feasible – to the point of incredulity no less – and he was reminded again of certain doubts and fears implanted by the swarthy gentleman who had lately departed the car. Supposing Jay *had* answered an advertisement, been vetted, chosen, and transferred across Europe to lie on a belt of white sand and be fucked in the rushing tide (wasn't the Mediterranean tideless?)? Supposing it were true (ie: that he believed it to be true), what then? But oh shit, oh God, oh fuck, it was – being gobbled – fantastic. And she worked at it so assiduously, the smooth movement of her jerking head unceasing and machine-like; the slippery lips sliding up and down over the tender glans penis, the prepuce having been pushed back and folded upon itself like a pram-hood. As for Jay, she loved the choking bigness of it in her mouth, the straining gape of her jaws that signified the grotesque violation and subjugation of her sex. She wanted to take, to accept, to swallow all its several inches as far as the pubes and in this way hold him captive in an oral-genital embrace.

'You didn't go to Cyprus, did you?' Gorsey Dene asked, stroking her hair.

Jay incorporated a shaking-of-the-head movement into the ceaseless up-and-down motion: an additional thrill.

'I didn't think you had, but I wanted to be sure. And I am right, aren't I, in thinking you were momentarily attracted to him?'

Jay nodded on her way down, was brought up short by the blunt head of the thing hitting the back of her throat.

'I thought as much,' said Gorsey Dene, settling back smugly with a smirk on his lips. 'Birds like you are always attracted by guys like that,' he observed. 'It's the sense of mystery they carry with them, the ambiguity of their shiftless lives. Isn't that so?'

On her way up, a nod.

'I've tried to cultivate it myself, without success. Trouble is, I'm too open, too transparent; too honest, in fact. I can keep nothing hidden whereas by definition a man of mystery must reveal nothing. Usually this is because they have nothing to reveal, but the world doesn't know it; false honours and spurious qualities are attributed to them through sheer ignorance and fear. And the pity of it is I cannot play that kind of game. I see too much, the most minute detail, to the very depths, everything. I perceive the shallowness of myself and others. Nothing is spared, nothing is sacred, everything is revealed. What a con-trick it all is, and- yet the obtuse among us lead the most successful lives. If they knew one-tenth of it it would send them mad.'

Jay nodded her head vigorously, sending Gorsey Dene into paroxysms of delight. He came in her mouth and she swallowed the thick stringy spittle of his loins at a gulp.

Queer chap, the dancer, Gorsey Dene reflected. His experiences, as related to them, put Gorsey Dene in mind of the drive with Tee when they too had stopped at an hotel for the night and been conducted to a room where he had made love to her long-limbed black body while he listened to the familiar sounds issuing from her throat. In the morning he had breakfasted alone, the hard-faced and solid-bosomed manageress striding through the dining-room in search of her kitchen staff. How strange that life should present one with these waves of coincidence as though working to a blind, inexorable pattern. Afterwards they had gone on to the Exhibition which even now, thinking back, depressed him, due largely to the amount of waste hidden behind the scenes. Had it really been worth all that spit and polish, that endless tuning of engines, the weeks of burnishing chrome, with the ultimate aim of deluding themselves (and others) that life was as clean, as uncluttered, as deodorised and hygienic as the glossy brochures made out? What about the tons of grease, the

mountains of oily rags, the *dirt* lurking in the workshops?
For every immaculate machine there was a waste tip to be
taken into account. All very well Alan Kimber strutting
about in his neat pale-green shirt and crisp cuffs, *but there
was a price to pay.* Cleanliness could not be achieved
without filth. Thinking back on it brought a smile to
Gorsey Dene's lips. They curved up in an attractive
crescent. He caught a glimpse of his own handsome
reflection in the glass over the speedometer. Tee had, in
many ways, been the fulfilment of all his dreams. With
her careless laughing ways she had been the first to teach
him what sex was all about. In the back seat of the car
with her legs spreadeagled . . .

There had been other times too, in Catford, and before
(or after) that the nightdrive with its squashed bloody
animals like patches of sticky black tar in the jouncing
headlights. The dance, also, where he . . . had . . . hadn't
Rhet Karachi mentioned something about a dance? Hadn't
the Pakistani jackal reminisced in gruff pseudo-masculine
tones about a similar experience? But who cared about
that figment from a nightmare. Forget him, he had been
and gone. Moving on to think about the forthcoming
assignment, Gorsey Dene wondered how the devil he was
going to research a paper mill. How can one possibly say
anything interesting about a paper mill? Perhaps the
photographs might give him a clue, for the photographer
was reckoned to be good at his job. (Photographers, he
had always found, were two-dimensional people, like their
snaps.) Thinking even further back — the photographs
having made the connexion — Gorsey Dene remembered
the shot of himself leaning through the window of the van
on the day of their return from Spain: tanned, shirtless, a
faint smile playing about his fine features. He had driven
three thousand miles with only one accident. The van had
been a bastard but prior to leaving England he had been
unaware of its fits and farts and sudden bursts of

temperament. The night in the Coach, for example, three days after Jay's departure abroad, when for the first time Pat had glued her eyes to his — little chubby Pat with the enormous dongers. Little had he known what lay in store for him *that* night! She had sidled across and engaged him in conversation:

'You have the most attractive eyes.'

(He knew this already.)

'Do you really think so?'

'You know it already.'

'Yes I do.'

As usual the narrow Coach was choc-a-bloc with bodies swilling ale and slipping on the floor. In the night outside the yellow lights cast a glow over the orderly town-centre, acres of clean tarmac gleaming faintly from the cinema to the bank. The van was parked in the street, steady as a tank.

Pat said, 'Are you coming to the party afterwards?' She had not, until this moment, affected him in any sexual way. It was her smallness that was so deceiving. But now he noticed that she had a regular pair of breasts and that her eyes were narrowed and watchful, ever-waiting for a juicy morsel to come her way. His several recent experiences with Jay and others stood him in good stead, for he was at the peak of believing in himself and his sexual prowess. Women, he had discovered, were not attracted by foppish sensitivity. The scrubbers of Oldham, for example, sought direct aggression in the form of a quick shaft behind the market stalls. Here in Rochdale the approach was no less violent if a trifle more circumspect. His problem (and didn't everyone have problems?) was that he had never learnt to treat women as human beings: they were at one and the same time above and below him. Pat, of course, was below. He felt that he could wreak his vengeance upon her.

Alan farted by, a beery flush working upwards from his neck.

Pat said, 'I've fancied you for quite a bit.'

Gorsey Dene didn't know how to take this.

'You do have transport?' Pat said, leaning against him.

'Sure,' Gorsey Dene said, slitting his sexy eyes. The dilapidated Coach was in uproar as eleven o'clock approached. Across the way the Pakistanis were being thrown out of the White Lion. He had never felt so powerfully invincible. The secret potent penis would this night be given its head; she would bow before it.

Little round Pat said, 'A number of people in this room are giving you stern looks.'

'Let them,' said Gorsey Dene with magnificent disdain.

'Are they friends?'

'Of a friend,' he qualified, knowing himself to be a perfectly handsome specimen. (It was his life's ambition to be constantly the centre of attention: it was no more than he deserved.) 'You have a husband?'

'He travels a lot.'

'Is he as tiny as you?'

'Smaller in fact.'

'Diminutive.'

'We make an ideal couple.'

'You must get on well together.'

'We would, if he didn't have a craze on Kim Novak.'

Why she should deem it necessary to trot out this useless piece of information Gorsey Dene couldn't fathom.

'And tonight, of course, he's away.'

Tiny Pat nodded, her protruding eyes looking up at him. Swollen with lust no doubt, Gorsey Dene surmised. She was a hot little potato who, unlike most women, would not be ashamed of her large breasts. They were sexual weapons in the conquest of the male member. Some women hated carrying them around — as a traveller who finds his freedom hampered by encumbering suitcases. The movement of her sweater indicated their rise and fall. Gorsey Dene smiled at them conspiratorially.

'But let's go to the party first,' said Tiny Pat. 'We'll buy a bottle of Scotch and share it. You do have transport?'

'Of a sort,' Gorsey Dene said. 'It's a van.' He looked at her. 'With a bed in the back.' He then said something funny and they both laughed. She had small teeth, white, sharp, and the interior of her mouth was a red maw.

The landlord put a ragged towel over the pumps and shouted into the crowd. Alan and a gang of them bellowed in chorus, silly and drunk with beer and laughter. Gorsey Dene smiled secretively at Tiny Pat; he had wicked eyes.

'Are you married?'

'Yes.'

'With children?'

Hesitation. 'Yes.'

'How many?'

'Two.'

'My husband is away.'

'You said.'

They went to a party in one of the six tower blocks.

The walls were made of compressed cardboard and the doors and window-frames were green and unseasoned. The party was a blur to Gorsey Dene and with the raw whisky became a sickly merry-go-round of grey faces in which eyes burned fiercely as with fever. Smiles grew lop-sided, laughter more shrill; pandemonium reigned. A friend of Jay's faced him in the hall and hissed in his face, adding that she had always known him to be a cheat, a weakling and a charlatan. Gorsey Dene regarded her with his drunken blind eye, imperious of and almost oblivious to her presence. Why should this friend of Jay's concern herself with affairs which did not concern her? Jay had gone, departed, out of harm's way, and was none the worse off for not knowing of his nefarious activities; he had to play the field while he could, before his faculties broke into little pieces and dropped into hell.

Tiny Pat dragged him by the armpit and in the instant

that her fingers touched him he had a clear, sharp vision of life: it was a labyrinth. His experiences coiled back in a series of dizzying spirals, curves and convolutions to childhood, to the golden magical past; and, incredibly, the entire structure culminated in his being alive Now. The past had no other purpose than this. He looked into the air and it appeared to be singing with the actuality of the moment — buzzing with molecules which this instant were alive, and even as he looked he knew that this aliveness in the air was in this place as far advanced along the path of time as anywhere in the universe. Here in this hallway! Alive and living now! His forehead was pressing against the frontier of all recorded history, against the furthest advanced point of the world's civilisations. All the great men who had ever lived were jammed behind him, their lives of no more significance than that he was alive and now (it had all been for him). He looked about him and the fabric of all he saw creaked with disbelief and all but fell apart. And even as he watched and listened old molecules were dying and new molecules were being born and he was being pushed along with them on the peak of the crest of time, living a moment the world had never known before. Tiny Pat's fingers were closing on his arm, a unique event in time and space since creation. What happened next would be unique too, and what happened after that, and after that, and that, and that, and that. And if he stood still it would be unique, and if he moved it would be unique, and if he laughed, cried, vomited, died, it would be unique too.

Tiny Pat pulled him from the hallway into the living-room where bodies sprawled, abandoned by their owners, each in a frenzied haze of alcohol. She thrust him against the wall and pressed her pubic bone into his groin, which to Gorsey Dene seemed a distant seismographic pain on the far side of the planet. He was possessed by lust and his penis unfurled and rubbed its sensitive tip against the coarseness of his inner clothing, and as it hardened emitted dewdrops of semen. Heat and music and semi-gloom enveloped him. Could this, he wondered, be a moment of actual life? For it truly astonished him that each instant of existence was not a substitute for, not a facsimile of, some other instant of real existence, but the actuality itself. Why could he not be in a million places at once? His life, it seemed to him, was only a fictitious preparation for the real thing yet to come — which was why all the events of his past experience had about them the quality of myth. His life was a story, a narrative within the confines of book-covers, and he longed to step out from the pages into a world that was real and live and non-fictional; and more than this, he was depressed by the notion that being in one place at one time precluded the possibility of being anywhere else and doing anything other than what he was doing. A trillion permutations from which he could select only one. It was unjust; sickening and unfair. He had to be doing all things in all places all at once; anything less was unjust; sickening and unfair.

Inside the bathroom he slammed shut the flimsy wooden door and shot the bolt. The floor was shiny-slippery with urine and footprints and they went down on it, incoherent and insensible with blood-red clawing madness, inner black space spinning behind their closed eyelids. He rammed his hand between her legs and she touched the hard lump in his trousers. 'Jesus Fucking Christ,' one of them said, and the other said, 'Fuck Cunt Dick Me-Me-Me.' Her head was up against the door at an unnatural angle; he was kneeling in piss-wet trousers inside her legs, his crutch aching to burst with the suffusion of blood. Her skirt went up and he smelled her. Then crashing on the door, hammering on the door, fists on the door . . . people trying to get in. Somehow they were standing, opening the door, walking out. Gorsey Dene jerked her into the living-room to the accompaniment of laughing jeers.

'Hot for a hole and an end,' Alan tittered.

'Bastard mean bastard,' hissed a friend of Jay's.

'Suckcuntwatdickmenow,' Tiny Pat mumbled.

Gorsey Dene fell backwards onto the divan with his legs open. He was fatigued and puking ill. Sweat on cold face. Tiny Pat rubbed herself on his knee, making greasy the place between her legs. She leaned forward, both palms pressed on the same spot, supporting herself. In a blank dream they went to the lift, into the lift, down in the lift, into the tingling night air, inside the vehicle, along the sodium-yellow-lit road in the direction she indicated.

'You do have transport,' gripping the edge of the seat, swaying.

'Didn't. I. Say. So.'

'I fancied you a bit now.'

'Yesss,' his eyeballs rolling up into his head as each successive sodium-yellow light appeared, passed over, disappeared. An effort, it really was, to fix his eyes on the road ahead.

'Husband away,' Tiny Pat said, holding the seat.

Gorsey Dene twisted his head to look at her. If he closed his eyes they would die. Was death unreal as life? If he closed his eyes would not die they would not, no: exchanging unreality for reality not be called death. In any case was same difference. They alive now but might as well be dead; if dead might be more alive than live. More live than alive. More life than life.

'Attractive your eyes.'

'Yesss.'

'Husband travels alot.'

'Small as you.'

'Smaller – ' giggling, choking '– than me.'

'I Deal Couple.' The engine ran in his head. Light coming, light passing, light passed, light gone, light coming, light passing, light passed, light gone. Light gone light gone light gone light gone lightgone lightgone lightgone. Gone.

'Married you aren't you?' Holding the seat.

'Yes.' Light coming, light passing, light passed, light gone.

'Two kids.'

'Yes.' Light coming.

'Me one. Husband away.'

He lit a cigarette and waited in a side street while she went to see all was quiet. At two o'clock there were few people about (there was no one). He began to shiver, till she appeared at the end of the alleyway and beckoned to him. Arm in arm, hips bumping, they crept through the backyard and into the house, stumbling up the steps. Inside the house it was warm and middle-class: Tiny Pat offered him a drink and staggered away, leaving Gorsey Dene to stare down at his hands. He smoked another cigarette, went upstairs, came upon her emerging from the bathroom in an underskirt. She pointed to a door and he went into the bathroom. He came out of the bathroom and went through the door, a bedroom in which she was lying in bed. Without a thought about returning husbands and vicious attacks and kicks in the groin and breadknives in the belly he stood at the side of the bed and took off his clothes. The bed was frilly pink, as was the dressing-table coverlet, the carpet thick to his toes. Tiny Pat's head, from out of the fluffy eiderdown, gasped when she saw his big stiff dick with its angry raw end. Then making him stand for a moment with it sticking out over the bed she pressed it down like a lever with her forefinger so that it recoiled upwards and reverberated before returning to its original hanging stiffness. He got in under the eiderdown and put his arms and legs round her chubby little body, the stiff hard thing sticking into her soft folded belly.

'Lick My Tits, Lick My Tits,' said Tiny Pat.

As he did she brought her knees together, gently trapping his hard and weeping prick, then rotating them so that it was rubbed, pressured, squeezed, held and released until Gorsey Dene had to say:

'Don't. I will come.'

Their wet gasping mouths worked at each other, slavering orifices with tongues and teeth. Tiny Pat felt his wet big thing protruding into her and — a surprise for Gorsey Dene — pushed him onto his back under the eider-down and went for it. In desperation (there is no other word) she sought him with her mouth, almost hurting him, and he had to appeal for gentleness and consideration. But her curly-hair head burrowed at him like a mole seeking refuge underground. With the pads of his feet he stroked her thighs, then hooked his toes between them and explored the slippery hairiness and hidden warm wetness. Her shut eyes squirmed and bulged with unexpected pleasure. She tried to speak but could not due to the heavy weight in her mouth; instead strange incomprehensible sounds of gluttenous appreciation gurgled in her throat and hummed in her nostrils. Gorsey Dene put the palms of his hands to her fatty breasts and pushed her away and she rose up spittle-hung and eyes threequarter lidded.

Tiny Pat waited dull-gazed and stupor-ridden for the next move. The softly-furnished hushed bedroom waited too, with its pools of pink lamplight, quilted headboard, and velvet curtains brushing the deep carpet. Not for very long though, for Gorsey Dene was still rigid with alcohol and impatience. He stood astride her and she lay back looking up at his hairy flanks which joined forces at the pulpy bag and straining muscle, the end of it taut with blood and the barrel swollen with purple veins. By stretching to reach up she gripped the stem and hauled herself upright, caressing his inner thighs with her cheeks and pressing the length of it with her fingers into her hair.

'Fuckcuntwatdickmenow,' Tiny Pat whispered to his flesh.

'How much, how much,' Gorsey Dene crooned.

'All, all, all,' Tiny Pat said with a muted cat's cry.

'You want everything?' Gorsey Dene said with mocking sternness.

'Everything, all, everything, yes.'

'Too much for one little girl.'

'Fuck. Cunt. Twat. Shit. Shag. Dick Me. Dick Me. Dick Me. Now.'

'Everything? All? Inside?'

'Pleasepleasepleasepleaseplease,' as a single word.

Gorsey Dene put her down on the covers, placed his knees on either side of her head and leaned forward on his elbows, looking down the tunnel thus formed to where the tip of the bulky hot thing was touching her lips. Like a good little girl with eyes shut tight she opened her mouth and swallowed him in. Held firm between tongue and palate, Gorsey Dene felt himself jerking with involuntary spasms and an ejaculation escaped his lips. It was difficult for Tiny Pat to contain him: she hung on with frequent moaning sighs. Then he swivelled, using it as a central pivot, and faced the other way, lying flat down on her to immerse his face between her legs and insert his tongue into the several folded layers, to flicker and dart in warm juicy recesses.

Later he was to discover that his back was raked with scratches. This had occurred when he had mounted her in the usual position and emptied the product of his testes inside her. And those same scratches were to remain with him as they journeyed south, the four of them, putting out tractor fires and staying overnight between strange white sheets with the van parked and loaded outside. In the brash morning light (which he now fondly remembered) they had eaten breakfast whilst watching the reflection on the ceiling of the glinting coffee-pot, butter dish and dome-shaped condiments. Rubber-soled waiters had sidled to and fro, bringing this, taking that. Fortunately for Gorsey Dene the scratches were healed before he had to bare his body to the foreign sun; Tiny Pat's handiwork remained

his secret alone, for having left her crumpled up beneath
the covers semi-comatose he had hastened away, never to
return. Via the person referred to as a friend of Jay's it
was conceivable that she might have received word of the
incident, but rising up now from his loins, mouth stickily
compressed and throat working, she showed no signs of
jealousy nor gave any hint that anything was amiss.
Besides, what had *she* been up to in another country?
Photographers were everywhere, and not to be trusted;
dancers too were undependable and should be watched
with a stern, unrelenting eye.

They decided to abandon the plan to find an hotel for
the night and set off once again on the interminable drive.
The growth, Gorsey Dene became aware, was blossoming:
it probably encompassed a goodly portion of the left-hand
side of his face by now.

Jay flounced her arms and lit cigarettes. The dark
whining car filled the silence, until Gorsey Dene said:

'What happened between you two?'

'Which two?'

'You and him.'

'Me and the photographer?'

'You and Rhet Karachi.'

'As you were here the entire time I fail to see how
anything could have happened.'

'Not the entire time,' Gorsey Dene corrected her. 'I got
out at one point leaving the two of you alone. Lots might
have happened – could have happened – and probably did.'

'Nothing happened,' said Jay in a voice thin with
impatience. 'He jabbered on about his experiences, that's
all.'

'His so-called experiences.'

'Don't you believe anything anybody says?'

'No –' Gorsey Dene said, and hesitated. He wanted to
say more but what was there to say? He didn't believe
anything anybody said.

Jay suddenly emitted a snort of laughter. 'He did tell me one amusing anecdote. You know the girl he was after, in the hotel, at the show, and finally at the dance? Well —'

'I remember very clearly,' Gorsey Dene said.

'Well apparently he eavesdropped — with a friend — on the girl and the bloke she was with. They were in the corridor —'

'The girl and the bloke?'

'No, *lis*ten: Rhet Karachi and his friend. They were in the corridor listening. It was a scream. They could hear them talking but couldn't tell what was being said because of the traffic —'

'Traffic?'

'Yes, traffic. In the road outside. Great thundering lorries giving off clouds of black smoke. And the record-player was on too, which didn't help matters.'

'So what was so screamingly funny if they couldn't hear anything?'

'Be*cause*, if you'll just listen, they knew that this bloke was under the impression that she was with him —'

'Wasn't she with him?'

'Of course she was with him; I meant under the impression that they were alone and that no one else was in the running.'

'Was someone else in the running?'

'Rhet Karachi!'

'And his friend?'

'No, just Rhet Karachi. But this bloke didn't know that. He didn't even know they were in the corridor laughing.'

'How did they know?'

'How did they know what?'

'How did they know that this bloke didn't know they were in the corridor laughing? If they were laughing he might have heard them.'

'He couldn't have.'

'Why not?'

'They were laughing soundlessly.'

'Laughing soundlessly?' Gorsey Dene said with a look askance. 'How can anyone laugh soundlessly? If you're laughing you're laughing.'

'You don't understand,' Jay said with a deprecatory shake of her head. 'It is possible. With kind of short giggles and bursting gasps. Wheezing rather than laughing, from the chest.'

'Anyway, go on,' Gorsey Dene said.

'Well, the real laugh is yet to come.' Jay broke off to snort. 'While this bloke was distracted by something-or-other —'

'Probably the lorries.'

'Possibly. Or maybe the record. While distracted, she snuck out —'

Gorsey Dene utttered a brief, sharp, one-note laugh. 'Snuck? You mean sneaked.'

'That's the word he used.'

'He would, the pimply Pakistani transatlantic twat.'

' — snuck out and came into the corridor where Rhet Karachi and his friend were leaning against the wall fighting for breath. This guy didn't know: he was under the impression she was still in there with him — you know? And all the time — well, part of the time —'

'Wait a minute, wait a minute,' Gorsey Dene said. 'Do you mean to tell me that this bloke didn't know she had sneaked out?'

'He was dumb; Rhet Karachi made that plain.'

'Not that dumb,' said Gorsey Dene. 'Nobody's that dumb.'

'Oh well, the room must have been in semi-darkness then.'

'That's better.'

'So okay, the room was in semi-darkness. But just think of it: this poor schmuck sitting there all alone thinking the girl was in there with him when all the time she was in the corridor laughing with Rhet Karachi and his friend.'

'You might think it funny,' Gorsey Dene said, 'but I don't,' his previous good humour disappearing.

'It wasn't my story,' Jay reminded him.

'You think it funny though.'

'Vaguely amusing, yes. It is, you can't deny it.'

'Depends from whose point of view you're looking at it.' Gorsey Dene lapsed into slience, struggling with the wheel for a while. Why was it that women were attracted by the cheap, the instant, the sensational? He felt a black mood engulf him. His own past was littered with experiences that would have knocked Rhet Karachi's into a cocked hat, but he didn't go round boasting about them. No, it wasn't his way; he preferred to keep them to himself.

The moorland dividing Yorkshire from Lancashire began to rise up before them. The late-night air had turned chill and wraiths of mist slid about in the headlights, parting with a flurry as the car passed through them. The red tail-lights glowed redly in the flurrying mist as the car ascended the tops. More memories awaited him.

Jay slumped sullenly smoking, her massive thighs flattened into ovals against the edge of the low seat. Doubtless she was thinking of the photographer, wishing she was back lying on the soft white sand with the azure-blue wavelets lapping her ankles. Or could she be imagining herself as the girl in the semi-darkened room, sneaking out to press her choking face into Rhet Karachi's quivering shirt-front while the bloke sat staring into gloom and listening to the hiss and crackle of some old 78?

More and more did it seem to Gorsey Dene that life was a *non sequitur.* Occasionally, every once in a while, he might catch a glimpse of . . . something — a sudden shaft of illumination revealing a crazy pattern of logic — but more often than not it was a dark, murky, impenetrable mystery. Was it that he was blind and they could see, or the other way around? If he did have sight, what was he able to see? Only the mystery apparently. And they, in their blindness; what did they see? He put his hand to his face in the darkness and felt the lump growing.

II

The ice and fog got worse the higher they went. The car slithered about on black glassy patches, and Gorsey Dene experienced little tugs of fear at his heart. Up here in the clouds it was easy to forget that the rest of the world existed — indeed, it required an effort of imagination to realise that it did exist. He was all alone with Jay, enclosed in a foggy cocoon, while below in the valleys was an improbable world filled with spurious memory traces and doubtful happenings. For example, behind them, Immingham; ahead, the Corn Exchange. And if he were not extremely careful the whole dreary charade would begin all over again.

It seemed to Gorsey Dene that he had inhabited many lives. He was a host of different people — each one a self-contained legend. His childhood, adolescence, young adulthood were old crackling newsreels forever being re-run for the benefit of somebody or other (probably the participants). They were outside of him, separate, so that somewhere in the universe an endless succession of Gorsey Denes was enacting his past, present and future. At the moment he was fulfilling one such role. Elsewhere another Gorsey Dene was lying in a cornfield with a train in the green distance; yet another was sitting at the bar of an Islington pub listening to a fantastic yarn. And still another was kneeling in damp grass with shivering flanks waiting to pierce an object in the darkness. One more was at this instant in the Corn Exchange recovering from a long fitful drive, and several were engaged simultaneously in unspeakable activities.

Even these moors contained his ghost: those idyllic summer days roaming the tops with the girl of his dreams, pausing in the hollows to kiss and cuddle and exchange lovers' confidences. She was red-haired, or to be more precise, gingerish. She wore thick glasses; her body was large and ample, and to please him was in the habit of wearing a dress without underclothes. Now the moors were covered in hoar-frost but then they burned under the sun and the tough grasses were flattened by the horizontal breeze: it gusted the dry bracken and made patterns as it scurried over the subtle undulations. Gorsey Dene loved to watch the wind chasing itself, planting huge invisible footsteps to the horizon. He often liked to note inwardly the fact that the terrain suited the people hereabouts, matched them in mood and termperament, just as it made an ideal backdrop for his bleak and empty personality.

The girl's name eluded him for a moment. Gorsey Dene frowned into the featureless night. He did recall — in the dim tangled past — an Oldham pub wherein they had sat clasping hands, her distorted eyes peering bulgingly out of the thick lenses of her spectacles. After a while a chap came in and sat with them, a peculiar little fellow with a sharp face and thin white hands. The fellow had been perturbed, Gorsey Dene recalled, about the incidence of violence in the town-centre: something to do with wrecked flower-beds and splintered benches. Though why this should concern *him* more than the rest of them had never been satisfactorily explained; he had not been coerced into becoming everybody's social conscience. That the chap was paranoiac there was little doubt. The way he slunk in avoiding the eyes of the people and sat staring into his glass as if too timid to straighten his spine and square his shoulders. Gorsey Dene had felt very superior that evening, and Sharl or Merl (Vyl? Ral?) or whatever her name was had teased the poor wretch unmercifully, hinting that he should have visited her and had failed to do so. He gaped at her like a stranded grouper, lifting and lowering his eyes, grasping and ungrasping his glass, alternately flushing and growing pale. His shocked face remained clear in Gorsey Dene's memory to this day.

(Jay was singing in a low untuneful voice, obliterated by the car's hum. The underside of her face was lit by the greenish dashboard glow. He felt himself becoming randy again.)

It seemed that he was continually coming up against such half-formed people. Why, he hadn't to think very hard to conjure up half-a-dozen empty vessels: spineless nutcases who needed attending to. Perhaps it was the circles in which he moved, for he did move in circles. This was why he had to make a conscious effort to alter the direction of his life; were he not eternally vigilant it was conceivable that very soon he would discover himself driving a green van towards a 2 a.m. destination, beer-wet around the knees and with a girl (Pee? Tat? He never could remember names) seated beside him. As if this particular nightdrive was not enough of a nightmare to be going on with.

When he cast his mind back his number of trips and returns was phenomenal. Yet what struck him as most odd was that he couldn't pinpoint the place where the switch had been made: where precisely had he been halted, shunted into sidings, and sent on his way in a new direction? The cypher eluded him. In an orderly world he would have progressed from A to B to C to D, but somewhere along the line a substitution had taken place, a swap had been made, and he now found himself with a mind and in a body he hadn't set out with. So where, in fact, were *his* mind and *his* body now? In the pub later that same evening – to take a specific example – had he been the one to take Verl, Shyl, Mal, Rarl (or whatever) up on the moors and make love to her gross body? It couldn't have been him after all, because his recollection was of the moors in sunlight. Or what about the occasion when he had lost his way in a maze of dirty chambers and mildewed passages with the low, hidden growl of plant machinery as an accompanying background noise? That had been him, hadn't it? Yet he couldn't remember ever having found his way out. Again, was it possible that the youth in the Manchester bar, the boy in the Islington pub, and the man in the Oldham pub were one and the same? But no — they had had different experiences, had told different stories. Then was it feasible that one of them was really himself? Which one of the many characters he had encountered was really himself? At present he was heading towards a destiny that belonged to somebody else, and presumably somewhere (in the past or future) that somebody else was employing his mind and inhabiting his body. The trouble was, it was going to be extremely difficult to locate that certain person. How did one go about it? Where to begin the search?

It was with a sudden spurt of nervous shock, a cold tightening of the heart, that Gorsey Dene realised something else. Were it to be totally and factually true that he wasn't himself, then none of the things he recollected as having happened to him had actually happened to him: they belonged to somebody else. The entire box of tricks, the whole charade, the complete mess — none of it appertained to him at all. He should never have undertaken the Immingham Drive; Jay was a stranger to him; none of his memories were memories at all, but transposed fabrications. Was his name really Gorsey Dene?

Perhaps the only way to solve the mystery was to spot a slip, a mistake, a snagged thread in the weave. At some stage he must have abruptly (and without realising it) found himself in a predicament that didn't make sense. Somewhere or other there was a threadbare patch, the frayed strands of which permitted access — or at least gave a clue — to his real life in the real world . . .

They were still in the clouds. The banks of mist rolled against the windscreen: the beams of the headlights struck the palpable white stuff and were swallowed up by the myriad billowing specks of moisture. Jay was sitting numbed and inscrutable. Gorsey Dene didn't love her after all; he didn't love any of them. His flawed personality subsisted on imagined slights. He prayed that Jay would not speak, for he could no longer give any credence to anything that was said: she was sure to add to the confusion by trotting out what was expected of her. Words had no substance; neither had people's emotions. Therefore — as the communication between people and the people themselves were vain tokens signifying nothing — his only recourse was to indulge himself in surface show, which he did. A bright word, a clever phrase, a mocking smile composed the sum total of his humanness.

'Gingy,' said Jay suddenly.

'What?'

'It's a gingy night. A real gingy night.'

(If he had invented her she was fast getting out of hand.)

So many things remained to be explained. He had lived up all his experiences and there was precious little more to tell. Yet in all this he had still not come close to the central core of his dilemma: an analysis of his moral cowardice in the face of humanity. Certainly it was unjustifiable, a sin, a shameful weakness, but the fact remained that had he not had a mind to comprehend such a condition and the sensibility to care about it he would not now be suffering the torture of self-despisedness.

Surely somewhere — *somewhere* — there was a bright, windblown world of towering cumulus clouds and endless blue vistas, a world of sunshine imagination instead of never-ending purple-black horizons spewing flame? Did one really have to regress into childhood and its golden visions to escape the bleak, unrelenting present? He felt the future to be devoid of meaning, a hard blank wall; it was as if his nose was pressed against it, and behind him the weight of the past was crowding him, compressing him, pushing his nose against a hard blank wall. He was teetering forward on the balls of his feet, his arms circling backwards at ridiculous speed, grotesquely unbalanced and yet with nowhere to fall. A man attempting to walk on all-fours on water would not have demonstrated a more hopeless and untenable plight. And still, in the darkness ahead, unimaginable nightmares awaited him.

They began to descend rapidly, slipping occasionally on the glassy patches — deadly black areas with the minimum coefficient of friction. Jay lit a cigarette from the stub of the old one and threw the stub out of the window. She could sense (perhaps by the smell) the ambivalent impulses working within him: desire and repulsion in direct confrontation. It brought to mind an occasion when she too had been engaged in civil war; hitting her knees with her fists and banging her head against the window leaving a tangled imprint had seemed the only viable course of action — or reaction. Creely had been unmoved that evening, she recalled, putting the car carefully into gear and driving with precise, unhurried movements along the motorway. She had never trusted him, not even then, and her suspicions had been confirmed by the letters Pat had written to her. Also he had been egotistical in the extreme, overbearingly confident that he had been the first. She had never disillusioned him, and, to the best of her knowledge, Alan — despite his habitual drunken loutishness and lack of tact — had never let the truth be known. She shuddered now at the memory (that night at the German student's) when, whipped to a pitch of frenzy by his lewd comments and crude behaviour she had suffered herself to be taken from behind in the cold box bedroom (Creely was still downstairs): caught in the act of bending over the bed to pick up her coat, and Alan not even bothering to work her up but merely moving to one side with thumb and forefinger the thin strip of her knickers and sliding his burning cock right up. She had gasped and choked and been unable to move. With a few jerks and a final grunt he had finished her off. So much for virginity.

'You're very quiet,' Gorsey Dene said.

'I'm thinking,' said Jay.

'What about?'

Jay smiled to herself in the darkness. 'Things.'

And what about this one, Gorsey Dene, Jay wondered; had he suspected — or was it a suspicion of a suspicion? — her dalliance abroad? The advertisement had been too good an opportunity to miss — though that was not to say that she had not had qualms. But the chance to travel, expenses paid, to the hottest countries in Europe had been the decisive factor, overriding all other considerations. At first he had overawed her: he was so knowledgeable and understated: the complete sophisticate. His tanned hair-covered hands with the square-cut nails thrilled her; and his authoritative manner and staccato mode of speech made it seem as if he knew precisely what he wanted out of life. He rarely, if ever, spoke of his ragged toothless wife back home in England, and this again was typical of him, sweeping from his mind with an impatient gesture anything which obtruded into the special spacetime warp he had perfected for himself. He spoke disparagingly of most people, not out of malice or envy, but because beside him they appeared to have no purpose in life — were motiveless creatures swayed by non-Euclidean tendencies and irrational whims. This had been new and exciting to Jay, fulfilling her wildest expectations that life could be, and was, a continuous miracle. His UNICEF assignment had left plenty of time for eating, drinking, lying on beaches and making love, all of which he accomplished with style and ease. It was he who had first taught her how to do a mouth job.

Through the mist to the left there appeared a necklace

of lights, fading, becoming brighter, fading, becoming
brighter again. It was a mill in the valley — or what had
been a mill and was now a dye works. To Gorsey Dene it
signalled home: the first outpost on the Lancashire side of
the Pennines. To Jay it was simply a scattering of fading,
brightening points of light down there in the darkling
valley. She was not conscious of their meaning anything;
the cold curling mist, wisping at the edges, had lulled her
into a dreamlike state in which the real world was a
transient, lightly-blown phantasm. It was similar to the
feeling she had had when reading Creely's letters specifying
his experiences with various girls: hearing of them at a
distance in a sunny land had made them seem unreal,
though she did not need to be convinced of their
authenticity. Indeed, it was just like him to have stumbled
on a situation where a girl taking a bath should invite him
inside and wrap her legs, wet and faintly steaming, around
his thin, surprised body, pressing her shiny naked breasts
against his palpitating chest and start to sob and gurgle
the whole sorry story of how she had been left in the
lurch, unloved, uncared for, the thread worn clean away,
and the only constructive plan in her head that of suicide.

'You are quiet,' Gorsey Dene interposed.

'Is there an obligation to talk?'

'No, no,' he amended hurriedly.

The car slithered downwards in the silence.

A little later Gorsey Dene said, 'The moors send chills
through me.'

The moors, Jay thought, remembering another letter in
which he had recounted a daylight experience: rambling
with a girl and her beau — the jerk of a boyfriend going off
alone into the brown-grey distance whereupon the girl had
forced herself upon him, murmuring lewd phrases as she
unbuttoned her blouse. Jay wished that she could have
been that girl, imagining herself taking the initiative as the
gingy schmuck trudged haplessly though the bracken and

stubborn grass. She always felt that a slight release of tension at the base of her brain would enable her to be far more ambitious and outgoing in her attitude and approach to life; an instantaneous slackening of moral inhibitions would allow her to undertake quite dazzling projects of staggering proportions, opening up a whole new realm of exciting possibilities in which she was the leader and not the led. And she could clearly visualise Creely lying back as the girl (whoever *she* was) lay atop him, the two of them smirking and sniggering as the speck of the boyfriend vanished beyond the undulating horizon, the hot contact of their flesh all the hotter because of their illicit coupling and because the moorland breeze was always cool even at the height of summer.

The car juddered over potholes, scrambling her thoughts. How far must Gorsey Dene have walked that day? Had his legs refused to stop, ploughing steadily onward over hill and down dale? Inconceivable, of course, that anyone else could have found themselves in such a ridiculous plight; but as for him —? Her two girlfriends, it was true, had never seen anything the least bit worthy in him. He had been a laughing stock, what with his burning eyes and petulant mouth, and they had hidden their collective amusement behind glasses of port and lemon, occasionally digging the other in the ribs in girlish complicity. But then that was typical of them: their wide and varied sexual experience had hardened their sensibilities to the point of crude insensitivity, and it wasn't to be wondered at that both Val and Shirl invariably fell about when confronted with a particularly ludicrous and despicable specimen of the male species. Women, Jay had come to realise, were the toughies. Gorsey Dene might regard himself as attractively virile but she had inside information. Pat's letter telling of his clumsy attempts that night in the flat she had read with smug satisfaction, showing it to Dmitri who passed his eyes lightly along it and smiled once, the implication being that one could not be too much concerned with the abortive fumblings of other, lesser persons. He had, it appeared, cornered her in the pub — probably the Coach, Jay surmised — and trailed meekly after her to a party, boring her with infantile sexual innuendo and plying her with neat whisky (an obvious ploy) from a pint bottle. During this time Pat had made a number of desultory rejoinders, seeking escape in vain. Later, practically having coerced her into accepting generous measures of liquor, he inveigled her into a position of extreme indelicacy, thrusting his knee between her thighs and moving it backwards and forwards with increasing rapidity, Pat's response being one of astonishment mingled with derision: she had never been 'made' in her life and didn't intend to relinquish her good name and reputation to a man with a petulant mouth. However, worse was to come. The whisky had begun — in spite of her watchful and defensive posture — to have the desired effect, and almost without realising it she found herself grappling with him in the pitch-black confines of, of all places, the bathroom. She could not remember how they came to be there, only that he used brute strength to push her to the floor, wet and slimy with rubber-soled imprints, and attempted to wrench loose her suspenders, in the process tearing her underclothes. All might have been lost — all very nearly *was* lost — but for the intervention of the others who hammered on the door in answer to her cries for help. They grasped him powerfully, his trousers round his ankles, his white pimply flanks quivering, and threw him into the hallway. From the fourteenth floor balcony they had leaned over and watched him limp away, Pat wrote, while she herself in a state of near collapse had been administered to by a man with cold, creased eyes and snarling nostrils. Where he had got to since was not of the slightest interest; she had written only out of a sense of duty and a desire to have the truth made known. No doubt

Jay would know what inference to draw and conclusions
to arrive at from these events.

The drab moors under the shroud of mist were now
safely behind them. The car was once again within Gorsey
Dene's control, proceeding sanely along lighted streets.
They passed by closed and barred shops, passed darkened
rows of terraced stone houses with the street lighting
reflecting in their dead windows, passed garages with
desolate forecourts: all of this silent under the yellow
street lights; the stone, the tarmac, the concrete garage
forecourt working hard at it just to exist. Behind and
above the clean-paved well-lit streets the moors waited,
biding their time.

Gorsey Dene said with plainly-felt relief, 'Nearly there.'

She could see his hands on the wheel, illuminated by the
passing lights, but not his head. Her back and buttocks
were numb from the drive — encased, to all intents and
purposes, in thick hard rubber which placed sensation at
one remove, so to speak. The feeling reminded her of
states of drunkenness when the face is foreign to the
touch, almost as if one's fingers were covered in woollen
stuff and thus prevented from making naked contact. It
brought to mind also her departure abroad: a snowblown
airport carpark with the tip of her nose deadened and
disembodied pressed into Creely's icy cheek. Flakes of
snow had scattered their lashes that day, making the world
seem magical and wonderful, each of them enclosed in
warm clothing, huggable and bulky. (Three days later
he was off to Spain.) Then standing at the broad slanting
windows they had looked out to the aircraft semi-obscured
by the flurries of snow; and Jay had started to cry even
while telling herself that his callous, shallow heart was
undeserving of it. It was the end of an era, the close of a
chapter: *that* was what made her cry. She would never
see him again, or, if she did, he would be different, not the
same, unrecognisable, another person.

'This is Saddleworth,' Gorsey Dene said inconsequentially.

'Is it really,' Jay said. 'Well I never. Would you believe it. I'll go to the bottom of our stairs.'

'We didn't manage to get an hotel after all.'

'Doesn't look like it,' Jay said, opening a new packet of menthol cigarettes. She felt utterly depressed. When the nightdrive had begun it had been exciting, a fast mysterious ride in the dark, a man close enough to touch; but now it was merely the end of another era, the close of another chapter.

His letters too (Gorsey Dene's letters) had been, like him, inconsequential. They had been so pathetic in fact that she had burnt them after only a cursory scan. In lieu of a sense of humour and native wit he had taken to calling her by the names of certain popular film stars as though by so doing she would be endowed with their qualities and flattered by the comparison. In truth the gimmick bored her stiff. It was weak, mean-minded, and devoid of any innate natural charm. For a start she didn't look anything like Kim Novak, having the wrong eye-colour, hair-colour, height and build. Just who did he think he was trying to fool?

Now with Dmitri it had been very different. She could see his brown face with the gentle mocking sneer, the indifferent eyes, the restless hands with the square-cut nails. *He* had known what he was about, treating her as capably as he handled the Pentax and Nikon. When she had had to leave (or felt that she should leave) he had seen her on her way under suffrance: the epitome of self-assured callousness. And that was how Jay liked to be treated. What was the point of a soft-as-shit man?

RK — as she preferred to call him — had had more than a taint of the bastard in him too. They had met in Trieste Station as the Trans-Orient Express squealed and rattled over the points on the start of its thirty-two hour journey to Calais. By the time it had reached Milan Central they had established an easy, bordering on the intimate, relationship; Jay had been glad initially to have someone to talk to, though it wasn't long before the snide, flippant, insidious streak in his nature began to attract her deeply. They shared a lunch pack that RK had bought, galloping down the platform the full length of the train to a man in a white coat and striped hat pushing a trolley: bread, chicken, fruit, cheese, jam, a curious kind of compressed meat which neither of them wanted, and a small bottle of weak red wine. In Brig they were joined in the 2nd Class compartment by three Swiss and one French, all women. The French woman was merry with drink and made certain remarks about one of the Swiss ladies who, it transpired, was a devout Catholic. She produced from her valise a brilliantly-coloured picture of the Archangel Michael whom the French lady insisted on confusing with Michelangelo, a wicked glint in her eye. The Catholic woman's companion was a girl of tremendous proportions who sat with arms massively folded and scowled straight ahead from beneath glowering brows. Throughout this exchange Jay and RK, seated opposite one another by the window, had secretly smiled into each other's eyes, a conspiracy of amusement, and, approaching Lausanne, two minutes precisely before eleven o'clock, had walked together along the swaying corridor in search of a couchette.

The train stopped in the station and fell silent. Outside it was deathly quiet (even the silence was muffled by the snow) and calmly beautiful. The hard clear station light bathed the snow-covered ground-level platform in perfectly even intensity. Jay leaned through the window, craning her neck to look along the train, and Rhet pressed his pelvis into her buttocks. She felt the hard lump grinding into her and the fluid of her bowels shifted. Then his hands went underneath her arms and clasped her breasts. His warm strange breath fluttered in her ear and

she felt her chest straining for air; should she or shouldn't
she? The dilemma was academic, since Jay's method of
deciding whether to accept or reject an experience was to
sample it first and decide later.

The sampling completed, they lay and talked about
their lives as the train passed through Vallorbe, Dole, Dijon
and arrived in the dead morning light at Paris Lyon. It
was during this period that she recounted the events of the
previous months with Dmitri — a story that Rhet had
scandalously re-told in the guise of an anecdote about a
supposed photographer-friend. She might have blushed for
shame (she wasn't at all sure that she hadn't blushed) had
not Rhet's manner of telling it tickled her sense of humour.
Gorsey Dene's very innocence made the incident that
much more hilarious: the gingy dupe's suspicions had been
thoroughly off-beam and his ineffectual perturbations had
been a sight to behold. But RK had sailed close to the
wind in describing her in such detail — a single slip of the
tongue would have been fatal, consigning the two of them
to a miserable, lonely fate, stranded at the side of the
road with nine pieces of luggage. As it was she was snugly
ensconsed in the passenger seat, her travels intact and
securely lodged in her brain: a series of events, happenings
and experiences that she might return to again and again
in future times.

'Is it good to be back?' Gorsey Dene asked, though she
only just succeeded in deciphering the question; his voice
was oddly muffled. Perhaps he was sickening for a cold.

'Mm-mm,' Jay replied inconclusively.

'Of course you'll be used to the cold, won't you?'

'Mmm.'

They were stopped at traffic lights on a deserted street.
The buildings seemed to be asleep, slumbering under their
shadowed eaves. A solitary glow reflected on the polished
floors behind the glass of Woolworths. Disjointed
fragments of the traffic lights were smeared wetly on the

tarmacadamed road: everything was still.

Used to the cold, Jay thought with a secret silent tremor of humour. If only he could see the colour of my body . . . just as Creely had seen it in the depths of the cornfield on that sunshiny day with the insects whittering and hopping among the close-packed stalks. Marks and weals had remained on her back for a lengthy period of time, joyful reminders of that day when – yes, she had to admit it – she had very nearly been in love with him. Any man who treated her as he had done deserved to be worshipped. The impact had been virtually instantaneous, from that first motorway cafeteria meeting in the early hours of the morning when she had found herself sitting opposite him. The look of his hands had made her desire him at once, and the soft, haunted, assured expression in his eyes had confirmed the rightness of her judgement. And yet it was neither of these things specifically – nor any other specific thing – which gave him the intense attractiveness she felt for him. It was none of these things and in a sense all of them. Not the colour of his eyes nor the shape of his head nor the manner in which he conducted himself; very simply it was that when she looked into his eyes she knew immediately what he was, and what he was accorded with what she herself felt inside. At once she knew what to talk about, without any hesitation or uneasiness, and the way in which it should be expressed. Neither, at the same time, was it necessary to utter a word: they could have remained silent, nicely at ease, and yet maintained a communion of spirits. To this day she still retained a visual impression of the stark setting against which they had faced one another, the bare halls crowded with shuffling people moving forward half-a-shambling-step at a time, the cruel fluorescent lights, the dirt and rubbish of social transaction covering the grime-ingrained floor, the squares of the windows like shiny black mirrors reflecting the chaos inside – all of it a waking nightmare in which he had been a dream-image with beautiful hands and expressive eyes.

Trust Gorsey Dene to spoil it.

Blundering in like a drunken rhino (yet mole-like in his demeanor) he stood over the table and insisted that he knew her, or, more correctly, had known her, calling her Ryl, to which she would only respond with blank-eyed amazement. He trotted out some incoherent tale of their having lived in adjacent rooms, babbling away ten-to-the-dozen with flecked lips and flickering eyes, intent on convincing her that he was who he said he was and that she, sometime in the dim-remembered past, had occupied the room next to his.

'I remember your room clearly,' he had said, leaning earnestly over the table, his bloodless knuckles kneeling on the worn formica. 'It was always so neat and bright, like a new pin. Cosy too. You had lots of warm colours and soft fabrics.' He breathed excitedly. 'There was a big bow window in your room that looked out over the main road. It faced east so that the sun came into it in the morning. It was a room that caught the morning sun; a morning-sun room. Mine was at the back,' he ended lamely.

She had looked into Creely's eyes and smiled gently, dismissively, and he too had smiled, reading her thoughts. The clatter and bustle of the cafeteria continued, surrounding the two of them in a cocoon of tranquility. Gorsey Dene had – typically – appeared not to notice it, neither did he seem aware of the effect his lumbering intrusion had had. With flushed face and soft lips a-tremble he stood waiting for further response far longer than any reasonable hope might have led him to expect. In short he was a plain nuisance. But being a person on whom the ground rules of behaviour and decorum were completely lost it was futile (they both knew it) to raise the point or press it home. Anything less than an especially deadly bomb would not have achieved the desired effect.

Evenutally he did go, and it was to be several months before Jay came into contact with him.

She watched his puny hands on the wheel; had it not been for their control of the car they (the hands) would have been powerless. The wrists were thin and hairless. Above them his head seemed a dark shadowed bulk, disproportionate to the rest of his body. What a queer specimen to have become embroiled with. Never, in all the time of their acquaintance, had she experienced the magic thrill, the breathless battering-ram shock of absolute oneness with him. Even the small private jokes were passed carefully from hand to hand, levity measured out in prescribed doses. He was totally alien, this Gorsey Dene, an unknown entity, an android. She doubted, sometimes, whether he was really human. While others communicated directly he did so via an unseen gallery of appreciative wags who greeted his sallies with unheard applause and bestowed adoring and unqualified approval. Thus the second party, the recipient of these gems, was merely a tiresome adjunct, a conversational appendage to the main proceedings, ie: Gorsey Dene talking for the benefit of his own self, the role of the other person being that of the butt, the sounding-board, the foil. Were she this instant to feed him a line he would strive mightily to turn a triple somersault, confusing himself and confounding them both with a dazzling pyrotechnic display signifying nought.

The lights changed from red to green. The question was, where was Creely now? As last reported he had left his wife and children and driven off, never to return, and knowing him he would almost certainly stick by his resolve. Perhaps he had looked in the evening paper and found a flat on the south side of town and was even at this moment preparing a makeshift meal in a grotty basement where the sun never shone. Did that fit the pattern? Jay asked herself. Was he likely to shut himself away from the light like a ground-burrowing mammal? Strange things happened to the human mind under stress. Perhaps (it was feasible) he had gone clean off the rails, was now a hopeless psychiatric case in desperate need of care and attention. For it was an odd thing that as she had grown in confidence and aggressiveness he had faded into insignificance, become a pallid simulacrum of his former self, almost as if he had deliberately effaced himself and lost all traces of personality. In some respects, towards the end, he had become so insignificant and featureless as to resemble a grease spot. *But where was he now?* Jay wondered, worrying the question as though an answer might materialise out of the thin, dark, rushing air. Would it ever be possible to find him in the outer suburbs of Manchester or wherever he had scuttled to? Indeed, were she to locate him, would he still be recognisable? Tales of people disappearing without trace, of changing shape, of being lost in a sterile limbo were not uncommon —

They were passing now through Oldham. The quiet streets were interrupted by the scudding roar of the exhaust banging back and forth from building to building. The night sky seemed very low, a matter of a few feet above the tunnel of yellow light in which they were travelling. Jay said:

'You must be tired after the long nightdrive.'

There was barely a flicker of response; a grunt perhaps; nothing more. Jay said again:

'You must be tired after the long nightdrive.'

This time a definite movement of the shadowed bulk of the head and a sort of a croaking form of reply — in the affirmative. He must be tired, Jay thought, after the long nightdrive. Several minutes passed without further sound. There was nothing more to say. Then, so faint as to make her doubt her hearing, Jay thought she heard something. Out of the corner of her eye she tried to watch him without his being aware of it but all she could see was a vague black bulk merged with the dark interior of the car.

She turned her head fully to stare but could see no more.
She had the feeling that something was crouching there in
the darkness, waiting, and occasionally whimpering to
itself.

III

But how was he to make sense of all this? Of course he had
a plan (who didn't have a plan!) but the trouble was he
didn't believe in plans. He believed in very little, in fact;
hardly anything at all if the truth were known. He had
once believed in success — until he had had a taste of it —
but it soured the mouth, as it must do of all those who
aspire to rise above the level of the merely superficial or
do not seek the tedious thrill of continuous masturbation.
But yes, on reflection, and to be honest, he did believe in
some things: loneliness and despair, both of which he had
experienced one Friday evening last summer. Come to
think of it, the events of last summer had been terrible —
because he realised for the first time in his life that his
life was finite. Strangely enough, what made him realise
this was that on that certain Friday evening his life had
stretched away endlessly into the infinite distance:
featureless, grey, without hope. *That* was what made him
realise his life was finite.

Now, this moment, looking back, he saw nothing but the
huge incomprehensibility of it all. The real and imagined
slights had festered in his brain; they had made him
perceive the universe in strange and wondrous ways. And
far from alleviating the condition had had the effect of
exacerbating it to the point where even this mystical,
magical nightmare (the past) seemed in retrospect to have
been a happy time. The misty golden future had been
transformed into the leaden ever-present Now. Things were

not going to get better, only worse. Not so long ago he had thought himself on the brink of understanding: safe and sound in his pocket were the rules of how to behave, how to react, how to navigate sanely towards death. But with the advance of time and the addition of several billion electro-chemical connections in the brain he found himself staring out of empty eye-sockets at a future without alternatives. The path was downward all the way, culminating in a dark skyline of spewing jets, in the lost galleries of a paper mill, or, even more terribly, in an empty back room upon whose walls through the slats of a venetian blind the sun imprinted a blood-red grid. He was trapped inside his own head.

What exactly had happened on 'that certain Friday evening last summer'? And what had happened since? Had anything happened since? Apparently not, outside of his own head. He was a character in a novel in which nothing ever happened. The people sat and talked about nothing; they travelled back and forth to no purpose; they didn't develop or progress in thought or in action; their lives were not lives in the accepted sense of the word but resembled particles whose main characteristic was that of non-volition. Neither did they exhibit an awareness of themselves as imaginary beings: they were transfixed in the stasis of perpetual motion; yet whenever he had encountered them they had presumed to be doing something and going somewhere. He too tried to behave in this way, but to no avail. He thought of himself as a man whose spirit was unclothed, perfectly transparent and naked, and that to enter into any kind of intercourse with these people they would first of all require him to decently cover his bareness and muffle himself in warm, constricting, woolly comforters.

His one great talent lay, and had always lain, in antagonising the largest number of people imaginable. Indeed, it was quite possible, given the opportunity, for

him to antagonise the world. Whereas others had the
innate gift of identifying with, relating, to, etc, etc, ever-
widening circles of people he found himself in the
ludicrous and paradoxical position of deliberately seeking
their antipathy. Paradoxical because on the one hand (like
every human being) he sought and required the approval,
liking and friendship of others, while on the other he had
come to regard that approval, liking and friendship as
misplaced — as, in fact, the expression of a sentiment
towards himself that was undeserved; and that once they
knew him fully would inevitably and rightfully be replaced
by aloof withdrawal. Thus, in order to remain truthful to
himself and to achieve the correct state of affairs as
quickly as possible, he circumnavigated the social
pleasantries by abrupt, boorish behaviour. To such an
extent did this philosophy engage his thoughts and actions
that he came to dislike and distrust *instantly* anyone who
showed him the slightest courtesy or displayed signs of
approval. And he carried forward this attitude with such
expert conviction that before long his facial expressions,
his manner of speaking, his physical presence — in short,
his entire personality — became immediately abhorrent to
the vast majority of people. This was a situation developed
to a nice degree, for it drove him deeper into the closed,
airless shell of melancholia and had the net result of
strengthening his resolve to excite open and active hostility
— which he achieved with unequivocal success.

The simple truth was — having reasoned it out through
many a sleepless night and many a nightdrive — that he
knew himself very well: every insipid impulse, base motive
and selfish deed; and how, knowing himself for what he
was, could be foist this spurious product onto gullible
mankind? How could he look into other people's eyes
when he flinched from gazing into a mirror?

Yet 'that certain Friday evening last summer' continued
to haunt him. He could not rid his thoughts of all its stark

significance. (That he did not know quite what the significance was did not lessen the terror.) What he did know was that it had broken him in two; his spirit had been smashed and his personality destroyed. The sun, he recalled, had been a flat red disc low in the sky: an omen. The shadows of the people had stretched thinly along the pavements and into the gutters; the perspiring tar road had exuded a heavy heated odour. Everywhere he looked he saw normality and strangeness intertwined and inseparable, residing in the same objects and in the very fabric of the air. At the first pub he came to he drank a double brandy straight down, attracting the stares of the landlord and the lone customer on the bench seat. The unreal evening daylight made the three of them seem like pale, silent, motionless fish in a tank of antiseptic fluid.

The newspaper crackled in his hand. He bent his head to look at it, avoiding their gazes. The print sharpened, swam away, sharpened again, disappeared. He drank another brandy and as he drank it it occurred to him that he was living his life. He was existing. So — again the shock, again the sudden lurch in the chest — he wasn't play-acting after all. He was a real man with causes and actions and consequences. Sweat appeared on several parts of his body at once. Why, he thought stupidly, he had been alive all the time : he had been alive : his life was not a dream : Tee, Val, Marl, Shirl, Pat, Ryl and Jay were existing at this moment. This was a truly dreadful thought because it meant that he had invented none of them.

Setting off from the pub (having consumed the brandy and deserted my wife and children) I drove light-headedly to Manchester. Blue fumes rose from the cars. The city was abashed in the unaccustomed evening sunlight, nervous and jumpy at being caught unawares; usually by this time she was decently clothed, the ugly details of night hidden in darkness. I passed by the Corn Exchange, a sooty-black edifice of impressive size and bulk, little windows glinting high up in the turrets and towers. People worked behind those windows for most of the days of the year, slogging away their lives in offices with dusty parquet floors and cheap wooden desks. The plumbing clanked and in winter rainwater and cold melting snow dripped from the ceilings.

After driving round aimlessly for some time I stopped at a pub which by the look of it was due to be demolished. It stood amidst acres of rubble − piles of reddish-brown bricks crumbled at the corners and broken in two − arranged in symmetrical rows as though at one time they had been houses containing people and separated by streets. Holes had been worn here and there through several layers of lino, like converging concentric ripples, and the bars were several-inch-thick solid wood rounded and smoothed at the edges with the faint tracery of grain showing beautifully. Each room was divided by frosted glass panels bearing scrolls and legends; the wall benches were of buttoned leather, dried and cracked.

I sat with my black cone-shaped Guinness and felt the world slide about my ears. It was a slurring noise, like a slowed-down gramophone, and the end-of-week laughter on this Friday night sounded maniacal as though the few hours' pleasure alloted them had to be compressed into hysteria.

As for me, the one vision that preoccupied my mind was of the down on my little boy's back. His miniature shoulder blades merged into the narrow upper torso: the hollow of the back, prior to the buttocks, covered in soft blond fleece. Was there anything in the world so precious? Yet I had gone out of my way, deliberately and with malice aforethought, to smash and destroy that very thing − the culmination of a series of capricious and irresponsible whims that on the evolutionary scale placed me no higher than a blind burrowing creature in the grip of driving instinctive forces and selfish greed. Perhaps (a consoling

thought) we have to become bad in order to distinguish
it from good. For how can a person be 'good' if he has no
knowledge of what it is to be bad? I had willingly
committed an entire catalogue of sins despite the fact that
my intention was to lead a good, decent, fruitful life. Not
'in spite of' but 'because of' my good inner self I had
wilfully indulged in many bad things; yes, for only in this
way do we acquire the beginnings of a moral conscience
and learn to weigh the difference between right and wrong.
A person who never seeks to do evil is neither morally
'good' nor morally 'bad'; he is merely amoral, and probably
a dolt into the bargain.

By the end of the evening I had drunk myself into a
maudlin semi-stupor. Of the alternatives before me none
seemed viable save that of locating a resting-place for my
weary head and body. There are occasions when all we
can do is lie down and sink exhausted through time and
space into embryonic slumber. The roads were awash with
moonlight; in both directions drunken cars zoomed and
sped, rocking on their springs like wild animals and
squealing with fury when stopped by traffic lights. Inside
was as though there was a great silence throughout the
in ritual mating manoeuvres, a kind of stately symbolic
dance of skulls. I knew, or could guess, what was going on
beneath the eye-line where glass gave way to metal. In my
own compartment things were vastly different: I had only
my trusty right hand, the left one being fully occupied
with steering and the changing of gears.

The Guinness had begun to affect my head, which was
aching and bursting. Where would I find a bed at this time
of night? The bloated sun had, of course, by now
disappeared. Nothing remained of it but a memory to add
to the many others. And that was partly the trouble: my
mind was choc-a-bloc with memories, spilling over with
them. Man can never aspire to eternal life; the weight of
remembrances would send him mad. The night took on a

kind of screaming-like intensity — me alone in it with only the sounds of my heartbeat and respiration and the crackling wax in my ears for company. I was sure that if I listened carefully I would hear the exudation of sweat. It was as though there was a great silence throughout the world and that my bodily functions were filling that silence with gurgling trickles and thuds and softly weeping seepage. What it meant was that my eyes and ears had turned inward, forsaking the dark outer void and alerting themselves — standing on tip-toe as it were — for the phenomena which evinced a warm, living, breathing being. They were looking and listening, in fact, for the only reality left: the incessant drone-like beat of the body. It is at such moments, in the dead still of night, that we must face ourselves and scrutinise our fingernails, know the shape of the callouses on our feet, recall which teeth are crooked and which are straight, recognise the fatty swell circling our waist and the rough, pimpled flesh on our lower buttocks and thighs, acknowledge that we are ugly and ignoble people (every last one) and deserve all that we get.

I would have to stop soon. The world was going to sleep and I remained at the wheel. I needed a woman exceedingly badly but I knew that all the women were gone. Pat was married, Val was diseased, Tee was in Reading, Jay was . . . etc, etc, etc.

It was then that I realised I was going to die. It was an immediate seizure at the back of the throat, an instantaneous convulsion of the pharynx at the thought that my life would not go on for evermore. I was finite and — something even more terrifying — ageing by the second. This instant, this very instant, would remorselessly vanish, never to return. Death as a cold-blooded fact did not worry me: it was the impact of non-being, of not existing, of not experiencing an infinite series of alternative futures that made the breath solidify in my lungs and the blood

rush and swirl through my body. We are all headed on a
disaster course, fragments of a dream in search of a miracle.

On a road fringed by trees I stopped and looked at the
houses set back behind stone walls and unkempt undergrowth. Surely the damned must live in these many-roomed
blocks of dingy brick, the vagrants and strays each in their
separate boxroom abodes, uniquely and yet collectively
living out their senseless lives – of whose number I was
soon to become one, a digit, a cypher, a zero. And yes, as
if to confirm the prophecy, several of them had cards in
their shabby windows advertising vacancies, and it will
come as no surprise when I tell you that I found myself on
the gravelled path approaching a door above which a
suitable epitaph might have been, but wasn't, engraved.
The looming, curtained house awaited my knock, smug,
silent, anticipatory. I knocked, and the ensuing silence was
followed by a muffled shuffling of feet and an occasional
flip-flap of tired and workworn slippers. The woman stood
there, not old but old-looking, wiping her greasy hands on
a dishevelled pinny and staring somewhat fearfully into the
darkness. I must have seemed to her as nothing other than
a bulky silhouette, faceless, without identity, and no
doubt frightening too. She led me along the passageway
and into a room festooned with washing, and her husband,
a Geordie, rose up out of his fireside chair and turned his
back on the TV set. The screen showed the retrieval of a
capsule. The man was pleasant enough: brisk and to-the-
point but friendly and humane also. He rummaged in a
drawer for a rent book and a key tied to a large wooden
block and waited patiently as I signed my name to the
cheque. The fact that he was a denizen of hell didn't seem
to phase him in the least – nor that a new inmate should
appear in the night out of nowhere. Had he studied my face
closely matters might have been different, but he didn't.
And besides, the room was heavily-shadowed, with the
limp hanging sheets and damp flaccid woollens dissecting

the air above our heads and chopping the room up into areas of light and dark so that it was difficult to make out features, or, indeed, the lack of them.

The little Geordie woman stood obsequiously by, hands and arms of wrinkled and sagging flesh wrapped in her apron. She was looking at me and yet not looking at me at one and the same time; studying me by default, as it were. My only hope was that her eyesight was not in good repair or that the obtruding sheets sufficiently masked my head or even that she was accustomed to receiving such specimens as myself at all odd hours of the night.

Still woozy from the Guinness I misheard something the Geordie said but gathered from his expression and general manner that the transaction was completed and that I was now signed, sealed and as good as delivered. All that remained was the purely mechanical ritual of installing me in the room they had chosen to be my new home. This was not in the same building: it was, in fact, in the next block along, and it occurred to me that perhaps the Geordie and his wife were the custodians of the row — handers-out of rent books and keys to an entire streetfull of lost causes, hopeless cases and soulless wonders. In any event we picked our way from one building to the next through the sooty rubber shrubbery, him unlocking the front door with a Yale key which he then silently handed to me while giving me to understand that henceforth this was to be one of the accoutrements of the office, a privilege and responsibility both. I put the key in my pocket and staggered as the weight of it dragged me down.

The passageway along which we stumbled (it being impossible, or very nearly so, to walk, what with various anonymous objects underfoot) I need hardly describe. It was the passageway to hell. On the way we passed by an open door and through it I caught the fraction of a glimpse of a cheerful, flickering fireside, easy chairs, a table in the recess of a bow window, bright prints and pictures on the

walls, a lamp casting a cosy circular glow in one corner, a
shelf of books, and on the floor a clean, richly-coloured
carpet. There was no one to be seen but I deduced that it
was a young lady's room and one that (it being at the
front of the house) would receive the full splendid glory
and dazzling benevolence of the morning sun. Naturally
the rooms at the back received no such thing.

However, as I've said, it was the merest glimpse, and we
quickly passed on to a door that in the dim yellow light
might have been any one of a number of colours — brown,
green, black — or a mixture of all three. The Geordie led
the way, pushing the door with his shoulder to force it
over the uneven floor and torn lino, switching on the bulb
hanging from its bare dangling wire, and literally having to
peer through the 60-watt gloom to establish that this shit-
hole was, as he knew it very well to be, vacant. As for me,
my head was splitting at the sight of it: the dust, the
debris, the discoloured wallpaper, the inch-thick grease-
covered stove in the alcove, the scarred grey sink that had
once been white, the rubbish-littered table and single
crooked chair, the venetian blind with its buckled and
broken slats, and the bed, a folding one, at this moment
upright against the wall with its springs showing and
caught in them the accumulated detritus of a slovenly,
damned life: cigarette packets, old adhesive plasters, a
squashed tube of toothpaste, elastic bands with tufts of
hair in them, a sock, a crumpled newspaper, the torn-off
strap of a bra, bits of string, beer bottle caps, used tissues,
and everywhere dust.

This was to be my new home and a suitable place it was.
Here I could live out my life out of sight of humanity, lost
to the world, a furry subterranean creature (the
transmutation being almost complete) existing in deaf,
dumb and blind obedience to the terrors at work inside
the monstrous growth of my head. That the Geordie had
not reacted to my appearance I could only attribute to the

weakness of his eyesight or the poorness of the light. Not that it mattered: he would never again see me and I would never again see him. The future stopped here; there was to be no future, only the timeless Now in this cave, this hole, this burrow of a back room. Here I could mull and paw over my wretched heap of memories, snuffle amongst the remains of real and imagined slights, stick my snout between my legs and knaw away uninterrupted at my own pathetic vitals. The Geordie could not have received the slightest intimation of this, for he pottered about turning the taps on and off, stamping on the lino with his heels, rocking the chair back and forth, and tugging at the cord which operated the venetian blind. It didn't work of course. Then he put the rent book and the key attached to its block of wood on the table and turned to face me, from his expression seeing nothing of my head and shoulders other than a vaguely defined bulkiness covered by a fur-like material. I said nothing, waiting for this final contact with a human to be brought to its conclusion.

'You'll be wanting other things,' said the Geordie, as though suddenly aware that I had not brought with me any of the items necessary to maintain the minimum standard of existence. 'Cutlery, cups, plates, bedding – a bit of food – and cooking utensils such as saucepans, a frying pan and so on. Do you have any of these things with you?'

'I shall be all right,' I replied. 'I will be all right.'

'Mmm.' He tried to look at me more closely but then gave it up as being either too much trouble or none of his business. He turned away, almost tending to shrug slightly. He had been about to make a gesture of some kind, reaching out to establish a point of meaningful contact, but had realised that it was futile anyway and would not achieve anything.

'Oh, before I forget,' he said. 'The bathroom is next

door and so is the lavatory. Be careful not to use too much
hot water and watch out for the overflow in the lavatory.
The cistern leaks too.' He stumbled over something going
to the window where he tried again, unsuccessfully, to
operate the venetian blind.

'Are there any towels?' I asked for something to say.

'No, no towels. No soap either.'

'Can't be helped. Doesn't matter.'

The Geordie came back to the centre of the room,
standing beneath the bulb pouring out its yellow light.
There were shadows everywhere, especially in the murky
recesses of the room. He seemed to see it for a moment
with new eyes, rotating his head slowly to look at the bed,
the table, the chair, the sink, the stove, the floor-covering.

'Not much,' he said, 'I must admit' − a wan smile
playing about his lips. 'You could smarten the place up a
bit, I suppose, but at the moment there's nothing here to
bring joy into anybody's life. The trouble is you get people
here for only a short while, a week or a day, like the last
one. Came and went and hardly saw him.'

'You won't have that trouble with me,' I said. 'I don't
intend leaving.'

'You're going to make it sort of your permanent base,
so to speak?'

'Such as it is.'

'Yes.' He paused, then repeated, 'Yes,' having a last look
round as if wondering what he could say to put the best
possible complexion on things. 'It is a bit of a dank dark
hole,' the Geordie agreed. 'But you'll be safe here. And in
the evening the sun shines in through the venetian blinds.
The one who had it before you − or should I say was
going to have it − was a queer fish. But he upped and
went, leaving in a hurry. *Doubtless you remember him?'*